THE LADY OF SERPENTS

THE VAMPYRICON

THE LADY OF SERPENTS

DOUGLAS CLEGG

ACE BOOKS, NEW YORK

THE BERKLEY PUBLISHING GROUP
Published by the Penguin Group
Penguin Group (USA) Inc.
375 Hudson Street, New York, New York 10014, USA
Penguin Group (Canada), 90 Eglinton Avenue East, Suite 700, Toronto, Ontario M4P 2Y3, Canada
(a division of Pearson Penguin Canada Inc.)
Penguin Books Ltd., 80 Strand, London WC2R 0RL, England
Penguin Group Ireland, 25 St. Stephen's Green, Dublin 2, Ireland (a division of Penguin Books Ltd.)
Penguin Group (Australia), 250 Camberwell Road, Camberwell, Victoria 3124, Australia
(a division of Pearson Australia Group Pty. Ltd.)
Penguin Books India Pvt. Ltd., 11 Community Centre, Panchsheel Park, New Delhi—110 017, India
Penguin Group (NZ), Cnr. Airborne and Rosedale Roads, Albany, Auckland 1310, New Zealand
(a division of Pearson New Zealand Ltd.)
Penguin Books (South Africa) (Pty.) Ltd., 24 Sturdee Avenue, Rosebank, Johannesburg 2196, South Africa

Penguin Books Ltd., Registered Offices: 80 Strand, London WC2R 0RL, England

This is an original publication of The Berkley Publishing Group.

First edition: September 2006

Library of Congress Cataloging-in-Publication Data

Clegg, Douglas, 1958–
    1. The lady of serpents / Douglas Clegg.—1st ed.
    p. cm.
    ISBN 0-441-01438-0
    1. Vampires—Fiction. I. Title.

PS3553.L3918L33 2006
813'.54—dc22
                                        2006017153

PRINTED IN THE UNITED STATES OF AMERICA

10   9   8   7   6   5   4   3   2   1

For Simon Lipskar, my agent,
for everything he did to make this novel
a wonderful experience for me.

With thanks to Ginjer Buchanan, my editor, for her insights and
her involvement in making the Vampyricon a wonderful experience; thanks to Leslie Gelbman, Susan Allison, and everyone at
Berkley/Ace. With special thanks to Raul Silva.

Visit www.Vampyricon.com

"*I met a traveler from an antique land*
Who said: Two vast and trunkless legs of stone
Stand in the desert . . ."

—Percy Bysshe Shelley, "Ozymandias"

◆ CHAPTER 1 ◆

◆ 1 ◆

WHEN the war exploded within a few hundred miles of the buried city, I knew that a hunter would come to that sacred place called Alkemara. Cities to the east and west were afire. Great plumes of smoke rose from distant lands. The mortal realm had begun finding the buried kingdoms at last, those remnants of the Ages of the Serpent and the Veil. Wars of the past century had exposed the tombs of lost kings and queens and priests of the three faces of the goddess, the bones of those years of my youth, and the ashes of the thousand or more years before even my birth. Bombs and satellites and all the weapons of warfare had unearthed the most sacred places of the Kamr priesthood.

I was born during the years of the Crusades, and now witness the wonders and terrors of the twenty-first century. I found Alkemara during those wars of my youth. Now, others find it during the current wars. I see omens of a New Dark Age descending again, and I see the medieval world rising up as if it, too, had only been sleeping.

I sense a tearing at the Veil that separates this world from the Other-world.

It has happened before.

War and its destruction drive those who seek me out. Though I have come and gone in the mortal world for centuries—and learned from travels and from a very late education—my tombs are many, beneath great cities and fallen kingdoms. Those who are left of my tribe sleep in the deepest places. I retired to one of the ancient sacred homes of the vampyre when I felt the world turning dark again. I was sure no mortal would find us, as had happened in Prague or Berlin, but it is always bombs and fires and destruction that expose our nests. We move on. We inhabit caverns and catacombs and those tomblike kingdoms that have yet to be found, keeping to the fringes of human awareness until the Serpent calls us. Until the spirit of the Serpent guides someone to us.

When the bombing erupted, in those cities distant to my tomb, armies and spies and supplies in jets roared over the empty lands. Several pilots noticed strange pathways along the desert, as if a trade route had once existed there. The pathways, covered during even my existence, had a serpentine shape. Along the mountain cliffs, beneath centuries of erosion, there were indications of two great monuments, faces carved upon them.

Some mortals, through religious fanaticism, decided to destroy these enormous monuments, for they seemed to represent pagan gods. Whenever fanatics find ancient knowledge or art or the hint of history that does not involve them, they seek to obliterate it. An international cry went up to save these newfound treasures. The monuments were of a god and a goddess, both nameless, both unknown to any books of mythology or history. The first archaeologists and historians at the site ascribed the artistry to Hurrian and other lost peoples who traveled these desolate desert paths thousands of years before.

I had not seen these monuments when I first came to this place, for so much was buried then beneath a cataclysm's touch. Yet, I knew them, for they represented the bringers of eternal life to my own race. They are of the Great Serpent and the three-faced goddess who is called Medhya, Datbathani, and Lemesharra. The face of Medhya would be set in a grimace, for she is the dark mother who brings terror in the night; Datbathani would wear a gold mask of the Queen of Serpents; and Lemesharra, who had protected the city of Alkemara until its fall, was the magnificent giver of life to the dead. The Great Serpent has no face, but all vampyres may see their faces in his. He is the serpent of the earth, the guardian of buried places, and the protector of secrets that separate this world from the world beyond the Veil.

When a British team of historians announced that they believed the ancient city of Nahhash once existed in this dusty place, it was only a matter of time before the trucks and tents and shovels and students and government supervisors would arrive and begin plundering.

An ancient manuscript by a mad monk of France resurfaced.

In it, the city of Nahhash had another name—Al-Kamr-Amon—and was called by this monk, "The Lair of Dragons."

This manuscript came into the possession of a wealthy archaeologist and professor of antiquities who had been traveling the desert for the past few years. She led a team of experts who studied ancient maps. She funded an extensive archaeological dig deep into the deserts of the Middle Eastern world. She was one of many who sought the origins of this place, and of these statues that seemed like a giant gateway into the valley between mountains. She believed they indicated a site "greater than the city of Petra," as she told the *International Herald-Tribune* in the one interview she granted. "And the ruins found in France, at the Taranis-Hir dig."

But I knew she hunted more than ancient ruins.

She hunted me, though she did not understand why.

♦ 2 ♦

I had fled the great city I had become comfortable within, and returned to the buried kingdom.

Surrounded by a nest of my tribe, we gathered to protect it from the exploration. Others hunted the temporary settlements to scare away teams of engineers and archaeologists who had camped a mere hundred miles from the entry to our buried, broken city of Alkemara. We had seen so many lost kingdoms fished from the sea or from beneath volcanic ash to be dissected and put on display in foreign museums, while all the sacred energies of these places were destroyed.

These had been our hiding places in troubled times. They were vanishing as the modern world dredged them up from mud and ash.

We positioned ourselves to slaughter any who found their ways through the serpent-holes along the cliffs that gave entry into the valley that existed within the mountain, with its milky waters and city of the dead.

But I could not slaughter the woman who led a small expedition through the narrow caverns and twisting drops.

When this archaeologist opened my tomb in the walls of Alkemara, I knew her by her eyes and by her hair and the shape of her face.

When she spoke, I heard the voice of someone I had once known in my first century of life. It is amazing how the human voice passes through the bloodline—how codes of life continue from one generation to the next, for hundreds, perhaps thousands, of years.

I saw in her eyes, also, a longing for me, as if for some youth she once loved and lost. I had been a dream to her, until now. A face seen at a window, years before. She combed her fingers through my hair and brought her lips near mine as if desiring all that I was and all that I knew.

"Natalia," I whispered, and wished I had not said her name.

I had just reminded her of a night, long ago, when she had been a girl of seventeen, sobbing in her room, looking up at the rain-spattered window.

Yes, I whispered as if in her mind, *I knew you would find me here.*

• 3 •

T HE nest of vampyres in the surrounding tombs descended upon her assistants, their wings blocking escape as they took the mortals and drank deeply from them.

I soon had her in my arms and would have drunk her dry as well, had I not heard her speak—had I not noticed the face of this woman, so familiar, as if she had come from a past century.

"You will stay here with me," I said.

"Will you kill me?" she asked as she lay beside me in my coffin at dawn. I embraced her as if we were lovers. She did not struggle against me, though I smelled her fear. My wings spread, folded around her body and mine, forming a cloak to warm us in that cold place.

An embrace of darkness.

• 4 •

A young vampyre, Daniel—whom I had brought into immortality six years earlier when he had begged for death along an alleyway of Prague—sealed my tomb each morning and opened it at sunset. The tomb was a generous size and had many scrolls and oil lamps by which Natalia might read. Food was brought for her, and freshwater as well as wine, when she desired it. This was the place in which the Priest of Blood himself had once been entombed. I slept in his crystal bier, and frequently thought of him as I closed my eyes each day.

I told her if she tried to harm me or to escape, she herself would die in the bargain when Daniel came to release me from the crystal coffin at night. "He will tear you open and pour your blood into the throats of a nest of vampyres," I said. "And you have no defense against them. So do not try to harm me, for you only destroy yourself by doing so."

I trusted she would not raise a hand against me, despite her fears. Perhaps this is the arrogance of the vampyre, but centuries of immortality bring out a sensual quality to our eyes and our lips, and our visages are sweet to the mortal eye—though a less glamorous slickness covers our skins during the day. We retain the vitality of each life we drink, for fertility and the erotic essence are in the blood more than in flesh and bone. Few mortals who still feel the charge of life within them can resist us. We do not need to build spiderwebs or traps, for the men and women from whom we drink seek us out though we remain hidden from others.

Likewise, I told her I would drink some of her blood, just a cupful each night, in exchange for what she sought from me. When I leaned into her to press my lips at her throat, or raised her wrist to my mouth, I felt her submission to me. She was here for the same reason I had come to this place. It was her destiny to find me.

In the small tastes of blood I took from her, I tasted my mortal memories again—for the blood of the living brought back my own mortality. I felt her desire for me. She longed for a forgotten ancestor—a lost bloodline.

I glanced up at her face as I sucked gently from the wound. A flush of pink came into her cheeks, and the rims of her ears darkened with a rush of blood. The distant look in her eyes told me she had gone into a place of pleasure and even shame. Her lips parted slightly, as she gasped, and gasped, and gasped, until she groaned beneath my ministrations at her throat.

Her arms wrapped about my waist, and I felt her animal heat as her hips ground instinctively against me. She whispered as her half-lidded eyes took me in, "You are so beautiful, so beautiful." Yet it was not me she saw, but the flesh of an ancient vampyre, which blinds the mortal eye.

Beauty traps many mortals, just as I had once been trapped by the vampyre Pythia, whose unconscionable beauty haunts me, still, after centuries. I was taken as a vampyre just past my nineteenth year. I still seem a strong, muscular youth of that age. Mortal men and women often could be drawn to my youth—the essence of life at its peak. It is the illusion of the vampyric flesh itself.

Natalia burned as I held her, a fever in her blood that I could taste. I felt something deeper there than the lust of the flesh.

She wept against my neck as I healed her wound with kisses along the soft pale flesh where I had moments before torn my entry. She held fast to me. She whispered, "I saw you when I was young and in love with a man. You took him away from me. It was you. You at my window. I have hunted you since then."

"I have watched you since you were a child," I said. "As I watched your mother. I wondered who of your line would find Alkemara again."

· 5 ·

IT was true—I had been at her window one night, in the rain, several stories above the ground several years before though it barely seemed like several nights to me.

She was not yet eighteen, and the man she loved was a mortal predator who would have destroyed her.

And I had watched Natalia Waterhouse since her childhood, as I had watched the generations of her family before.

The man named Vieri Montealegro pursued Natalia only for her wealth and family connections; the Waterhouse fortune was vast and crossed continents.

When I grabbed Montealegro in my embrace, I drank from him until dawn, until the silk sheets of his bed were flooded in his life's essence.

After I departed his bedroom, my curiosity about the girl of seventeen overwhelmed me. I rose upward to her bedroom window to see her. I wished to see her, just once, as I had seen her mother and her grandmother before her.

For a moment, I suppose, she saw me there, outside her window, my great wings spread out like a dragon angel in the rain, my cloak drawn over my form yet my face visible.

I knew it was a risk to be there, but I had protected this bloodline as no other among the mortal realm. I could smell the blood of its descendants, and this one, Natalia, was special.

I was curious about her, this descendant of that line, looking so much like one I had once known in that ancient century barely remembered even by the hidden ones of the earth. It was as if the one I had known in my early century had lived in the blood, to emerge in Natalia's face, the reincarnation of a woman I had once loved.

What I saw tore at my heart, but she lay upon her bed sobbing as if the world had ended for her when her false lover had been killed.

When Montealegro's body was found, she must have known that her grandmother's stories of the vampyres were true.

Perhaps this, more than anything, had set her on her course of studies, crossing between the occult and mythology and the histories of buried places.

◆ 6 ◆

ONE twilight in our shared tomb, I awoke to see her standing over me.

As my eyes focused, I saw she held a scroll in her hand, half of it drawn down, the parchment torn.

"This tells of explorations by the ancients," she said. "Of traveling the world, the entire *world,* thousands of years before the discovery of the Americas. This could rewrite all known history."

"History is a half-truth, written by conquerors," I said. I rose, pointing to other scrolls. "Those are tales of the other races of beings who shared the Earth with mortals, though the originals of these scrolls were destroyed in the fires of Alexandria's libraries. Once, there were many species of what you would call humans, not just the ones who blanketed the Earth these past several thousand years. There were technologies before my birth that rival those in existence in this century. Histories are burned and buried and revised. Conquerors turn the gods of the vanquished into demons. Do you think legends you have studied were born from lies? For you see me here now as you saw me at your window when you were seventeen." I allowed my wings to unfold from my shoulder blades. "I, too, am legend, as all the tribes of Alkemara are legend, though you see us now as true."

After I had drunk from her, just before dawn, I passed her that manuscript of my first years upon the Earth. This tale ended in my capture, and the capture of my companion, Ewen, by the whispering shadows of the Myrrydanai, and of our imprisonment in an ancient Roman well, cast there by the power of the Myrrydanai, sealed with lead and silver to keep us from escaping what would seem a tomb for many years.

That night, after she had spent the day reading what I had written of my youth and my first journey to Alkemara, she begged me to drink from her as if her offering was a way of thanking me for this newfound knowledge.

◆ 7 ◆

DURING those nights together, I took her up in my arms into the curved cavern that held the magnificent fallen city.

Ever upward we flew, into a sky full of jeweled stars beyond the slender opening of the mountain that covered Alkemara like a shell. She held tight to me, overcoming fears of falling, of dying.

By the eighth night we spent together, I brought her into the experience of the stream itself, that current that runs among the immortals of the world.

I told her that she was the first living mortal to feel it course about her, to feel the connections between those of my species and hers.

She whispered that I had given her the greatest gift of her entire life.

"I will give you more than this," I promised. "For there is a secret of Alkemara that has been meant for you. It has been held here for centuries until one of your bloodline returned."

✦ 8 ✦

W E sat up along the steps at the entrance to the Temple of Lemesharra. She gasped in wonder at monuments and the fallen cityscape, the walls, the houses and chambers, the carvings of glyphs along columns. But most of all, she was shocked by the beauty of our tribe, many of whom flew above us, out into the night for their hunt. "I knew you existed," she said. "But I didn't fully believe it. But now, there is a race. Not merely a few of your tribe—but a population."

"Perhaps a million or more of us, for even I do not know of all of my kind. Some of us are . . . different from others. Some come from the west, and their history is another path that was not known to my tribe for many thousands of years. In some centuries, there are fewer of us, but we flourish when the Veil is thin."

"Is it thin now?" she asked.

"Yes. I can feel its fabric stretching. There are shadows that seek to return to the earth. There is much still hidden from the world of mortals," I said. "Much that is unseen or unnoticed. I have lived among your cities for centuries, as have others of this nest. We return here in times of trouble, or in times of omens of the descending dark. This is a sacred place to us and will remain so."

When she first arrived, Natalia had several boxes and satchels, as well as supplies brought in by her workers. These now lay strewn about the entryway to Alkemara. She asked that I find a particular satchel that had been among her belongings when she and her assistants entered Alkemara's realm. I called to Daniel to find it and retrieve it for us. He returned with several boxes, as did other vampyres, bringing them to the steps of the temple.

Sifting through these, Natalia lifted up the brown satchel, unbuckling its stay. "I want to show you something passed down for many years," she said. From within the satchel, she brought out a small pouch. From it, she drew a dried purple flower. She set this on the step between us.

"The graveyard flower," I said. I pointed over the crumbling walls, many miles from where we sat. "It still grows there, among the bones. It is native to the ancient city, Myrryd, which lies in ruins not yet found by mortals. Merod grew the flower here, again, having rescued it before the city of his birth was destroyed. An alchemist once stole it and carried it to distant shores. It was not meant for mortal use."

She reached into the pouch and withdrew what looked like a wolf's tooth. A tiny hole had been drilled through it, as if it had been worn as a charm. She held a small, rounded talisman in her hand. On the back of it, strange symbols as of some ancient prayer. On the front of it, a cracked mirror.

I looked these over, turning them in my fingers, remembering the battles I had once seen, remembering the shapeshifting Chymer women, speaking with the dead, calling up spirits to aid them, and running as wolves in the night.

"This." I held up the wolf's tooth. "Wolves were plentiful in those days. The dead and dying covered the battlefields of the world. Wolves and wild cats developed a taste for human flesh, for it rotted at the edge of the forest. They were a terror. This tooth is from someone who shifts, and becomes a wolf through sorcery. There were women who had once been nuns—anchoresses—who had . . . changed when plagues came to the land. When the Veil tears—"

"This 'graveyard flower'? Is it merely a memento, or does it have properties?"

"You're a scholar and a scientist," I said. "You have tested this?"

She nodded. "It seems to be some throwback of the poppy, but with properties of a carnivorous plant. A fly-trap, perhaps."

"These are a bit of poison, really. When in the ground, it will curl about the finger and prick the skin to draw a bit of blood. For the vampyre, its nectar is a powerful drug that gives us second sight or draws us beyond the Veil itself." I picked up the dried purple blossom and pressed it to my lips, inhaling its slightly bitter rose odor. "This has no nectar left in it. It was called the Sang-Fleur by the French — the blood flower."

"And to immortals, it brought visions?"

"What does not kill us opens our eyes." I picked up the small, rounded mirror with its spiderweb cracks. It was only a bit larger than my thumb. "A highborn of a certain kingdom would wear this about the neck, an amulet. It is the Disk. In Taranis-Hir, it protected one from the winged devil. Do you see the writing? It is a prayer that simply says, 'Virgin of Shadows, Mother of Darkness, Keep Us Safe.'"

She looked at the statue of Lemesharra. The two vipers that entwined about the statue's sandals, each with a different goddess face, all aspects of Medhya herself. "Why would a people pray to a mother of darkness?"

I thought a moment, and said, "Because they are frightened by the terror that comes by night, and the shadow by day. Because plagues killed many, and winged devils blanketed the skies. Terror makes captives of many." I picked over the objects she laid out upon the crumbling steps. "I imagine with these things, you also found maps. Passed from your great-grandmother. Passed from her great-grandfather. Passed down so far back in the centuries that no one knows the name of the person who first held these things in her hands."

"Her?"

I nodded. "I knew the original owners of these objects, Natalia."

After a minute of silence, she said, "Yes. One of the maps is of this place. Of this temple."

"Which is why you found it so quickly, when for centuries men have sought it in vain," I said. "Why now, Natalia? Why are you here?"

She reached down to the satchel and drew out papers wrapped in plastic. The first was a map to Alkemara—it had once belonged to the alchemist, Artephius. She turned the map over. On the back was written, "The tomb of the Maz-Sherah," with a legend key to the map.

I turned the map over again. A rounded star had been drawn at the place where my tomb rested. The ancient language of the alchemists had been scrawled about the parchment, and designs for machines and devices had been sketched upon it. The mapmaker had known exactly where I would be in a future century. Artephius had done this so that one of the descendants would find me. "He had known I would come," I said. "Long before I was born, I was meant to come here. And Artephius had *known*."

"It is this map," Natalia said, "that drew me to the study of the ancient world. When I was a little girl of eight, I found it among my mother's papers, locked and hidden away as if it were a treasure map. I had stolen the key from the small silver purse that she kept deep in her middle dresser drawer. I tried every strongbox and trunk I could find in our house, but the key fit nothing. One afternoon when my parents were in their studies, I knew I had a few hours to hunt. At the back of a wardrobe in the false attic of our house, beneath piles of carefully wrapped clothes and stacks of paintings from my mother's youth as an artist, I found a wide mahogany box with filigree inlaid upon it.

"When I looked at the silver clasp of the box, I saw it was in the shape of a wolf's head. I opened it to find documents and titles, money from other countries that had no doubt been collected as some ancestor traveled the world and came, eventually, to London at the start of the twentieth century. I found these things, and they captured my imagination. I often looked at these objects and this map in particular. One night, my mother caught me as I pored over these things. She was furious that I had gone through her things. She told me she kept them, as she did those amateur paintings of her early years as a struggling artist, purely for sentimental reasons, but they were private. I asked her why they were locked away. She told me that children break and destroy things. She didn't want to bring these out until we were older and less likely to damage them. She made me swear that I would never again go to this wardrobe or this box. I took that oath, but broke the promise almost immediately. She had hidden the key again, and I could not find it, but I went to the wardrobe. Sifting through those paintings of her girlhood, I saw one of a beautiful man. I could not tell if he was seventeen or twenty, but he looked as if he had been cut from sinew and muscle. His lips were thick, his eyes narrow, and his hair covered his forehead and fell down nearly to his shoulders. I had never seen such a young man as he before. My mother had captured something from memory, and had painted it—this young man who looked dangerous and alluring, and became my dream as a girl. It was you. I knew the moment I saw you, at the window. Do you remember? It was your portrait. She also had seen you in her life. You had . . . guarded her?"

I kept my eyes steady, for I did not wish to speak of her mother to her. Her mother had seen me by accident—I had not wished to reveal myself to her. I meant only to watch the bloodline and protect it from harm until the one would come to find Alkemara, when the Veil had grown thin again.

She continued, "I imagined the map from memory, and tried to draw it several times. I begged my parents for a world globe for Christmas. When it arrived that year, I searched it for this city, this country, but could not find it. I became obsessed as a teenager with history.

When I entered college, I quizzed my professors and signed on for any digs in the Middle East, in hopes of finding this place. I spoke of this map, and generally received the smirks of colleagues and professors, as if I had a map of El Dorado in my back pocket. As my studies grew more serious, I begged my mother for the box and the map. She told me I had imagined the map, or that it had been a child's drawing. I was able to fund my doctoral work working for rich men who sought out treasures from the lost kingdoms of the ancient world. I went on hundreds of digs and studied pieces of ancient documents and worked with translators on what seemed long-dead languages unknown to many. I eventually found a manuscript in which you are mentioned by name. It was within the urns of the Taranis-Hir dig. Aleric Attheffelde. Aleric, Falconer. The monk who wrote this—Brother Micahel—mentions a 'lost century.'"

"That is what it was called by those who remembered," I said. "But it was not entirely a century, though it seemed it. Please, continue. This monk fascinates me."

"Micahel's papers were considered fraudulent and heretical. He was later brought before an ecclesiastical council and tried on charges of witchcraft and murder and sodomy."

"He was sentenced to burn," I said, nodding. "But somehow, this never came to pass."

"Brother Micahel had written an account of this lost century. Within it, he spoke of several plagues of nearly Biblical proportions—of a stinging pestilence, of fire from the sky, of what sounds like earthquakes and tidal waves. He writes of a changing climate as well—taking place over a mere two years. He drew creatures with tentacles as long and thick as oaks, and of something called the plague maiden, though I am not sure if this is a creature or merely the mood of his age. Much of his manuscript rotted or was destroyed, but these pieces are intact. He mentions the city of Taranis-Hir, and a Lady White-Horse who practiced what he called 'bog sorcery.' He claimed that this age of mankind was in chaos, and was neither of the Devil nor of God. He brings up the heresies of spirit-possession by 'shadows.' And this." She picked up the cracked mirror amulet. "The disk, and upon it, a small, curved looking glass. Yet the pieces of this puzzle are missing. You have the answers, don't you?"

I touched the objects on the steps again, as if they brought me some comfort. "How did your mother come to pass you these things?"

"She died. I . . . could not be there . . . but my cousins sent me some things she had set aside for me. I received the box and its key after her death, along with a letter from her. She knew I would pro-tect it."

"Will you?"

She nodded. "But I must know of this time. This lost century. You are the Maz-Sherah. The meaning of the word is ancient, but it roughly means 'messiah.' Your kind is mentioned in the old myths of this area. There are both Arab and European accounts during the Crusades of the 'winged demons of Hedammu.'"

"Hedammu was buried beneath a new and shining city," I said. "A tourist city."

"I know," she said. "It was there—when I worked with Professor Clarendon—that I found this."

She drew a small jewel box from within the satchel. Opening it, she withdrew a flat yet slightly curved piece of gold, as if a shard from a plate. She placed it in the palm of my hand. I did not even need to look at it, for I felt its power.

She said, "It's not from the area of Hedammu. It's from thou-sands of miles away. Within another tomb of your kind. We found hundreds of bone fragments of the dead, but no ordinary bones. We found the skeleton of a female. In her mouth: teeth like a saber-toothed tiger's fangs. Outstretched, connected at her shoulder blades, wings like . . . a pterodactyl."

"Or a dragon's," I said. I let the small gold piece drop onto her lap and rested my hand at her throat. I felt the warmth of her pulse. The thought of her blood comforted me. She drew my hand from her throat, brought it to her lips. "It is an ancient resting place for our kind, and the one from whom this gold came had asked to be taken there, to rest with her tribe." I glanced up into her warm eyes. "You know more of this than you say."

"In her letter to me, my mother wrote of an ancestor," she said. "And in Micahel's manuscript, her name appears on a list of the damned, along with the name Aleric, Falconer, the Maz-Sherah of the vampyres. You. Alkemara. Merod Al Kamr. White Robes. So many others."

"And you wish to hear of these times that have not been spoken of in hundreds of years? The age that shrouded history from the eyes of those who came after—when the unmaking of the world had begun. You, Natalia, were guided to Micahel's manuscript as you have been guided here. It is important you hear of those times, particularly in this world now, for the Veil grows thin again. Somewhere, someone seeks to tear it." I reached over to her, clasping my hand over hers.

"I am not afraid of you," she whispered. "And I am not afraid of death. But I want to know all you know of this time, and this place."

I opened my shirt, to expose the mark branded upon my flesh.

I brought her hand to it so that she could feel the ridges of it.

"It was engraved with a branding iron upon all of us in the prisons," I said. "And would not heal. Do you see?" She seemed to recognize the same markings on the rounded scar that she had seen on the back of the mirror disk. "It is a talisman of an ancient age. You were drawn here, Natalia, by something more than war and artifact. You were drawn here because the blood of an ancient race flows within your body." I brought her hand to my lips. "I can smell your past within you. The blood of one family is distinct from other blood. The blood that courses through you still holds the vibrations of that Age of the Serpent and the Veil. And this," I lifted the broken mirror up to the emerging moonlight that shone through the crack that ran along the cavernous mountain peak above us, "was the sixth plague of that age, for a dream of a disk that shone like a moon's corona appeared to many over several nights. Dreams get into our blood, Natalia, and do not leave. This dream infected all who slept and all who existed in that time."

I began the story of those years of my captivity, and of those who came after.

Each successive dawn, before the sun found me, I drank from her as payment for the tale of my existence, as Scheherazade was once paid for her tales with the promise of survival until the following night.

I write this from the telling of it. I write what I know, and what I learned from others in that century, hundreds of years in the past.

◆ 9 ◆

I awoke from the Plague Dream as if an enormous explosion had occurred in the world, though it was a whisper sent through many of us.

The sounds of the dying on the surface of the earth, and the cries of war and of terror; the earth itself trembling and changing; the climatic burning and freezing; the Veil ripping further, as any fabric will tear and tear and continue tearing once a small thread has been pulled; while I, and my companion Ewen, drank from each other's throats that we might not go into the most dreaded of deaths, that hell within the particles of flesh, that vampyres call the Extinguishing.

It was the Age of the Serpent and the Veil.

We believed in our gods and the Otherworld, then.

We feared them, as well.

◆ 10 ◆

EVEN among the undead, the vampyres of the Medhyic line, there is disagreement over our beliefs and our gods. Silver, they said, destroys us. Mirrors do not reflect us—for having no soul, we cannot have a reflection. Drinking from other vampyres was believed to destroy our race.

Yet, I have sustained silver daggers to my body.

I have seen more than my reflection in a mirror—I have seen another world.

I have known of a mirror forged from gold and glass and silver and shadows caught between the Veil that separates the worlds. Broken, its shards passed into this world, taken by the Priests of Blood and Flesh and Shadow, hidden within the artifacts of ritual. When the Priest of Blood took me into the visions of the Veil, it was through the Glass itself—that shard of the Medhya's mirror that remained embedded in the Veil, showing what is and what is to come.

Yet all of this was mere legend to me, in captivity, once the Nahhashim staff had been stolen from me. Once the shadow priests had taken over the mind of my beloved, Alienora.

Once the earth itself trembled and the lost age began.

I spent years in a prison beneath the earth, and shared my blood—tainted with the graveyard flower's nectar, called by some the Serpent's Venom, by others the Flesh of Medhya—with another vampyre, that we might survive our captivity.

Even the legends and prophecies of our kind may be interpreted many ways.

Merod Al Kamr had said to me in his tomb at Alkemara, "There is a final prophecy you do not know, Maz-Sherah. It must be broken. It is of the end of all mortal life and the destruction of the Veil and the Glass, a time of monsters and madness. The only hope is to raise the Nahhashim. Only the possessor of the staff may do so. Sacrifices will be made. Sorceries will burn the skies. Many will extinguish. Many will fail. The staff is the source. You cannot let any other take it from you. You cannot give it. Keep it close at all times, for within it is something more powerful than even the Veil, though I do not know what it may be . . . Medhya is gathering skins of humans, and her Myrrydanai swallow souls. They create an army of the spirit, using the Veil itself to bring the shades and banished demons into a monstrous existence. Even now, they whisper in the minds of men, and seek to destroy those who have touched the Maz-Sherah. They are unleashing the Old Gods as well, the giants and the beasts held back by the Veil for thousands of years. One day, the war will begin, and you must lead our tribe and protect the flock of humanity both for their sakes and for your own. You must protect those from whom you drink life, or life will be no more."

This is the only truth I know of my existence—these words of prophecy from the Priest of Blood, Merod Al Kamr, spoken to me in a lost century, in the buried city of Alkemara.

But it was through visions when I first became vampyre that I learned of those other sacred objects that I would need to possess to fulfill my destiny.

The mask, from which the piece of gold still exists, was only one of them.

◆ 11 ◆

YOU have heard of my early life, until late in my nineteenth year, when a vampyre called Pythia, a Pythoness of ancient days, brought me into immortality.

You have read my first testament of how my companions and I followed the Serpentine Path to the buried kingdom of Alkemara.

You have heard of Merod, the Priest of Blood, whose very existence lives within me, though I had yet to unlock the secret of it. I returned to my home in Brittany, to Alienora, my beloved, who had given herself to the whispering Myrrydanai shadows. The shadow priests threw me, along with my beloved friend Ewen, into a deep and ancient dry well where once I myself, as a boy, had found a vampyre of many years, sealed in a prison of silver and lead.

Though I tell this story of the Serpentine Path within the Vampyricon, I am but one vessel among many that holds its essence. In those days, in what is now called the Medieval Age but was for me the Age of the Serpent and the Veil, I slept in a well of demons. I had been trapped by the maiden I once loved. She had turned to sorcery and to the shadow priests, who had come with the great whisper of plague. Above me, the earth itself trembled, and the shadows of the Myrrydanai possessed much of the mortal realm.

We existed in a time of legend.

In that age, new monsters would be born. I saw them, in a dream.

In the dream, the Virgin of Shadows came to me. She was but a halo of a maiden in darkness.

The Virgin of Shadows spoke of tidings from the Dark Madonna. She told of the White Robes, who would come as shadows from the holy night. "These are angels who will guard and guide you," she said. "Do not fear them, you who are pure in your offerings and who honor your king and queen. The White Robes see what is within your soul, and you shall have no fear. But those of you who harbor secrets and transgression, who break the laws of this world and the next, you will live in horror of their retribution."

She spoke of the great cataclysms of the Earth, and of the plagues released from the hand of the eternal against the transgressions of mankind.

The Virgin of Shadows spoke of heresy, and traitors, and those Old Ways that needed the torch of purification. She spoke of the apocalypse visited upon earth for a thousand years. "You see the signs of this end of days," she said. "For, have not winged devils crossed the skies? Is Hell not unleashed from below? The Great Crossing comes. The White Robes bring sanctity to your lands. Turn to the Disk for your soul's protection." Above her, as she spoke, the golden Disk shone with an aurora about its ring. "Hear ye all nations of mortal life: the House of White-Horse shall be the earthly home of the spirit. It shall rise up, a new and shining kingdom, from the ashes of the plagues. It shall arise at the edge of a humble forest, in Brittany, from the ruins of a Roman city and a queen's barrow. All honor the Lady White-Horse, and the White Robes who stand with her."

I was not alone in having this dream.

It was visited upon every man, woman, and child alive in those years, for a thousand leagues in each direction from where I lay in captivity. Perhaps it had even been dreamed of across the seas, in those forgotten continents, unknown to those of my country. Inquisitions to root out this new heresy had begun, but the plagues themselves wiped out the inquisitors; Rome denied the divinity of the dream, but many ignored the Pope's decree, for they felt truth in the dream of the Disk and the Virgin of Shadows. They saw the cataclysms—the fires across the sky, the frozen seas, the fertile orchards turned to wastelands in a season, the hand of winter that held the Earth in its grip for many months beyond the season. Medhya, the Dark Madonna, had cast her shadow across all of mankind.

She had come in plagues through the Veil itself.

The dream of the virgin came to all who were vampyres, descendants of the bloodline of Medhya, and of the father who guarded the Veil between worlds who was called the Great Serpent.

Within that dream, the Disk itself. It was round and silver some would say when they saw it in a dream; no, round and gold like a mask, others would say; like a halo of a saint; like a rounded pit of an ancient well, others would guess.

To just a handful of us who saw the Disk in our dreams, it was made of a fiery gold, with the face of a Gorgon at the center.

A mask within a corona of light.

It was the second face of that terrible goddess from whom the Priests of Blood stole power. The first face was called Medhya, the Dark Madonna.

This second face was Datbathani.

The Lady of Serpents.

During the plagues that rode with the whispering shadows, thousands in Europe died within the space of a year. The first plague was of insects; the next of ice; a fever brought fire beneath the skin that ate flesh from the inside out; the death cry, which sounded over all the Earth; the fifth plague was the great shattering that attacked bones beneath the flesh and broke them; and the sixth, the dream itself, which infected and brought fever to many. It was prophesied by the shadow priests that a seventh plague was yet to be released, but the White Robes held it back with their rituals of purification.

Thousands more turned to the Disk and its dream to protect them.

Many men opposed this new sect of worship and saw in it a true heresy. And there were those in the world, as well, who sought to end the rule of the White Robes and the Baroness who had arisen, as if queen of an unknown country, from the dust of my homeland, a place now considered sacred to the Virgin of Shadows, the Mother of Purification.

Wars began. England fought, and Normandy invaded the barony. The Anjou sent a battalion with the blessings of the Pope as a special crusade. These armies were driven out by devils and plagues and would not return to oppose the White Robes again.

A reign of terror began to spread to other lands and other kingdoms. It moved with the plagues, and created fear and panic among many. Of your age, you know the inquisitions and the burnings that came into being a hundred years after my first age—but in these years lost to history, there were threefold more.

Along the roads, men were crucified; women were burned in special festival nights. Any outsider was suspect, and many were arrested as traitors.

Drawing from princes and children of barons and dukes, none of whom were first sons of their own kingdoms, the new Baroness Enora—once known to me as Alienora—and her nobles brought them into the new city as Knights of the Disk. With them, many soldiers of other lands were conscripted, promised both freedom from the plagues and blessings in the hereafter as rewards for service. A monastery arose where the abbey had fallen, and these monks were little more than a death cult, with their blue smoke incense and flagellations and sacred skulls and bones drawn from the ashes of purified heretics.

It was a tumultuous time, and few could escape the influence of the White Robes. These creatures of shadows, the Myrrydanai, had drawn human skin across their faces. They wore the radiant cloaks of priests so none would know their true nature, yet all felt the shadows of these creatures when they brushed by.

My dear Natalia, I was not alone in these times, for others gathered at this crossroads of the mortal and immortal, vampyre and human, just as I bring you into the stream now. Even those who were my sworn enemies told me of their meetings at the crossroads. I bring you news of these events as they experienced them, as I knew them. As no mortal before you has heard the tale.

First, I will tell you of a creature of rags and ash who disturbed the stream itself and caused it to rise that I might feel it in my prison beneath the earth.

In my visions I first saw this creature. The Sight is like a theater of the mind—the film plays, but in three dimensions, and you enter it, you observe it and move around the people who inhabit the vision, yet you cannot touch or interact with them.

But behind your eyes, in your mind, it burns its images and sounds into your memory. I had thousands of visions that drove me mad, of what the hounds of Medhya had done to the earth.

I saw, in such endless visions, the new city rise above the earth with its many white towers.

I saw the magnificence and terror of it.

I saw the new Dark Age come, brought on by the whispers of the shadows as they tore the Veil and ripped the skin of the world.

BOOK ONE

OUR LADY OF CROSSROADS

"That orbed maiden with white fire laden,
Whom mortals call the moon."

—Percy Bysshe Shelley, "The Cloud"

I
AFTER THE PLAGUES

◆ CHAPTER 2 ◆

◆ 1 ◆

THOUGH I was captive, still I had visions of what lay above me. These were like waking dreams, and would come to me at twilight or before dawn. Sometimes it was as if I flew across the sky and looked downward at the Earth and its people. I watched the shadows bring darkness from the other side. I saw with their eyes as they rode the mists, spreading pestilence in their wake. Though I speak of this now, I saw much in the visions and learned more from others later, but I shall tell you of these sights and wonders as they existed.

The forest of my birth had been drawn back against rock and cliff, a skin pulled back to expose the skull of the Earth, torn by fire and by cataclysm. An age of early winter descended, casting ice across lakes and frost that would not let loose the tree root until brief summer's arrival.

The earth had been carved out; mines plundered. Where a modest castle of a distinguished baron once covered a low hillside surrounded by other hills and fields and village and abbey, now a walled city and seven white towers arose like the upturned fangs of a giant wolf. Taranis-Hir, it was called, though I would not learn of this until later—an ancient name for the slopes upon which the city was built. The hill had been a burial mound of a long-dead queen of the land, her reputation all but lost to history by the time of my birth. The barrow of her grave and its attendant chambers encompassed three low hills. They had been dug by the quarriers, cutters, and hewers, their treasures plundered from the many chambers of the necropolis beneath the old castle. To the south, the quarries became mines. To the north they dipped below the Akkadite Cliffs. The caves beneath— much of the land had caverns underground, carved by buried waterways within that ring of what had once been my village—were opened and made useful for this new citadel. White caelum stone had been brought up from the barrow passages and chipped at by artisans and craftsmen until it seemed as shiny as a milky crystal—some said it looked like ice itself. Silver and iron had been mined in the area, creating desolation where woods had previously grown wild. These metals became a major trade, while the foundries attracted laborers from the fields and forests who had lost all during the plagues.

Taranis-Hir resembled no other fortress or city in all of Christendom. Its high walls gleamed with the native caelum stone, and its pinnacled towers dominated the horizon from all vantage points of the forest and surrounding cliffs. The smoke from its foundry and furnaces blackened the air with great plumes. It was a city of pilgrims and vagrants, merchants and soldiers, alchemists and priests; and the foundrymen who worked on the transmutive metals of the alchemist from the East, with his sciences and calculations, the architect of this city; and the scarred beggars who cleaned the furnaces and foundry, called ashlings for their appearance.

Some believed the furnaces that burned eternally in the white towers were Hell-Gate itself—but these were the Akkadites on the far cliffs of the lands. Few of them ever entered the walled city that had arisen after the six plagues, for many had already been put to the sword and the pyre for such a journey. Those Akkadites—or any traitor or heretic or foreign enemy—who did enter the walled city, could be found—if alive—in the Barrow-Depths awaiting the block or the Illumination Nights; or in the hanging cages that were strung along the outside walls, over the canals, slowly starving to death as winter came.

These visions came to me, for I had been once touched by the Veil, and through it I saw more than I desired as I lay with my companion in our rounded subterranean prison.

I saw the stranger who would come to us, though I could not see her face.

I did not know if she meant to destroy us, or to free us.

◆ 2 ◆

IT was eleven years into my captivity. In my visions, I saw daylight for the first time in years. Even in my mind's eye this brilliant light nearly blinded me, yet was tempered by shadows that existed in that land.

Captivity had sharpened my ability for the Sight. It had become stronger the more years that passed, though sometimes it reduced to a glimmer rather than a full-blown vision. Yet this one vision, of a strange maiden of rags and ashes, and her seeking of the necromantic sisterhood stood out, was overwhelming to me, and had the quality more of physical reality than simply a vision.

I saw the great belching black smoke from the furnaces that towered over the walls of the city as if half the kingdom were on fire. A dark plume eclipsed the seven towers and rose into the air where, it was believed, the ashes of the dead sought Heaven. Ash fell like snowflakes upon the streets. Some of the motes of gray ash blew out toward the abandoned lands, and some may have reached the Akkadite Cliffs that rose far to the north of the kingdom.

Far below the smoke, within the outer walls where common folk plied their trades down alleyways within the maze of low streets of the citadel, a creature wrapped in rags strode with purpose through those places of whores and beggars and the merchants of disease and death.

"This murderer's head! This abomination to the New Kingdom!" a one-handed swordsman shouted as if to the dead man's head thrust upon the pike. He pointed with the end of his forearm, which had been fitted with a small hand-sized trident. "This man betrayed his own son! He betrayed our Lord and Lady! He betrayed the White Robes! He has defiled the Disk! He betrayed the people of our land and defiled the memory of those who died in the six plagues! Many nights did he spend in the cages, and you saw him and heard his blasphemy if you walked along St. Taranis bridge, did you not? Before I cut off this head, I cut off his hands! And his feet! And still he cried out his heresies! To suffer such a fate, surely his crimes were of the worst, the darkest, the most devilish of crimes against our city!"

The swordsman crouched to gather up the coins and rings tossed to him, and to wrap up the salted cod and loaf of bread. He muttered mostly to himself, "They don't come out so much after the frost."

Why? I asked the Priest of Blood who dwelled within me, *Why do I see this now? Why do I hear the voices? Let me see others, those I care for, let me see what has happened to the Forest women, to Alienora, and show me the grave of my child that I might mourn. Do not show me this dirty place with its blackguards and knaves.*

Yet I received nothing but silence, and the vision of the swordsman and alley continued as I lay, eyes closed, in an ancient well.

Behind my eyes:

When the narrow, crooked street emptied, the swordsman sat on an upturned barrel as if hoping for something more. A beggar-woman played her sorrowful songs down at the end of the street, right where it turned off onto the next lane.

By twilight, the lone creature in rags came, offering the swordsman several good coins—the just tribute for the relics of the dead, he told her solemnly, pointing his trident hand at her. Echoing through the chill, the beggar-woman at the street's end sang of some lost love and of the times before the Akkadites and before the seas turned to ice and before the White Robes themselves.

The ragged creature glanced back at the singer at the entry to the backstreet. "You are Thomas Cutter," she said.

The swordsman nodded. "Executioner, pig-butcher, and merchant-soldier. And . . ." He glanced at the executed man's head. "Merchant of other items."

A maiden in rags, I thought, as he watched her. *A whore, perhaps. Why must I see this vision? Merod? Do you show me what I must see, or does my mind's eye wander aimlessly because of the torn Veil itself?*

"A beautiful voice," the ragged one said when the singer had stopped her beautiful song. "But she sings of such sad things."

"Her voice may be pretty," Thomas Cutter said, "but she is a blight. Sorrow needs no singer, they say. I miss the *trouvères* who once wandered here. When I was a boy, the language of love was in the songs. Now, it's sorrow and bitter snow." Thomas Cutter drew the head from the pike, thrusting the trident-hand into the thick of the neck. He glanced this way and that to ensure he would not be observed. "I want more than coin for this head, miss," he muttered. "It's my own head should anyone squeal about it."

"What you wish, I will pay," she said, her voice as soft as rabbit fur.

He grinned. "Let me see your face, pretty one."

When the stranger drew the cloth from about her visage, I still could not see her. I watched as if floating in the air just above them.

Cutter gasped. "Eh, you," he said, his lips curling as if he'd bitten into a sour apple. "Enough, enough. You could have warned me. I've seen you in the Barrow-Depths, my dear. Dancing for rings and trinkets. I did not think you would leave the foundry in daylight. I don't deal in ashlings much."

Ashling. The word was unfamiliar to me, though I knew that girls who worked the hearths in castles were called ash-maids. This intrigued me further, for there seemed something familiar about this ragged woman. Her voice, too, tickled a memory, though I could not quite place its origin. Had I met her before?

"I am called many names," she said. "Ashling is merely one of them."

"You furnace wenches all have the mark upon you. Do you look for scraps here, ashling? You a Deathmonger?"

"No."

"Good thing," he said. "I'd not sell you a head for a day and a night if you were." He said this in such a way that it sounded precisely as if he would sell to any Deathmonger who came along. He glanced about to make sure no guard stood by, nor the overlookers who reported such black-market selling as this.

He looked up along the rooftops, gasping, as if he'd seen a shadow cross the sky.

For the barest moment, I was sure he somehow could see me— though how could this be? I lay in the bottom of a sealed well, deep in the earth. My mind traveled through visions, but my body could not exist in his view.

Do you see me, Thomas Cutter? I was sure he could not, but was there a ghost image of me there, in the air, just above them? He looked right through me.

"The Morns like day's end. Chilly. In the summer, they're scarce, but with the frost . . . Morns love the cold, the quarriers say. They should know, down in the barrow-ways with them at dawn." He shivered. "Couldn't do that kind of work myself. No, no, no."

"The day passes too swiftly," the ashling said, also glancing upward, staring right into me yet not seeing me. *What did they watch for in the skies?* I wondered. *What are these "Morns"?*

She glanced back down at him. "Still, it's early yet, and I imagine your hook would give a Morn a scrape it would not soon forget."

He removed the small trident from the lifeless neck. "A trident, ashling. Not a hook. I can't stand hooks. I look at it sometimes and almost feel like these are fingers now. Look, you see? Are these three prongs not like fingers?" He waved the trident around, near her face.

"Was it a plague or a transgression?"

He shrugged. "A hand in the wrong place means a hand on the block, don't it? Had to hack off my own hand, ashling, that I did. It were law, and the White Robes stood about to make sure I did it good and proper. Everything's a risk, though, ain't it?"

She held out two more coins. "Is this enough?"

"To have so much," Thomas Cutter said, "you must be grasping at pockets somewheres."

"I am favored by the more fortunate who see my . . . condition . . . as reason enough to give me tokens of their pity," she said, passing him the money.

"Whoring pays well," he muttered as he looked at the bracelets that jangled at her wrist and the twelve rings upon her left hand. He flicked his tongue at his lower lip as if he could eat the bracelets. She let the cloth fall across her wrists, covering them.

Thomas Cutter lifted the dead man's head by the scalp.

Eyes shut, mouth open, tongue hanging.

I could not recognize the man's face, for it had rotted enough to obscure the more telling features.

Cutter chuckled to himself, shaking his head slightly as if remembering an old joke. "Once knew this poor bastard, I did. He were good with sword and horse, quite kind to some, rough to others. You would never believe it, ashling, but I once rode alongside him in the hunt, when I was barely more than a lad. Did not think he'd have turned against us."

The ashling drew a rough sack from the many folds of her cloak.

Thomas Cutter put the convict's head in the sack, tying its end strings carefully. "For some foul ritual, no doubt. Are you an *Akka-dite*? I don't serve no Akkadites here."

"I am but an ashling," she said, "burdened with scars of the fevers."

"If it's witchcraft, I can't know. You understand? If it's some foul magick, I still expect the head back as is. As is. No carvings, no tattoos, no bits of flesh missing. And don't let them that flies find you with it. They may not be so forgiving as Thomas Cutter, swordsman of Taranis-Hir. I expect to see you back here soon, ashling. Yes?"

"You shall see me again, Thomas Cutter, as surely as the sun rises across the western wood," she said. The ashling took the sack from him and tied its strings about the corded belt beneath her outer cloak.

Before she had walked far down the alley, Thomas Cutter whispered, "Return it to me before dawn, or it will be *your* head on the North Gate pikes next."

• 3 •

I N the Sight, I followed the ashling as she went down the lane. As the ashling passed by the beggar-singer, she drew a ring from her finger. She tossed it into the singer's lap. "It is sweet to remember the past," the ashling said.

The singer nodded and thanked her by singing of the time before the trembling land and the burning rocks, when the countryside of the Bretons flourished in springtime; and of the reigns of the Duke, and the kings of France and England and the legendary queens who brought courtly love to the kingdoms; when the wars were distant and fought for holiness and honor; when winter was but a short season, and the harvest a long one full of dancing and joy; when the ships sailed the seas and returned with treasures; and of those legends from many years past of King Arthur and his knights and his unfaithful queen, of Prince Tristan and Isolde, in the days before the Disk, before the White Robes, before the plagues; in the days when the marshes were thick, the Great Forest was endless, and before the winged devils came from the sky.

◆ 4 ◆

T H E ashling wandered the alleyways until she came to the road be-yond the wall, paid her tribute for passage, gave her destination as "the fields." The guards scrutinized her, but when she showed her face, they let her pass as if she had offered them death itself. She waited at the edge of the western canal for a boatman.

"How far?" the boatman asked as he drew his boat to the shore. He was an elderly man wrapped in the thinnest of cloths, shivering from the cold.

"As far as can be gone," she said. She passed some coins to the old man and boarded his boat. The man sighed as he nestled down be-tween the oars. A near-tropical steam came from the waters. All around the edge of the canal, black pots filled with the caelum stone and dry wood burned. I could only guess this kept the canals from freezing over.

I tried to look about, to see others, to see more of the city around this—but my vision only allowed me to watch the ashling below.

"Few of your age survived the early plagues. Do you remember the old times?" she asked.

The man looked at her, as if trying to guess the intent of her question. "Before the plagues. And the dream."

"These were marshes," she said. "And thick woods."

"Before the storms and floods." He nodded. "Before the earth shook beneath us, and the cliffs thrust into the sky. Before the sky rained burning stones. Before the barrows were quarried and . . . before the towers grew." He grinned, his teeth worn down to nubs, and the light in his small eyes seemed clouded with sorrow. "Before canals. I was a herdsman by trade. I buried my children and my grand-children. Three sisters I buried as well, and a good wife. Now the sheep

are scarce, cattle are few, and what's not scarce is in there." He pointed
to the walls of the city. "You had the fever?"

She nodded.

"And yet you remember?"

Again, she nodded.

"You would do well to forget. The world is unmade, though
many pretend it has never been different. Still, no use looking back
over what has passed, whether it be kingdoms, loves, or death." He
was quiet during the journey toward the Forest, as if he were afraid
of her memories. Then he spoke a few words in the old language of
the Great Forest, derived from the speaking stones when all had to
go into hiding for survival in a previous Dark Age. It was said among
the crones that the tongue came from the elementals—those energies
that arose from wood and stone and fire and air, yet took the shape of
spirits of the Forest such as the Great Stag of Cernunnos, the Lord
of the Wood, or the Briary Maidens who appeared in desperate times
to simple folk out along the thorny briars near wooded mists. It was
called the Nameless Tongue, for it was older than mortals themselves. *"Aiyen-athet,"* he said. *"Malis-brana." To you, maiden, the
swiftest ravens.*

"You risk much to speak this blessing," she said.

"I am seventy years and have outlived any I care to live for," he
said. "What do I fear of the Illumination Nights? My time draws
near. I would drown myself before any Morn could take me."

"Do you wear the Disk?" she asked in a whisper.

"Only when I must," he said, quietly.

She smiled at him, and he at her, though they did not speak again
until the boat had stopped. There, among the winter geese that gathered along the bank, the boat docked against the rough-hewn stones
that formed steps up to the planked landing.

At the shore where the canal broke off and narrowed on its way to the Lugh River, a boy stood by—a shadow against the growing shadows of the day, half-hidden behind a clutch of trees.

"The swiftness of the raven to you," the elderly man said as he looked up at her from the boat, offering a knowing smile.

"And to you," the ashling said, as if these words meant more than their apparent worth.

"You seek the moon-child?"

The ashling nodded.

"There he is—see him? Among the white balmaren's branches, he watches for you," the boatman said, pointing out the strange boy. "He takes you to the den of wolves, no doubt. Tell me, is your business here dark or light?"

"I could not yet tell you, for it would bring you harm, my friend," she said. She turned to walk the slender path that had vanished into the Forest, many miles from where it once had grown wild.

She turned and called out the name, "Mordac!" and the boy came running to her side.

• 5 •

THE early winter had worn away at the forest floor, and frost thickened the leaf-covered earth. The grotto had long ago dried, its basin now filled with offerings from pilgrims and wanderers. To this windswept wasteland, the forest trees had drawn back as if in grimace, their roots exposed. Intertwined in their twisted roots were the bones of the dead. The purple flower—the Serpent's Venom, which brought me the Sight from the Veil—and its nettled vine twisted in and through the bone piles, creating something like a path toward the cave door.

Hearing the shrieks from the sky (and though I tried to look upward to see what made such noise, I could not—but watched the earth and trees and the ashling as she moved), the ashling approached the cavernous home of the anchoresses. These women I had known as Magdalens, but they, too, had changed in the years of pestilence, and I would soon enough learn they had a new name for themselves—the Chymers, though I would not know from whence they'd been rechristened as such. No longer did they serve any saint of Christendom, for the human bones in their wild garden suggested a much darker worship.

I began to see—as I watched the ashling—that she had come to these women for some form of necromancy, for why else bring the head of a murderer to this bone garden?

A den of wolves, the boatman had called them.

The boy accompanied the shrouded maiden, his left hand tucked into her right. With his right hand, he clutched the sack that contained the head. His strange silver-gray hair fell long, covering his shoulders. From a distance, an observer might mistake him for a young wolf standing on its hind legs.

"I would have been lost had you not guided me," the ashling said, her voice barely raised above a whisper. "So much has changed in the western woods. I once knew these trees as well as my own hand, but now, it is . . . it is like a foreign land."

The boy nodded. He said a few words in the wolvish language, which amounted to not much more than snarls and yips.

"I am not afraid of them, Mordac," she said. "They are greedy. All who are greedy are cowards." From the folds of her rags, she produced several coins, as well as a handful of sparkling gemstones and several rings pressed down on her fingers. "They may be bought more easily than even the Barrow-Depth whores."

The boy grunted and huffed, but did not say a word. He pointed along the leaf falls outside the door to the stone chambers of the anchoresses. Bones and broken skulls, intertwined with vines, lay in stacks like wood for the hearth. Upon the vines, small purple flowers grew, their petals closed with frost. Each three-fronded leaf curled slightly, tiny nearly invisible nettles upon its stalk.

"The Sang-Fleur is not deadly to me," the ashling said. "It won't drink my blood. Look." She crouched, and ran her fingers gently over a flower's buds and followed the twisting vines through the pile of bones. The boy grabbed her arm to pull her back, but she shrugged him off. "Mordac, *watch*." The curled leaves seemed to shiver slightly as if a breeze had touched them. "The flower does not seek my life force, Mordac. It smells the plague within me. It knows that what is in my blood would wither its stalk, and soon its petals would drop one by one to the frosted earth. Do you know how the Sang-Fleur was brought here? From the distant wars? A city of the dead, where it grows. It is not meant to be here. This is poison to all but the winged demons themselves. And to me."

The cave's rounded oaken door slid outward, and when the ashling glanced up—I, too, saw the small, gnarled fingers of a Chymer sister, as if I looked outward from the ashling's eyes.

◆ 6 ◆

*T*HIS *had never happened before in the Sight.*

I had never been drawn into the body of one I watched in vision.

I felt myself sucked into the ashling, into her form. It was sudden, and felt as if the breath had been quickly drawn from my lungs.

I felt her body around me.

I felt the plague within her skin.

And yet, I did not know her mind. I dumbly watched through her eyes.

Did she know I was there? Could she feel me within her? I could not then answer these questions, nor did I understand how this was possible—actually to move into the body of one in a vision.

◆ 7 ◆

A T the open door, a thick-set woman stood, her cloak's hem muddy as if she'd been wandering in the low country bogs. She wore a plain-cloth wimple tight about her throat, and her scalp had been fitted with the nebula headdress that identified the Chymer sisterhood, its thick black cloth covering the head. The crown of her headdress was lined on the outside with a mottled yellow fur as if from a wild cat. It fell down the back of her neck and over her shoulders like a capelet. Her eyes were small and brown, and her skin had the wine stains of one who had suffered much with plague. Her forehead was slightly veiled to cover up the protuberance of her skull. Her teeth were sharp as a wolf's, but small and barely thrust out from her gums.

"I am Godwaina, the humble and gentle. I have served these caves since I was seventeen years old," the Chymer said, her tongue thick in her mouth as if she'd been chewing a dry strand of beef. "You bring tribute. Lovely." She glanced at the boy. "The little beast-child has returned." She wagged a finger at the boy. "You are not to steal food from us, nor furs, you pup." She glanced back up at the ashling's covered face. "Has he stolen anything? Killed someone?"

"He has guided me here."

"He is quite the rambling little moon-cub." Godwaina reached forward to grab the coins from the ashling's hand. "Very nice," she said, examining each coin, and pressing it in her teeth to check for clay. "Very fine. And such a pretty picture of Our Blessed Lady Enora upon it." She held the coin up to the fading cloudy light. "A likeness from a court artist, no doubt."

"I have more, if you help me," the ashling said.

"How much more?" Godwaina's lips drew high over her pale white gums. Her small teeth were stained blue from the *gonilde*-seed, which had properties of magick for those who spoke with the dead. She added, as if reciting from memory, "We are but a poor sisterhood and depend upon the charity of those more fortunate to continue our worship."

"I wish to speak to one who is dead."

"As do many who come to us," Godwaina said. "But do you not have a priest? A church? A White Robe? You are . . . you seem young, my dear. Are you from within the walls of the city, or without?"

"I am from within," the ashling said.

When the ashling drew the hood from her head, just a bit so the woman could view her, Godwaina gasped, and said, "Ah, you are one of the blessed. We pray for your kind each day and ask the dead for guidance in your protection."

I could not see the ashling's face, even so, for I looked out from her eyes at the Chymer woman.

Godwaina turned about briefly to call to her sisters. "One of the blessed has come to us, my sisters!" Godwaina drew out the small symbols of her sisterhood from the folds of her gown as she turned to face the stranger again. One was a long, sharpened tooth embedded in ingot, and another, a circle of silver, within which hung the mirror-disk half-covered in talismanic writings.

Godwaina kissed these two pendants. She offered them to the air as if spirits might see them and bless them, as well. She dropped the necklace back within her blouse. "Do you come as a servant of another?" she asked. "Do you come for some master's sake?"

"I come here for my own understanding, for much is lost when mortals die. This one did not live long enough to speak with me, though I sought him."

"You are blessed to find us," Godwaina said. She held her hand out to touch the edge of the ashling's face. "Some saint has touched you."

"Do not come too close, Lady Chymer," the ashling said. "For I bear a plague upon my flesh. I understand it is like fire under the skin to those who have not felt it."

The Chymer drew her hand back. She looked at the coins in her other hand as if she might drop them for fear of contagion.

"This plague does not pass by coins or rings," the ashling said. "If it did, many would be dead from my touch."

"Yes, your . . . entertainments . . . are known even by those as chaste as we. Your kind have suffered so," the Chymer said, but with a cold edge to her voice. "You carry the liquid fire inside your flesh."

"I am not one you should fear, good anchoress," the ashling said. She glanced up at the sky. "Just moments until nightfall, if that. I have already heard them shrieking."

Godwaina also looked over the tops of the trees where the sky turned muddy at its edge. She drew her hands to her lips as if eating a crumb of prayer. "Come in." She leaned over and poked at the boy's shoulder. "The beast-child cannot enter our sanctuary. He defiles all he touches."

The ashling turned to the boy. "Mordac, wait for me there, by the oaks. Do not fear for me. Watch the skies for Morns."

He passed her the sack.

The ashling combed her fingers through his thick bird's-nest of hair. "Don't let them find you."

Mordac growled at the Chymer.

As she followed the Chymer sister into the cave house, the ashling looked up and saw the year's first flakes of snow begin to fall.

Against the purple twilight sky, I thought I saw a vampyre, wings spread wide, as it glided across the lands beyond the city from high above the trees.

Why would a vampyre be here? And free? What had I seen in the sky? I did not know then what creature patrolled the air of Taranis-Hir, but it gave me some hope to see one of my kind, even if a silhouette, as night fell in the world above.

◆ 8 ◆

WITHIN the hour, seven of the Chymers had gathered about a low wooden table covered with the instruments of their trade. Some introduced themselves, and I recognized a few from my youth when

I had seen these anchoresses before they had changed into this necromantic sect.

There was an opalescent bone box, in which they kept a greasy ointment boiled down from the fat of hanged men's corpses, meant for rubbing on their bodies to ease possession by the dead. Near it, small pincers for drawing the spirit off the flesh if it refused to leave after the trance was done. And at the center, the necrolabe, a curious piece of metalwork through which the spirit of a corpse might be located in the body and drawn from its vapors using the curved and sharpened blade at its center. A few of the women had begun dipping their fingers into the bone box, passing it about. Others cooed and ahhed in their feeble and frightening ways when they saw the torques and rings and necklaces the stranger had hidden within the folds of her rags. "You are a robber or a whore," one of them said, her eyes beaming as she counted coins.

"I knew your price would be high, and I know the dead also desire payment," the ashling said. I began to feel as if the ashling were aware of me, within her, watching from under her skin, for she seemed to speak more slowly, and now and then she faltered as she spoke.

Godwaina glanced at the ashling, shaking her head, even as she wiped her cheeks to a shine with the bone-box grease. She leaned toward her, whispering, "When it comes to price, do not pay the dead. Do not feed the dead. They hunger, and you must not satisfy them."

The Chymers spoke in hushed tones of such things that most agitated them—the Morns who guarded the walls of the city, the accounts of a new plague spreading along the southern countries, and the harsh winter that had was upon the land.

Godwaina had drawn out the dead man's head from the sack. "Oh, it is dead too long, I fear," she gasped. She sniffed at it. "Twelve days? Fourteen? Surely the soul has fled."

"You speak with those who are dead many centuries," the ashling said.

Celestria, whose wimple sagged across her scalp to reveal thin strands of reddish hair, clapped her hands suddenly. "Sisters, we will try for this unfortunate one. We will invoke this spirit, and if the soul lurks, we shall find him."

Each sister kissed the head on the ear or cheek or lips as they passed it one to the other. A crude sort of ale that stank of fish and meal was poured from a pot into the dead man's mouth. Each sister drank of it, also, and they encouraged the ashling to sip the foul mixture as well. They brought out a small white clay bowl filled with the "congertail herb, sacred to the spirits," one said. A candle lit the herb into a bright blue flame. "Congertail grows wild in subterranean streams. It must be gathered by young virgins, then dried with great delicacy by the fire over many months. It is rare, and few find it, for the White Robes claim most of it for their own ceremonies," Godwaina informed the ashling as if to impress her. "Its scent awakens Death's handmaidens."

They each cupped the clay bowl with the smoldering herb, passing it to the next sister in turn—though, if one were too greedy, the sister beside her would grab it quickly from her fingers while offering a harsh word or two.

"The dead love the herb," Godwaina told the ashling as she pressed her nose close to the smoky bowl. "It draws them from the skull."

"The soul lives in the skull after death," another said, tugging the bowl away from Godwaina.

Still another added, "Some for days, some for months."

"Some for centuries," Godwaina said. "If they do not wish to leave the body, they may sleep there. Locked in the prison of the bones."

"Some believe they sleep until judgment day."

"Some believe the soul remains in the flesh and bones if not consecrated," Godwaina added. "Now, sisters, we must be good to the ashling, for she has brought us fine payment."

"Yes she has," one of the Chymers nodded, holding up several rings.

"Ashling, this is Celestria, and that is Ideyn. Mikaela is closest to the hearth, and here is Helewys, and Sweet Margery, who is favored of the dead," Godwaina said, pointing out each of her sisters, though they had already introduced themselves. The smoke of the burning herb seemed to make them giddy.

"Is Mordac's mother here?" the ashling asked.

The sisters—each of whom had been fumbling with needles and threads ("for the mind must be empty while calling spirits, and needlework is best for this"), or were pounding *gonilde*-seed in cups with rounded sticks—all fell silent.

"Morvethe? She is gone for now," Godwaina said.

"She prepares for the Illumination Nights," Sweet Margery spoke up, her voice a squeak.

"Do not bring that boy—her son—here again," Godwaina said, pointing a needle at the ashling. "The dead do not like him. We do not like him here. He is an abomination and brings shame to Morvethe."

"A terrible, terrible thing," Helewys muttered. "Giving birth to a . . . child like that. The shame of it."

They fell silent, and the ashling asked of spiritual matters. "Do you know how the spirit will behave?"

"We have all called the dead, and they are very predictable. Do not trust them much, or they will linger. Do not ever agree to pay them," Godwaina said. "They ask it, but you must threaten the spirit with damnation. You must threaten the spirit with remaining inside the body until it rots through. You, of course, cannot make this happen, but the dead are stupid and full of fear. They believe anything is possible, and cling to whatever hope is offered. Promise the spirit paradise, if you like. Milk and honey, pearls and jewels, and you will only release the dead when he answers your question."

"Most souls leave within a fortnight," said the largest and youngest of the Chymers, the one called Ideyn. "They go to the Threshold be-tween life and death. They are drawn there, you see. They do not like to linger, though there have been some that stayed."

Godwaina, drunk from the ale, turned to the ashling. "Why do you wish to call upon this spirit?"

"I have lost something dear to me," the ashling said. "This dead man knows where it is."

"I understand," Godwaina said to the others, silencing them all. "Inhale, sisters, let us go into our trances, for the spirit may not be willing if he is made to wait much longer in that rotting head."

Within minutes, most of them had already gone into their deep-ened states. Though some eyes were open, most of them closed soon enough as the trance began to overtake them, one by one.

Their drunkenness and smoking infused them with visions and delight as they moved further and further away from consciousness.

I could almost smell the congertail incense in the air.

The herbs stung the eyes as smoke thickened from their white bowls. Spirit tongues overcame the Chymers. Soon, the wild cries of birds and of cats and the howls of wolves came from their mouths. They had all gone into trance, and all wore ecstatic expressions.

Among them, Ideyn squatted on her haunches, inhaling the in-cense, the skull-drink dripping down her naked breasts as she tore at her clothing. As her shoulders shook and her eyes rolled up into her head, she spoke: "Who calls me from death's embrace?"

"I come to ask questions of the dead," the ashling said.

"Are we known to each other, or are you a stranger to me?" asked the dead man through the slack-jawed Chymer.

"Though I have seen you, we were strangers in life. It was at your execution that I saw you most clearly."

"What is it you ask of me?"

"I seek the hidden place where the winged devils are buried

alive," the ashling said. "And I seek knowledge of them and of their powers."

"I know this place," the spirit said through Ideyn's slack jaw, as if her body had become an echoing cave within her.

"Tell me where it lies, for much has changed these several years, and only the priests of the shadows know its entry. And you know it, for you tried once to bring them up."

"Tried and failed, for that was the beginning of my imprisonment," the spirit said. "I knew one of these devils when he was a boy. I did a terrible wrong to him, for I did not understand how dark the world would grow in a few short years. If I tell you where to find this well that has been covered to hide it from others, you must promise me one thing," the spirit said.

"I will promise you whatever you demand," she said. She glanced at the Chymers, all in their trances of pleasure.

"You live now in a kingdom of dread, daughter of ash. They are dragons with the faces of men," the spirit said.

"I do not fear winged devils," she said, glancing at the Chymer sisters, all of them humming and swaying as congertail incense flowed from the white bowl at the low table's center, as if it were the form of this spirit itself.

"Do not worry so much, little one, about these necromancers who called me from my sleep. They are deaf to our words while in their trance. Otherwise, they would surely slit your throat if they knew what you ask of me, and what I, in turn, ask of you." The spirit paused, and for a moment I had a feeling as if the spirit knew I was within the ashling. I had a sense that this spirit, through the Chymer, looked at me and not at the ragged maiden. "You may wish to change your mind before I tell you what I require from you in payment. Tell me, why do you seek these winged devils?"

"Vengeance," she said.

As she spoke this word, I felt something pull hard upon my form, as if a great warrior had hit me with a blow and grabbed me at the shoulders.

I was drawn back, from her body, briefly floating above her.

I saw the spirit himself through the head, through the jaws of the Chymer woman.

I saw him and I knew him, though his form was like colors of light through a mottled glass.

Kenan Sensterre.

But I opened my eyes, no longer in the vision of the Sight.

No longer in the lair of the Chymers.

Instead, I lay with Ewen at the bottom of a deep well, in darkness.

I gasped for air, as I had never felt such a vision.

I did not understand the true meaning then of what I had witnessed. In my mind's eye, many visions came to me, of the past and future. All were a maelstrom of images, of the Priest of Blood, of a gold mask upon the face of a naked woman, of the city of Alkemara in its glory as I had never before witnessed it. And some were the Myrrydanai shadows before their flesh had been torn from them by Medhya, the mother goddess of the vampyre race, when their skin was bronze and their eyes red with blood that pulsed within them, when they truly were priests of that Dark Madonna on the shores of a distant citadel at Myrryd, the kingdom that gave birth to the three priesthoods of Medhya—the Priests of Blood, the Priests of the Nahhashim, and the Priests of the Myrrydanai.

I saw this shore with its black sand and its towering cliffs, and the great city of Myrryd, nothing but towers that rose from gray mist into the sky.

In these visions, I saw Medhya herself, without a face, without form, yet I knew the darkness was her body, and I knew her blood, for it was the same blood that ran in my veins.

The same breath, the same blood.

Drawn into me and all vampyres descended from the Priests of Blood.

And I saw her other aspects, as if they were three sisters who stood together:

Medhya, Lemesharra, and the last, Datbathani, who was also called the Lady of Serpents.

I saw them in visions, and for many years, I could not stop the Sight as it brought these wonders and terrors to my mind.

But this final vision within that well was visceral—I felt as if my flesh had been pulled from it, into it, and I had parted from the ashling with a level of pain I had not felt before in the Sight.

Eleven years into my captivity, a stranger sought our subterranean prison.

It was the ashling from my vision, although I did not know if she meant to bring silver into my heart, to draw Ewen and me into sunlight to watch us slowly turn to ash ourselves, or if she had more terrible plans for us.

· CHAPTER 3 ·

◆ 1 ◆

I could smell fresh blood on this intruder for several nights before I saw her ragged form.

◆ 2 ◆

I hungered for mortal blood as a dying man hungers for life.

The years had been spent in monotonous captivity, with the interruptions of the visions induced by the Serpent's Venom from that flower's nectar, which brought mainly the constant and deafening lamentations in the world above us. Feeling the trembling of the earth, Ewen and I had lain together, at first plotting escape.

As the years passed and our energies ebbed, we simply waited for an eternal and terrible sleep to take us.

The lamentations took the form of death-singers, both of Christian and pagan hymns. The smell of death permeated the earth as many were buried and more had their ashes spread upon the ground.

Many nights I slept against my beloved friend, Ewen, after we sated ourselves upon our commingled blood, tainted as it was with that flower's juice. We wondered at the legends that had brought us here—at the fate prophesied by the Priest of Blood, Merod Al Kamr, whose words continued to echo within me, though I did not believe we would ever roam the night again.

I doubted we would ever taste the blood that would revive us.

The previous night, I felt something—a disturbance in the air. Though I had not felt the stream in years—that membranous thread that connects those of our species—it seemed as if a fly had touched the edge of the thinnest of spiderwebs with her wing. I felt this vibration; so briefly was it done that I did not know if I had imagined it or not.

I had not recognized the stream since our first night within the well, when, offering my throat to Ewen, we both sensed a fire that exploded in the stream as we broke one of the great taboos of the vampyre.

• 3 •

I thought I would go to my Extinguishing buried deep in the earth—while, above, in the world of daylight, shadows swept the land.

It was as if the skin of the world itself had been peeled back, unmasked, and brought forth the plagues from another world. The land trembled and shook, though our prison was encased in thick rock. The well vibrated with these shiverings, but neither my beloved companion nor I could know for certain what had become of the land above the seal of our tomb.

• 4 •

IN those first nights of our captivity I said to Ewen, as he drank at my throat, "Do you hear them?"

He drew back, looking up at the sealed roof to our round prison. He glanced back at me, his eyes shining with a reddish glow.

We had been drinking from each other, our immortal blood mingled with the juice of a small but potent flower from the necropolis of Alkemara, far to the east. It had been the only thing keeping us from the Extinguishing—the hell of a consciousness locked into physical death and decay. While this shared blood was enough to sustain basic energy, we had lost faculties and could not move as we did when we soared the night sky, nor could we sense the stream.

My love and affection for him grew in our captivity. I wanted to care for him that he might not hurt in this terrible time. I had spent too many of those first months in fury, crawling as far as I could up the curved walls before falling down again to the pit. I planned escape after escape. We used the old instinct to dig our ways out of graves as our brethren had done when buried, and yet it was rock all around— too tough, too perfect, to give way to hands that had become bloodied and raw in the process. I cared less for myself than I did for Ewen, and when we sat up together after bleeding each other for sustenance, we spoke of our childhood loves and of the world and of our hatred. We tired of each other often enough. We lay at separate curves of the pit some nights to avoid each other, if briefly. Some nights we spoke of those we missed, among the vampyres—of Kiya and Yset and Vali, and of the loss of Yarilo to the lamprey-maidens of Alkemara. Ewen's fear was enormous, from our earliest nights; I comforted him with what I began to believe were lies and false hope.

We began referring to the well as our Round Tomb, and all we had, in those days, was hope and fear and fury at the mortal world above us, unseen.

I did not tire of his beauty or his rough embraces or the pounding of our hearts as we lay together after drinking the blossom-stained blood. Many nights, we fought like tigers, as even mortal men do when trapped in a prison, but when the fight was done, it was to the harbor of his body that I sought my mooring.

I searched in vain some nights for any markings or weapons or holes in the rock that we might expand into escape routes. We clawed at the curve of the well to try to reach its summit, but did not have strength in us to reach even halfway.

Yet we heard the whispering of those terrible shadows—the Priesthood of the Myrrydanai, fleshless and of the substance of mist. They moved across the countryside above us, an army of fog, filling us with dread.

"It's them," I said, reaching to my throat to stanch the flow of blood across the wound that had repeatedly been torn and healed for more than a year's time. My fingernails had nearly become talons, and the filth of the place no longer bothered me. "Myrrydanai. More come through."

Ewen had begun losing hope, though I still believed in the prophecies. Men in war, when despair overcomes them, cling to each other, cling to their memories of home. The affection between Ewen and me grew, even as our energies diminished. We drank from each other, and we lay beside each other, and where he left off, I began—until it was as if he was the entire world to me. We had known each other since we'd been boys, and those recollections became our brief escapes. We spent many nights pressed against the curved stone of the well, whispering of our childhood in the Baron's castle that once stood not far from where we were imprisoned. We spoke of herding the swans and gathering the sheep; of the sun, golden and fiery on a summer's day of hard labor and little rest. We remembered lying upon the mats, near the hearth, with all the other boys who worked in the Baron's household, and how one boy was always the storyteller and would tell tales passed down from the days before the Romans, or after the Romans, or before the English kings, or of Wales and Cornwall, where many ancestors had come from. The tales of Arthur and Guinevere, and the Holy Grail and its purity. Sometimes, we spoke at night of our time in the war with the Saracen, and of my brother, Frey, who had been cut down in the last battle I would fight as a servant-soldier. Ewen spoke to me of what was in his heart, of how when I had left him and gone off to die at Hedammu, he had thoughts of his own death. How he had sought me out, and found a vampyre instead of the youth he had known. "I would go into Hell with you, my friend," he told me, and I joked that he indeed had done so.

The well was my place of mourning, though I could not tell Ewen of this for it would sink his spirits further. My soul was in pain, for I had spent my mortal youth with an idea of love, and of my beloved. I had truly loved Alienora de Whithors, the daughter of the Baron of my homeland. We had vowed our hearts and souls to each other, and though I was murdered and resurrected into vampyrism, my heart did not change. Yet, I had seen her commit an unspeakable act. I had seen her, in the Glass of the Veil, give birth to our son, and bleed him across a bog for the sake of infernal sorcery—the bog magick known to the Druids who disdained it. This magick brought terrors to the world. When I had come with Ewen to stop the Myrry-danai, Alienora had committed a brutal act against her young brother; though we vampyres may drink and slaughter and steal life from the humans, it is a thousand times more terrible to watch a human being do this to one of her own kind. And so I lay with Ewen, my friend and my beloved companion, and dreamed of her—of Alienora—as she was before the shadows surrounded her and took her over. Before she had ransomed her soul. My own soul's pain took solace from Ewen's ministrations as he drank from me. I wished to be drained on those endless nights. From loneliness and the need for heat, we en-twined together. Though we no longer felt the stream that connected all vampyres, we sought that connection in our embraces, and in our drinking of each other's blood, and in our early mornings, before the sun had run the world beyond our well, when he fell asleep in my arms, whispering of pretty memories and the nights of freedom we once shared.

"I thought at first we would escape this place," I told him, during one such dawn. I pointed to the strange scratchings and carvings on the wall. "I thought those must be some ancient language. I thought the vampyre who had once been trapped here had left a message. But those scratchings are his madness. His fear as he went toward the Extinguishing. Who knows how many hundreds of years he had been here before a boy had come out, believing him to be a gryphon. Had raised him for his final journey into that terrible oblivion."

"Will they destroy us?" Ewen asked, leaning back to the floor, wiping his mouth with the back of his hand. "I know they'll destroy us. We are no use to them."

"If they wanted to send us to the Extinguishing, I think they would have as soon as they had the Nahhashim staff."

"We are jackals now." He pressed against me for rest during the coming dawn. We were each other's grave and took some comfort in this. "We will extinguish here, like dogs thrown in a pit."

"I will not let you extinguish here," I said, "I took a sacred vow." I closed my eyes, remembering what I'd seen in a distant land, in the tomb of the Priest of Blood of Alkemara.

Above us, on the surface of the Earth, the Myrrydanai made their nest.

* 5 *

TALES were told among mortals that after the winged creatures with the faces of men had been captured, the end of days began.

Those who later remembered told of shadows that swept the dusty air one summer when a warm deep wind blew off the bogs and marshes. Miasma grew and festered; the unseasonal heat burned across the land at the edge of the Great Forest. Strange insects, with long needlelike stingers, rose from stagnant black pools and swarmed in the air.

These bog-flies were drawn to sweat and blood, and few could avoid their pincers and needle-sharp jabs. Local sheep were found dead, with thousands of stingers in them. A young child's lifeless body found along the drying marshes. A woman, fallen at her spinning wheel, a window open, the mark of the flies upon her. The stingers went deep. A baby might be found at dawn in its crib with flesh as blue as if he had frozen to death—but the handiwork of the bog-flies was evident.

As people mourned the dead innocents and set fire to the bogs deep in the Forest to drive the pestilence out, it worsened. Many turned to bog magick, once outlawed by the Church, for protection. But folk followed the example of the Myrrydanai and of the Baroness, who was revered as a living saint for she had been identified with the dream of the Virgin of Shadows. Within days, the sky turned black with bog-flies, and clouds of the creatures spread over the countryside. Villagers grew sick. The local water became tainted with dead insects; and from the water, yet more bog-flies emerged, until no well and cistern could be trusted. When the drought of summer ended, and the bog-flies died or flew to warmer climes, the plague seeped in through autumn winds. It was seen as a sign of heaven's displeasure with mortal man.

Winter brought some peace, though many had died, their frozen bodies stacked along the abbey walls, since the ground was too hard to break for proper burial. An ice storm passed through the following spring, and when the first new winged demons arrived in the night—after the two that had been captured by the young Baroness the previous year—they terrified even the local priests, whose crosses and sanctuary kept no one safe. Word spread that the devils had come to take over the Earth.

For eleven years, we languished and did not feel another vampyre in the stream, though in the cold season, we felt the whispering shadows come through the Veil and take hold in the world above.

And more than halfway through the eleventh year of our captivity, I heard the sound of cutting and scraping at the top of the well.

◆ 6 ◆

"SOMEONE'S here," I whispered.

It chilled me as I said it, for we both knew that we could be destroyed. The years had weakened us. We had no fight left and more despair than hope.

I looked upward, but could not focus. Though darkness was my light, my vision had become that of an old man.

All I could see was that circular platform, rimming the well's apex. Even this was murky. It seemed many leagues above, and I wondered if I only imagined a brief movement at the top of the well.

For three nights, I heard the noise, but had not mentioned it to my companion.

It was the sound of locks and chains being broken.

On the fourth night, when I awoke, something had changed.

The air in our prison seemed different—a brief cool freshness had come to the stale tunnel into the earth.

"Someone has been here," I whispered to my friend as he offered me his throat for sustenance.

After that, I began watching for signs of changes after we'd awakened in the night.

I saw small footprints.

I smelled flesh and blood, though I still had not seen anyone.

During the day, someone came to watch us.

Someone came to disturb our prison.

◆ 7 ◆

THE ashling arrived just as dawn flowed from the east through the darkening woods. The sun's light never penetrated underground, for there was no crack in that seal at the top of the well.

While asleep that day, I heard Merod's voice, not with sound, but the Sight again.

In these visions, I saw Alkemara again, but as Merod had seen it in the ripeness of his immortality. I saw vampyres covering the skies with their wings, and the Priests of Blood and of the Nahhashim and even those of the Myrrydanai that had not yet been enslaved by Medhya. I saw golden temples, and obelisks made of black stone that shone in moonlight. The city had not yet sunk into the earth, and it sat upon the crown of a great mountain. Atop the thousand stairs up to its first walls stood the statues of the Great Serpent and of Datbathani, the Queen of Serpents, the Keeper of the Venom. The statues were painted with gold and red and black, and garlands of flowers had been thrown at the feet of the goddess by mortals who had come with sacrifices to bring prosperity to them and their descendants. Musicians played along the boulevards, and in the long pools, black swans floated and children stood by the edges of the water, while vipers crossed their paths without stinging them. I saw it all as if through Merod's eyes, for this was the gift to me from him, that in my blood he would come, and in my flesh he would live, though I did not always understand these visions he sent, or why he was silent within me much of the time.

I saw a vision that haunted my nights. I could not wipe it from my mind. I had seen it before, when Pythia had pressed her lips to mine, when the Sacred Kiss had come to me, to bestow the death-in-life of vampyrism.

I had seen the Priest of Blood, Merod, with the Nahhashim staff in his hand.

Behind him, an altar—a stone table as large as a king's bed.

A female vampyre was there, her face covered with a terrible gold mask.

Upon the mask, the face of Datbathani, serpents entwined about her hair. The Serpent Goddess, called the Lady of Serpents by our tribe.

In my dreams, the faces changed.

Sometimes, Merod wore the gold mask, the same one I saw on the Disk in the plague dream.

Sometimes, Pythia wore the mask.

In each of these visions, Merod spoke the same words to me, over and over. "Immortality is not a gift," he said. "It is a sacred obligation, even unto the prey."

I tried to ask him: what is that obligation? Tell me what I must do. Tell me what must be done, and explain this vision of the gold mask and the altar and the Nahhashim staff—for I did not yet understand any of it.

Sometimes, in the waking dream, I stood beside the sacrificial altar and it was I myself, who wore the mask. And from behind it, I could see the Myrrydanai, their shadows swirling as they advanced. *"We see you, Maz-Sherah,"* they whispered, their voices like the sounds of snakes moving across dry leaves. *"We know you. You have given us the Nahhashim staff, though you and your jackals did not unlock its secrets. Bring us the golden mask of the Lady of Serpents. It was stolen from us by one who has abandoned her tribe. Your friend will live, and you will both be set free. If you call for us, Maz-Sherah, we will hear you and know that you are willing to bring us this gift. If you call to us, and worship Medhya, from whom your Priests stole blood and flesh and the secrets of the flower that is sacred to her, then you will save your friend whom you love."*

✦ 8 ✦

I forced my eyes open to remain awake as long as possible.

Ewen had already drifted off, his head against the bend of my elbow, his face stained by a smattering of my blood. He had a peaceful look. Despite the dryness of his skin, the way his hair had grown too long over him, and the breeches and tunic that had long ago turned to rags, I saw the beauty of our kind within him—and savored the taste of his blood still on my tongue, the touch of his neck at my skin.

I did not wake him, though I sensed the stranger descending into our lair. I had but moments before the sleep of day would draw me to its darkness.

My first thought was that there had to be two of them—one to secure the rope, and one to descend. Perhaps a dozen people stood at the top of the well, or perhaps just one. But there had to be at least one other person to help this intruder get back out of the well. My mind began spinning over this fact, for if I had that rope, perhaps I could escape. Perhaps Ewen and I could attack this intruder and climb the rope to freedom.

Yet, what awaited us above? The burning sun and our own destruction.

I had the power of an old man at this point—nothing in me for fighting, nothing in me for overwhelming even a mortal child. Eleven years of drinking our own blood had made me this way.

I smelled her as she began to descend, a rope wrapped about her hands. She seemed thick with a spice scent, of citrus from the southern climes, and the marsh-grass stink, as well. The unmistakable odor of cat piss also wafted in, as if she slept in a nest of felines in a barn.

That other smell, too, assaulted me like a fist to my nose, a wondrous wrenching stench.

I could smell blood through her pores—it was fresh and vital.

Instinctively, my lips grew moist, and I felt the thirst rise up.

A sliver of that purple light of a new day thrust downward like a spear. Though the light did not touch me, I could feel its burning at a distance.

Light was our enemy; darkness was our sight.

Why do you come, ashling? I wondered. *Are we to be slaughtered now? Brought up into the sunlight so that our skins might smolder?*

I had seen a vampyre killed once, like this.

I had seen what mortals do—for I had been one of them in those days.

I had brought the same terrible fate to one of my tribe.

Here.

Beneath the earth.

Raised him into the sun's harsh glance.

My prison—an ancient well made with such craftsmanship that it did not seem a well to me, but a rounded vessel for holding captives— built by the Romans hundreds of years before my existence. It had been surrounded by temples to their gods, as well as older standing stones that had been in the Great Forest since before time itself.

But all this had turned to ruin. The vine and fern of the forest floor had taken over the fallen temple columns and sealed many of the wells.

Somehow I felt the presence of the ancients in this well that had become my tomb.

And now, this mortal ventured down the stone curves to find the two winged devils.

◆ 9 ◆

I had not anticipated the seal at the top of the well to be made of silver, nor for its bottom to be upon a solid rock ledge. No amount of digging like a wolf, trapped, would free us; and my strength was so weakened that by that eleventh year, I could barely raise my lips to Ewen's throat for the week's ration of nutrient.

Yet I heard Merod's voice, comforting me, speaking through his blood to mine, at first warning me of Artephius, the unseen alchemist who had been powerful enough to entomb Merod Al Kamr, the father of my race. "He is the engineer of the destruction of mankind," Merod whispered to my blood. "He does not think it so, yet he has stolen the secrets of the Serpent and of the Dark Mother both. He is neither vampyre nor mortal, but may never die and cannot be destroyed by any mortal or immortal hand. I wondered, in my centuries beneath the halls of Alkemara, if he is the unmaking of the world in the form of a man. He is dangerous to all, and builds toys that slaughter and temples meant for enslavement."

Merod's voice, at times, seemed a symptom of my own madness. I could not tell if his voice was truly within me or if I simply imagined it that I might find intelligence and comfort.

Ewen had become nearly childlike during those years—like a baby needing the mother's breast as he drank from me. I worried for him, and fretted, but even the visions I had begun having were not shared with him—he was not able to see from the flower's juice—and by that eleventh year, I wondered why I had ever been chosen to be the savior of this tribe and why I had brought Ewen, dying, into this terrible immortality.

If the stranger had not come, I believe we would not have lasted another year together.

♦ 10 ♦

THE ashling scurried down into the well, clinging to a knotted rope, feet and knees scraping against the jagged rock edges.

As she touched the well's bottom—and we lay pressed together against the rim of the wet stone edge—I felt the heaviness of day and fought the sleep of the dead that called to me.

Ewen had already gone limp, his eyes closed, his skin shiny with the semblance of death.

My eyes weakened as they did when dawn came in the world above. I felt the drawing of narcotic sleep at my throat, at my wrist, at the back of my scalp.

She stood at the center of the well, and looked at the two of us as if with curiosity.

"Why . . . why do you come?" I asked, my voice soft and feeble.

She stepped back, gasping, as if she'd expected I would already be in the death sleep of dawn.

The stink of fresh blood was strong all around the mortal.

"Do not be afraid," I said.

She took a step forward.

Another step followed.

Finally, nearly touching me, she knelt beside me. Her hands moved about my face as if measuring, yet not once did I feel a touch.

"Why do you come?" I asked. "Who are you?" My voice, a rasp as the day's heaviness came into me. I was beyond fighting sleep—it would take me as a drug into its dreamless black chamber.

With the mortal still watching, darkness overcame me. As my mind shot into that sleep, I had the sensation of fingers touching the edge of my face.

◆ 11 ◆

WHEN next I opened my eyes, night had returned. The intruder had left behind two large sheep bladders full of some dark substance.

Blood. Human blood.

We had not tasted this in years. I had assumed we never again would.

"They may be poisoning us," I said.

"Poison or no, I smelled it as soon as the sun died." Ewen leaned forward, crouching near a bloated bladder. He sniffed at it, reminding me of a dog at a bone. He glanced back at me. "I will try it."

He tore at the bladder, leaking the blood into his mouth. He took great gulps, and his dried white skin seemed to plump slightly—and the blue veins began to fade quickly as he nursed. I saw his youth return in the blink of an eye, for he glanced over at me, grinning, his long canines extended as they would when drawing mortal nectar. His green eyes shone with luster, and what had seemed bruises upon his flesh now flushed pink and red beneath the skin. The talonlike fingernails fell away as if they were an overgrowth killed by poison.

"It is good!" he shouted, laughing. "It is *good!*"

We had just been handed a treasure, and yet I was sure a trap

surrounded this red coin. I crawled to the blood, lifting the second
bladder into my hand.

I sliced a fingernail to the edge of the bladder, and a drop of the
blood landed on my palm. I sniffed it—it reminded me of a new kill.

I tasted it.

To describe what I felt would be as describing what the dying
man feels when given the most delicious tonic for revival—to describe the opium addict when first he tastes of the poppy's syrup.

I felt reborn, just from that drop.

Ewen watched me, his youthful grin growing, his eyes brighten-
ing. "It's not poison," he said. "It's not!"

Within seconds, Ewen seemed drunk. "It's fresh," he said as he
passed it to me, his smile growing. "Fresh. From a maiden. From a
beautiful maiden. A strong maiden."

We both sat there in the early evening and drank, though I did not
understand why such a stranger would come to us and offer us sustenance. When I looked at Ewen as the hours of night passed, I saw his
youth and vigor again. His hair grew thick, and his eyes burned with
the passion of life.

The stranger's gift had renewed us, and still I was suspicious.

"It is a trick," I said.

"I do not care whether they come to kill us at dawn in our sleep,"
my friend said. "I feel as if I could face the sun and still survive it."

That night, with more strength in us than we'd felt in years, we
tested the power of our wings again, as birds might feel when their
first feathers come upon them.

Our wings spread out, feeling the stretch of new bone and skin,
then retracted. I had not felt them move in so long. The wings were a
gift from the Nahhashim staff—a power granted to us when we had
journeyed to find the ancient city of Alkemara in ruins. Granted to us
when Ewen and Kiya and I opened the tomb of the Priest of Blood
and met one of the prophecies in the flesh.

Even after that great staff of power had been stolen from me when we were captured, certain powers remained.

Our wings were beautiful, though not the wings of angels. They were leathery and oily as they emerged from our shoulders. There were legends that we were a race descended from dragons, and the wings attested to this mythology, for they added grandeur and terror to our form. Yet they emerged by our will, by thought. They were instruments of the stream itself, and would absorb swiftly back to our shoulder blades when we did not use them.

It was a joy to feel them move, to curve and bow their talonlike prongs.

It felt like life itself had returned to us.

◆ 12 ◆

I began having intense visions that night, one after the other.

In one, I saw a black orb that shone with an inner light.

I saw it in the hand of the creature who had first taken my life, my blood, and brought me into vampyrism.

To say I saw her would be a lie—for she came to me only in my mind.

She wore a mask like none I'd ever seen—not the gold mask of the Disk but of a dull green jade stone. It bore the primitive carving of a serpent upon it. The mask shone both green and silver, as if the dangerous metal were beneath the translucent stone.

It seemed I looked through it, to her face, through the moonlit water of a cavern lake, and all I could see were dark eyes.

She did not come to me as I had known her.

Pythia, the Pythoness, daughter of Alkemara, daughter of the Priest of Blood himself, Merod Al Kamr.

The priest who had brought the secret of our kind into being when he heard the words of the Blood upon singing grasses; and she, the one who stole my mortal life and breathed death and immortality into my mouth with her Sacred Kiss. She did not come to me as that unearthly beauty and terror, whose dragon wings unfurled as she saw within my being something more terrifying than her own monstrous vampyrism.

But in my mind, I saw her in golden robes, masked, with a crown of sharp long leaves of a plant I had never before seen. Intertwined with these were long plumes of blue and green, and even entwined through these were young vipers; her wings were like ice with the fire of the sun coming off their glistening tips; and there were serpents wrapped about her waist and arms like bracelets and bindings, holding her within a prison of the Great Serpent, keeping her trapped.

And there, in her hand, an orb made of a dark translucent stone—obsidian, a stone blessed by the Serpent, and within that orb, a swirling dark mass as if it held a world within its roundness.

In that vision, Pythia called to me. Called to me by the name of my destiny, "Maz-Sherah," her voice echoing through a cavern.

◆ 13 ◆

WE had grown stronger in just a few nights, because our mysterious young benefactor continued to deliver fresh mortal blood. We had grown back to the youths we had been when turned to vampyrism. I no longer felt like an old man with unending thirst. I felt vibrant, and a flush of rose coloring had come into Ewen's pale cheek.

"We are like dogs in a kennel," Ewen said, not unhappily. "They throw us bones."

"Not bones, but life," I said. "For what reason, I cannot guess."

"Perhaps Kiya has come with an army of our kind. Perhaps . . . we will be set free. Perhaps it is over."

"Over?" I asked. "What has changed? There is nothing but human darkness above us. We can only imagine how the world has shifted under their guardianship. I worry for Kiya and others of our tribe."

"When we felt fire in the stream, years ago," he whispered, "I felt them. Perhaps they are no more, and we are the last."

◆ 14 ◆

WITH practice, I could press my hands against the cold stone and move like a spider along its rough edges. Upward I would go, a few feet at a time. I managed to climb nearly halfway to the top before slipping.

Ewen followed. He had stripped himself naked for the climb, for he felt that cloth and leather held him down. I watched him scamper nearly to the top of the well. He called down to me, laughing as I hadn't heard since before his death.

I managed to move in a spiral up the edges until I crouched beside him.

Above us, the silver seal, surrounded by lead.

The feeling of silver—or quicksilver to be more precise, for it was the liquid form that held poison for vampyres—was as a miasmic fever might be to mortals. Or the stings of many insects coupled with weariness and pain. It made breathing difficult, and the throat clenched as if in a chokehold. My fingers began to slip from the slimy rock edge near the underlip of the well, and Ewen put his arm around my waist out of fear of falling.

Slowly, carefully, we moved back down the well.

"They mean to destroy us now," I said. We would go into the Extinguishing—worse than death itself.

We would live eternally, consciousness without movement, in endless thirst, until even our ashes retained this tortured existence until the end of time.

"But you are the One," he said as we returned to the bottom of the pit.

"They mean to destroy us," I repeated. "We will fight them. We are strong. We will fight until there is nothing left of us."

"They will come as cowards," he said. "All mortals do. At sunrise. When we have no strength. When we can do nothing."

That night, we slept side by side. Before day we spoke of the others we had lost or had not felt in the stream in many years—Kiya, who had remained at Hedammu, the City of the Dead, in the distant Holy Land. Vali, Yset, and those vampyres left behind in that distant land.

Other vampyres existed, but though we pushed our minds into the stream to feel their presence, there had been no response since first I'd felt a fire run through the stream—when Ewen and I broke the sacred law that no vampyre would drink from another.

For all we knew, we were the last vampyres in the world.

"If we are extinguished soon," Ewen said. "I want our ashes to mingle, as our brothers and sisters in the tombs of Hedammu remain together in the Extinguishing."

"Yes," I said. "But we will fight them, Ewen. We will fight."

"They know how to destroy us," he said, his breath slowing as he went into the day's sleep.

But I waited that morning, as long as I could.

I knew the ashling would return.

She had a reason for bringing us this blood, and I intended to find out why she had sought the dead to come to us.

And why she brought us fresh life to make us strong when we were the enemies of the mortal realm.

♦ 15 ♦

AGAIN, I knew the ashling descended into the well, bringing more blood. I fought sleep until the last moments. Again, the stranger came close to me, touching my face.

I lunged, grabbing her about the waist. She pushed against me, but I reached up for her face that I might see it.

There, within the folds of her rags, I saw a face I had not seen in many years.

Not since the maiden had been a strange child more than maiden.

She had been called the veiled one, for the hiding of her face and form.

It was that child of the Forest women, who was called Calyx.

She had plague marks upon her throat and shoulders, which gave her skin a translucent quality. Her face had been much scarred, but it had an opalescence to it, as if she were the color of the moon itself with all its mottling and shadows.

She pushed me back, and I fell to the ground from the weakness of oncoming day.

As I lay there at her feet, unable to resist that oblivion of sleep, she pressed her lips close to my ear, and whispered, "Listen well, for I have much to tell you. I am not alone. Others also wish your safety, though they loathe your deviltry." She glanced back up to the top of the well, as if those who helped her descend might be watching. "They have given their blood that you and your friend might find strength. The world is not as it was, blood-drinker. The guards will come for you at twilight. They expect you to be easy prey for their champions. Rise early and drink your fill. You will need your strength. If you are taken into the Barrow-Depths, whether imprisoned or forced into that chair of torment called the Red Scorpion, look for me. Know that I watch you. If you see me, do not speak until I speak first. If you escape, seek out the cliffs to the north and west that grew from the cataclysms. Look for the golden tree of our ancestors, and from there, the caverns of the skull. Do not trust anyone unless you see the mark of the Akkadite upon them. It is the shape of the leaf of that five-fingered herb, the shape of a child's hand." She drew the folds of her tunic apart, and there above her pale hip was the Akkadite leaf tattooed in blue and green. "Monsters more brutal than you have broken into this world. Many of your own have been enslaved and destroyed. The Veil is thin and weeps with tears of fire. No one is safe. If wolves follow you, you must lose them before approaching the caverns along the cliffs, for they are spies of the shadow priests and seek our hidden places. Beware the White Robes." Just as I closed my eyes, though I fought with every ounce of my being to remain awake, I heard her say strange words to me, "Beware the Morns."

These last words of hers echoed within me when I awoke hours later, just as the sun crested the far western hills. I roused Ewen. He was still groggy, but I managed to pour blood into him, and drank much of it myself before the seal above us turned.

We began climbing toward the top of the well. By the time our jailers had removed it and had begun their descent, we would have the chance to overcome them. I thanked Calyx in my thoughts for having foreseen this and bringing us sustenance. Ewen and I drew ourselves to the upper edge of the well, just as they had brought the seal up, its silver well away from us.

I glanced at Ewen, whose fangs gleamed against the darkness.

I looked upward, and saw for the first time in years, high above us, the early stars of twilight. I savored the blood that remained in my mouth, on my tongue, at the edge of my lips, and felt my teeth sharpening for a new kill.

I went first, drawing myself up over the well's edge.

• CHAPTER 4 •

I called to Ewen, reaching back to him, offering my hand should he need it. He grinned, fangs gleaming in the dark.

He moved swiftly upward, like a cat scrambling up the side of a wall.

I felt invincible, the blood brought by Calyx rushing like thunder beneath my flesh. It is difficult for those who are not immortal to understand this, as if immortality itself should be exhilaration enough. But I felt like a god, and it is when one feels godlike that one falls to the deepest depths, I suppose.

I leapt up from the well onto its thick stone rim. The rush of fresh air in my lungs was a shock. My eyes had been unused to seeing light of any kind, and so the vanquishing twilight seemed bright all on its own. Purple light edged the distant white towers, though I did not recognize them—they barely seemed of this country, let alone of the barony. I felt winded, yet excitement ran along every nerve of my skin. My wings exploded from my back to full span, curving and twisting as I moved them by will alone.

Nine men, some in armor, others in breeches and loose shirts and tunics, stood there with ropes and nets and small silver torques and cuffs. They had planted torches all around us, and the light briefly blinded me. I have no doubt they thought their work would be simple, expecting us to be weak and docile after years of captivity and isolation. When my vision adjusted, I could see their faces, which were terror-stricken, yet set upon their task.

I saw more clearly the rings of men around us. Behind the knights and guards, there were boys with nets. Beyond even these, archers stood, crossbows at the ready.

The clash of metal, the flash of swords drawn in the wavering light. Yet no one moved toward us.

As we crouched on the lip of that well, I looked upon the men we would drink from in moments and recognized two or three of their faces. These had once been boys with whom we'd worked in the Baron's household, in the paddocks and among the herds. I saw in their eyes no recognition, for we were their winged devils.

I glanced at Ewen. "Now!" I cried.

His wings went to their full span from his shoulders. He looked like a beautiful angel of death. We both knew we needed to fly, to get beyond this place—and find those other vampyres who existed.

Something stirred in my blood; my senses sharpened too quickly.

Beyond the knights and guards, I saw the shadows that had infected this land. Their darkness was disguised with human skin, and they wore long white robes. They had the aspect of elderly mages, yet their skins were loose and did not fit them well. Their eyes were empty; I heard their whispers like locusts on a summer's night. I wondered how mortals could be so controlled by shadows, but the power of these hounds of Medhya was great.

Two men sought to throw nets over us, while three others, who had no weapons, backed to the other side of the torches. The knights were brave, and came at us, two-fisted, with their weapons. Their swords sought our flesh, but I wrestled one from the first knight who attacked me, tearing his arm in the struggle. I swung the sword down upon his comrades; Ewen had already grabbed a guard and raised him into the oncoming dusk, shooting nearly straight upward as he took him by the throat.

A spear gouged my side, digging deep. I drew its owner into me, sending him to death's embrace. When I pushed him away, I removed the spear; others surrounded me, moving close, their daggers and swords and axes at the ready. I pushed at them with the talons at the tips of my wings, and grabbed up one who was close—but when I saw I had a trembling boy of fourteen in my hands, I threw him down in the dirt.

I heard the hideous sound of a ram's horn at some distance.

The circle around me took slow steps backward. Each man looked to the other, as if in silent agreement. They widened their circle, moving farther back, toward the torches and the Myrrydanai priests beyond.

I glanced up to Ewen who glided halfway down to me, ready to attack again. Beyond him, I saw what I thought was a flight of huge birds of prey moving swiftly across the darkening sky. Their wings seemed longer than ours, and they moved like arrows shot directly for us. I heard the cries go up among the men, "Morns! Morns!" Some shouted for the boys to duck, and others ran to lift the torches, as if this were the best defense from the attack of these creatures. Calyx's words—"Beware the Morns"—rang in my ears now.

I spread my wings and ascended into the night, toward Ewen. With the unfurling of my wings, and the swift movement upward along the invisible current of air, I again felt that grandeur, that sense of being untouchable by the lowly mortal realm, or by the pull of the earth. I saw the creatures heading for us as they blackened the sky. When I think of this now, it was like watching dragons—just as I thought of my own tribe as dragons when we took to the air with our leathery wings and bowed talons.

Their bodies seemed slick as eelskin, but with a mottled blue coloration. Their wings were like gray membranes pulled taut against the spinal cord, exposed at their backs, and tight as a drum to the spiny prongs that thrust outward. Their hair was white as moonlight, though some had shaved heads. They shrieked like hawks attacking in a flock. They grabbed Ewen in their long talons, as he tried to fly upward again. Seven of these creatures covered him, dropping him to earth as if easy prey.

I heard the mortals cry out, "Morns! Morns!" They ran, scattering to the winds with their fear of these beings.

Three of these creatures leapt upon me, wrestling me to the ground, gnawing at my arm to make me drop my sword. I snarled at them, snapping at their throats and faces and arms as they overpowered me. It was as if I were fighting wild cats whose claws scraped at my skin, digging deep beneath the flesh, shredding me.

I saw what had been done, though I did not understand how this was possible.

The face of the Morn who pressed down upon my chest, baring her own fangs, much longer than mine, her lips having been torn off around them.

Her eyes were white as if she were blind. She sniffed at my face as her viscous spittle drained from her mouth onto me.

There was none of the sensuality or beauty left of the vampyre I had once known.

"*Yset*," I gasped.

◆ 2 ◆

I had last seen her in far Hedammu, when I had taken leave of Kiya and others. Half of her head was now shaved. Scars spread across her scalp and brow as if drills and saws had gone into her skull. I saw blood pulse at her throat in a twisting of the veins, like the roots of a tree pushed out of place by rocks, turned in upon itself.

In response to hearing her name, she let out that siren shriek I had heard from the sky. She had become a dumb creature, a monster, a slave at the hands of the Myrrydanai. These others around us, holding Ewen down, were slaves as well.

Yset leaned down and swept her tongue across my face, as if tasting the salt. Her stringy white hair brushed my cheek, smelling like rotten meat. Her tongue was rough, and her breath, rancid. The stink of festering wounds surrounded me. Were these still immortal creatures? For they seemed to be slowly decomposing corpses rather than vampyres. What torturer had done this to them? What sorcery had peeled back their skins to reveal this beneath the flesh?

The other Morns at my arms and thighs also began lapping at me, as if my sweat was to their liking. Waves of revulsion and fury swept over me, but no matter how much I fought, their strength was greater, and their claws scraped at me as they held me down. Where were the Priests of the Kamr and the Nahhashim for their children? Where were our protectors?

The guards returned and secured a torque made of silver and bronze across my throat. Thin silver bracelets were wrapped about my wrists, and upon my ankles, cuffs of this same metal.

· 3 ·

THE boys with the nets came to us next, shivering with fear as the Morns watched them approach. The guards barked orders for them to cover us and hold us there. The Morns backed away from the nets, and when a ram's horn sounded again from some distant tower, they sprang up from my body and from Ewen's, and flew in a flock off to the west. The nets, which were thick twine interlaced with silver coins, were wound about us like shrouds. Though I struggled, the metal's vibrations overcame any fight I had in me.

While twilight slipped into dusk, and the sky overhead turned a deep purple shade, we heard other alarums and the sound of hoofbeats along the road. A few of the soldiers whispered of a lady. As I was drawn up, I saw Alienora, from a distance. The men called out, "Lady Enora comes!"

She stood upon a litter that resembled the old Roman chariots, and had no driver but herself. At each side of her were female archers, their crossbows drawn and aimed. This strange litter was drawn by two white horses, flanked by guards on all sides, sword and ax raised as if anticipating attack. Alienora had become some kind of goddess or queen to these people, not just a baroness.

I did not see her clearly, but noticed a shining coronet at her brow and great furs draped across her body. I heard her call to the guard, as if she were furious with a delay in some evening activity.

I could not even remember love anymore, for my last sight of her before my imprisonment was of a monstrous deed, unworthy even of the undead. The source of her power was bog sorcery and the Myrrydanai shadows.

In her hand, she clutched that staff of my tribe created by the Priests of the Nahhashim. It shone to my eyes—a luminous source from within the bones of the Nahhash priests within the staff itself— as a nearly blinding bolt of lightning might appear if held by human hands. This sacred object of the ancient Priests of Medhya was stolen from me upon my arrival in this land eleven years earlier. It was a source of vampyric power, handed to her by the Myrrydanai.

That staff was what I needed to have, again, in order to fulfill what prophecy remained. There were ceremonies then unknown to me; powers of the Nahhashim I had not unleashed from the staff before it was taken from me at my imprisonment.

A knight on horseback rode behind her litter. His horse was black and his robe deep red. He wore the armor of one who attends a great ceremony—it was bronzed and shone in the torches like gold. His helm was at his pommel, and though I did not see his face clearly, I recognized his voice as he shouted to soldiers who ran alongside him. "Clear out these devils!" It was Corentin Falmouth, my brother from my mother's womb and from the seed of Kenan Sensterre, the huntsman who had turned against me and sent me to the wars. His hair was cut short, and he drew his sword from his sheath as if to ride out to me and cut off my head himself. "Clear them out! Our Lady does not cross paths with the Damned!"

♦ 4 ♦

A black cloth sack was slipped over my head, covering my face completely. I felt as if I were being led to my own execution. *Ewen?* I sent the thought into the weakened stream, hoping he could hear me. Hoping he still breathed.

I felt cudgels slam into my back, and blows from the hilts of swords to my face and head. Guards and knights beat me down until I had no fight in me, nor did I think I would ever awake from this attack. I only saw the blackness of the cloth. Yet through this my head ached with questions and confusions—I had tasted freedom so briefly.

Where are you, Merod? Within me? Why do you keep silent now? Is this the torment before my Extinguishing? Were the thousands of years of your existence meant for nothing? Were the prophecies lies? Is our cruel mother, Medhya, whose blood flows in our veins, in this Earth of mortals? Does she tread upon her children here, and yet the prophecies of the words of the blood have no meaning? Where is our war that was promised? Why am I called Maz-Sherah at all? I have no power, no strength, no will. What is left to me to fight for? Our world is ending. The New Dark Age has come. The goddess from which the ancient priests stole the immortal blood and flesh and spirit now seeks to walk among mortals. I am nothing. I am no one. I am the undead resurrected, that I might watch the destruction of all humankind.

The pain of the beatings grew too much for me, and the silver at my throat tightened like a vise. I blacked out, trying to remember all that Calyx had told me in those seconds before day had come.

When I awoke, I found myself manacled with silver cuffs in an iron cage.

II

THE ARENA

◆ CHAPTER 5 ◆

◆ 1 ◆

I glanced from one end of the low-ceilinged room to another. The air grew thick with the stench of animal feces and sweat, while a faint odor of blood lingered, as if this cellar had been awash in it recently and had been scrubbed clean again. Other cages were in a circle around us—some covered with blankets and others too distant for me to see. The nearest I could tell, we had been imprisoned beneath a long, low corridor. Below the cages, interconnecting wheels descended in a pit beneath the planked flooring. Above us, a ceiling that seemed made entirely of a gray ash stone.

I crouched, and brushed my fingers through Ewen's fresh-cut hair. He looked as he had when, at eighteen, he had come into this world. The years that had passed, the anguish of our prison, the taint of drinking our own blood from each other, did not show. This small thing made me happy—for I felt we had some hope so long as we remained together.

His eyes opened, squinting in the darkness—light, for our kind, comes up slowly when first awakening. He laughed at the way my hair had been cut and drawn back from my shoulders.

"You're shiny," he said.

"You, as well," I told him, offering him my arm.

I drew him up, and we stood close together. If I had not had Ewen with me through all this, I think I would not have cared for my own existence. "I saw and heard nothing," I said. "They moved us, and washed and oiled us."

"It's like some kind of sacrifice," he said. He put his hands to my face, rubbing at the oil and some kind of paint they had put on my cheeks to make them slightly ruddy. "They want us beautiful and full of vigor—at least in our looks."

I nodded as he spoke. "And we can use this to escape," I whispered, unsure as to our privacy here.

A voice came to us from two cages away. What I had thought was a pile of blankets was a female of our kind though I did not recognize her. She turned to us, her cloak covering her features. "Many have tried to escape the arena," she said.

◆ 2 ◆

SHE drew the hood of her cloak from her face, and there, before us, was Kiya, the dark, stately vampyress who had first taken care of me in the distant citadel of Hedammu. Kiya, who had gone with us on the journey to the lost kingdom of Alkemara.

Kiya, whom I had asked to raise an army of vampyres to battle the encroaching shadows of this kingdom, before Ewen and I were captured. I had told her to find scholars and warriors and to gather those who would serve the Nahhashim staff and the Maz-Sherah. Now, her scalp was shorn of hair. Her dark skin shone from the oil she had been covered in; she looked more like a goddess. She stood before us in a long tunic embroidered with the markings of the Disk, and of those symbols of both Christianity and the bog sorcery that had become the low magick of Taranis-Hir. The tunic was white, split down the middle and tied with a narrow golden cord at its center. It was spattered with dried blood along her breasts and down her middle, as if she had recently drunk from prey or had herself been tortured. Upon her wrists and ankles, slender silver cuffs, nearly like bracelets, similar to the ones I wore.

As if remembering our last words in Hedammu before we had parted eleven years earlier, she said, "I waited for your call to us."

"I could not," I said. I reached through the openings of my cage, but could not reach her.

She nodded, slowly, keeping her eyes closed as if she did not want to look at me. "I went to the old cities and the fallen towers of Byzantium. I sought out the vampyres of the islands as well, from Crete to Sicily. On battlefields, I went to dying soldiers, seeking the ones who had been bravest and most ruthless. I stole into prisons at blackest night to bring good tidings to the doomed. Before their deaths I told them I could give them eternal life in this world if they would serve the Nahhashim and the Priest of Blood. To a man, they swore, for all were afraid of mortal death. I brought the breath into their lungs, and the Sacred Kiss passed to each for as long as I had the ability to offer it. And they rose again from the dead, and their thirst was great. They honored their oath to me and to our tribe. Still, I waited for your call in the stream. We all waited. I felt fire in the stream, and I grew afraid. I could no longer bestow the Sacred Kiss, and though our wings spread in the night, still we all felt the pull of the earth with them. But I did not give up hope, Falconer. Many took over merchant ships, for their wings would not sprout. The ships provided constant food for us, as well as a daily resting place. Those of us who still could fly guided them through storm and rough sea. Our first sign of the change was the sound like a dragon roaring in the distance and billowing smoke from many lands, as if mortals had set their homes and castles afire to cure the evil that had come. Plagues overtook them, and with their arrival, death and winter and despair. Entire villages were wiped from the Earth. Cities lost half of their citizens from fever and miasma. Many murdered their loved ones. Seas froze as if an age of ice were upon us, and yet the land might be warm as summer. When we hunted, even children who suffered offered themselves up to us. And then . . . the dream . . . the Virgin of Shadows with the great Disk and its corona of light. I despaired of you, Falconer, as we all did. We traveled the night, weakened by silence within the stream, drinking from too many mortals, rabid for the last drop of life from them, unable to satisfy ourselves. Here . . . the Myrrydanai drew us with the power of the Nahhashim. A year of war ensued, but all was lost. All . . . lost . . . There is no Maz-Sherah, Falconer. You are but a youth called Aleric found among the dead of Hedammu. All the legends and all we know of Merod Al Kamr— lost. The Serpent has sloughed his skin and left us. The Myrrydanai increase, and have stained the mortal world with their shadows. This Game was devised for us, and those who pass this test become . . . become Morn."

Finally, she opened her eyes to show me the one thing she could no longer hide. Her eyes were without color, as those of the Morns had been who attacked me earlier that evening. "I can still see," she said. "But they have torn at me over the past few years, Aleric. They take us and put us on a device of torment where we are burned and torn and bled. It has tiny barbs along it, and it pulls at your skin, and it moves you as if it is . . . a living creature. The Red Scorpion, some call it, for its claws are sharp, its sting is painful, and it is stained deep with blood."

"It writes the crimes of the vampyres upon our flesh," someone off in the dark said.

Another cried out, "Its stinger jabs and burrows beneath the skin."

"It is made," Kiya said, "to extract our essence."

"It is made to enslave us," said the one in the dark.

I had to catch my breath, for seeing Kiya, I felt an urgent need to hold her and to gather our kind together that we might fight this enemy that had imprisoned us all. "The stream is weak," I said. "I broke the law of our tribe. I mingled the juice of the Serpent's Venom with my blood that Ewen might live from me, and I from him. But we both felt the fire burn through the current connecting all of us."

"The stream exists, but it is weak as are all of us," she said. "We must accept our fate here. There is no escape as long as they entrap us with silver, torment us, and send us to the Game."

An eternity seemed to pass before she spoke again. During this time, Ewen and I watched others—movements of bodies in cages, shapes beneath cloth. I counted nearly twenty there—how many were vampyres? How many mortal? I could not tell. As I noticed flashes of silver at the ankle or wrist, I guessed these alone were the immortals of my kind and counted at least six.

"I am sorry that our meeting again is our ending," she said.

"Kiya," I said, and as I did so I became aware of others in cages. "What is the Game?"

She drew her long cape closer to her body. "Midias and I have fought in three previous Games." She glanced over at the vampyre near her cage. "He has fought bravely. We have . . ."

"We have *survived*," the one called Midias said with anger rising in his voice. "We came for you. For the Maz-Sherah. We felt the fire in the stream, all of us, but still we came. We saw the Dark Age descend. And tonight, we will kill each other, for that is the Game. Kill or be killed. Extinguish or live to the next Game." He made a growling sound as if ready to chew his way through the bars of the cage. "You, the Maz-Sherah," he said. "You, hidden away for years. Unable to escape your prison. You are no Maz-Sherah."

Other vampyres rose, and mortals stood in cages, as well—stripped nearly naked, be they man or woman. Their stories were many—some had been nuns and monks, others were peasants or local gentry.

At some distance, I heard the restless snorts and whinnies of horses, and growls like dogs. I could not fathom how so many creatures were kept imprisoned like this for a game.

"When your kind came, the Devil rode out with you," a mortal said. "The Devil owns this land now. We are forsaken by all that is good. We have only the dream and the Disk. And you monsters brought these plagues on your wings when you first came from Hell."

Midias laughed. "I'll drink you dry tonight, fool, so you can meet this Devil you love so much!"

"I would prefer death to this," the man said.

I felt a terrible wave of remorse for having brought any of them here. Had I not existed, Kiya and others would have remained at Hedammu and Alkemara—they would not have crossed the sea and land to come to this place, from which plagues were born. Instead, just as Alkemara had been inverted, so the world itself had inverted and was now ruled by shadow. It was because I went to Alkemara, I freed the Priest of Blood and fulfilled the prophecy of Medhya, that the Veil had torn, that the Whispering Shades had come into being in this world. It was because I had gone searching for power—and for what must not be found.

"The same alchemist who imprisoned the Priest, has built a machine of Hell," Kiya said. "It . . . changes us."

"We will soon be Morns," yet another vampyre, a female, said, though she kept her face hooded.

"I will never be a Morn," Midias said. "I will slaughter all of them before submitting to those treacherous shadows."

"The Morns have no memory of us," Kiya said. "Morns are empty shells, the meat of them dug out with pincers."

"Slaves to the Myrrydanai," Midias said. "They are the vampyres who find no rest."

"All of us will become Morns here. Or enter the Extinguishing."

"You demons!" a woman shouted from a cage not far from mine. She raised her fist upward as if imploring God's wrath. "You brought evil to our land! You deserve worse than death!"

"And we shall have it," Kiya said.

"What of this?" I asked. "These cages?"

"The arena is above us," she said. "These are the Illumination Nights. For the nights of the full moon, they celebrate with slaughter. We are the entertainment."

"We are the Game," another said.

"A theater filled with the kingdom of Hell, above us."

"An arena of blood," Midias said. "I have seen such games—in Rome, when I was young, before even the emperors came, I saw my people, Etruscans, pit slave against slave for entertainment. And as the great city rose, so its coliseum was built and great gladiators fought. This is what this alchemist has created. The trenches were dug, the stage built, the old theater risen, and the marshes drained for the Illumination Nights."

"It is a festival of murder," a mortal man said.

"The alchemist has maps and plans for such engineering," Midias said. "Like us, he is immortal."

"But not vampyre," Kiya said, still retaining the pride of our tribe. "Yet he has the essence of our breath within him."

"I have seen his handiwork before," Midias said, nodding. "For he once created great spectacles for Rome, and in the days when the ships of Egypt crossed the seas, he also was there. He may be as old as the Priests of Medhya. He may be but a thousand years old."

"Artephius," I said. The name brought chills to me, for this unseen immortal had linked his fate to mine. I had felt his presence in Alkemara and seen his handiwork in the bone and blood cellar beneath the inverted kingdom. Now he had come, like a plague himself, to entrap our kind, to bring some apocalypse to this Earth with the tearing of the Veil. And yet, I wanted to meet him and see what power he had.

"*Artephius,*" Kiya said the name as if it were poison. "He is sent by the Devil himself. He is the creator of the device."

"The wheel and table, with their torments, that draw us closer to becoming Morns."

"The Red Scorpion," Midias said, almost quietly.

Red Scorpion, I thought. Calyx had mentioned this, as well.

"What are Morns?" Ewen asked.

Kiya closed her eyes. "They are us. They are what we become in the Red Scorpion that the alchemist has devised. The torments may last for years, but in the end, when the extract is procured, the essence of our lives is drained. Our minds are fragmented. Our wills, gone. I have seen many become Morns. They walk in daylight and do not burn. They obey only their masters, and none other, and believe they are children of the alchemist himself."

"Neither do they rest, until their last bone crumbles," Midias said. "They hunt for transgressors. For vampyres. For the Akkadite heretics. For all who oppose the kingdom."

"Their wings are torn and retorn, and their tongues cut. They are a thousand times cut and ripped and their skin flayed, until, as it regenerates, it has changed in substance. It becomes tough and thick. Their youth and beauty are bludgeoned. Their brains are cut and examined. They are eyes for the Myrrydanai, who send them out like hounds to hunt for heretics and traitors and all those who oppose them."

"Morns are dirt. Better to be extinguished than to become one of them," Midias said. "Better to be torn by the Chymer wolves in the Game, than to become Morn."

"All of us will become Morn," Kiya said. "In the Game, they wear us down. They pit vampyre against mortal, or vampyre against those wolf-bitch Chymers," Kiya said. "The arena runs with blood after the

Game. The women of the Forest are burned at the week's end—for the festival of blood finishes with the witch-fires."

"We fight bears, as well," another woman said. "Sometimes. Sometimes, Morns."

"The blasted Chymers and their shapeshifting," a man said.

"God help me! Please save me!" a young maiden called out. "I do not want to die! I do not want to die!"

"Shut your trap, you whore," a man snapped at her.

"Please, God! Please, God!" the maiden moaned.

"If you don't shut your trap," the man responded, "I'll be the first to cut you. I swear I will."

"Aleric," Ewen said, pointing to the ceiling above the cage. "Look."

"Kiya," I said, ignoring Ewen for the moment. I looked at her white eyes with their slight discharge—as if tears had formed and would remain along her lower eyelids. What had they done to her? What tortures? Why do this to us? Why not just send us to the Extinguishing—what did this kingdom gain?

"We are all dead, Maz-Sherah," she said, so quietly that I thought she might be speaking in my mind, in the old way, as if we had the power again. As if we had the talents of vampyres within us, rather than the talents of jackals. But the silver cuffs kept us from our power. "These mortals do not even understand what is to come— once our tribe is destroyed here, Medhya will regain her blood. And her flesh. And her being. And the balance of life and death will be no more."

"It's beginning!" a man shouted. Several of the mortals in their cages began rattling at the bars, and moaning.

"What is it?" Ewen asked.

"They hear the wheels turning at the back," Midias said. "They hear the hum of the crowd."

"Like a plague of locusts," Kiya said.

• 3 •

I listened, but could not hear anything, for the mortals in their cages had begun this kind of lowing and sobbing that sounded too much like cattle. From cages beyond my sight, I heard the howls of wolves and the shrieks of some kind of wild cat.

Kiya's mouth widened as she, too, began crying out against the Game to come. Her teeth had been filed to nubs. They had not grown back, which I did not understand, for in our race, whatever was torn from us or wounded would heal and regenerate by the next nightfall—unless our hearts had been torn out, or our heads severed from our bodies. I did not understand this vulnerability.

"Look for the poison bucket," Kiya said, her voice desperate and sad.

"One's for poison, one's for silver!" Midias shouted. He leaned into the space between the bars of his cage. His white eyes squinted as he looked toward me, and as he clutched the bars, his cloak opened, and I saw the heavily muscled body of a man who could have been a beast in terms of his girth. He was big and broad, and I had no doubt that he could tear a man in half with his bare hands. "Look for the sacrifice. The first mortals to fight are Provacators. They will be easier to defeat than those who come after. The Essedar will fight from chariots—to gain advantage, look to the horses and not the arrows."

"Do not trust even the smallest child in this Game, Maz-Sherah," Kiya said. "Do not let yourself be taken."

"One mortal is sacrifice," Midias said. "The others are there to cut off the heads of the vampyres. They will try to take us down and trample us."

"Why do they play this Game?" I asked.

"These are funeral games before the great feasts," he said. "The Illumination Nights are for the burning of the Forest folk whom they call witch. We are their sport, for subduing demons gives them pleasure and raises their blood for the excitement of the Feasts of the Sacred and the Illumination Nights."

"How do we win?" I asked. The humming had grown louder above us. I smelled the fear and expectation of all who waited in the cages.

"You don't win!" a mortal maiden shouted from somewhere in the back. "We send you to Hell!"

"To Hell!" a man shouted from another cage.

I heard the grinding of gears and the squeaks of pulleys.

"The sacrifice!" Midias shouted, "The ring of fire! You must get to her!" He cupped his hands over his mouth to be heard, for the hum above us had turned to a roar, and I could not understand his other words.

It was beginning, this Game.

"It's opening," Ewen said, grasping my arm as he looked upward.

I glanced to the ceiling, then I felt the lurch of the cage.

Beneath us, unseen wheels turned rapidly with the groans of some mechanism.

Above, a trapdoor flew open.

The cage we stood within moved rapidly, hoisted upward in jerky movements.

I grasped the bars of the cage, and Ewen, as if he were my child, grabbed me about the waist as he half sank to the cage floor.

Kiya's milky gaze followed me as the cage ascended up, up, up through the trapdoor, into the night, into that deafening roar of an audience waiting for our entrance.

Waiting for our destruction.

Above us, chains and ropes were hooked across an overhanging bower made of thick masts, like fishing poles and nets, drawing us upward, while a counterweighted series of chains dropped into the cellar below.

The trapdoor, now beneath us in the floor of the arena, snapped shut. For a minute, I crouched in the suspended cage and looked out over what seemed a multitude of torches and hundreds of people all gathered in circles about me. Other cages shot up from their trap-doors as well.

Four cages had come to hang there, suspended from the bower above a rounded stage.

The arena was long and broad, and the tiered rows of seats sur-rounding it were packed. The torchlight was blinding.

My eyes watered as I squinted, trying to see how we might make an escape.

The effect overwhelmed our senses—vampyres are keenly sensi-tive to light and sound and smell, for they are important in the hunt.

From their tiered seats beyond the netting of the arena, the crowd chanted slogans. Drums were hammered at earsplitting levels, and the thick smell of incense coated us, its blue smoke drifting from large urns set along every few yards of the stage.

The stink of the herbs and smoke and the chanting and the drum-ming and the unbearable torchlight forced my eyes down onto our stage, unable to sense the extent of the audience or what weapons might be focused on us to keep us in our place.

"I am afraid," Ewen whispered as he clutched me.

I tugged at the silver cuffs at my wrists, but they gave me a series of shocks, like touching fire itself.

The bottom of my cage dropped, pulled by a chain from below.

• CHAPTER 6 •

I fell several feet to the ground—dusty earth, packed against the floor. Ewen dropped with me and landed on his left side.

I tasted the dirt in my throat.

A thunder roll of shouting and crying out accompanied the dropping of the warriors for the Game.

Lying on my back, I glanced upward to see what escape route I could find.

A net of some fine filigree was thrown across from one bowed staff to another, as if it were a rib cage with the net as its skin, covering it, holding us within. I had no doubt that the net had silver within it, or some sorcery of the Myrrydanai. They would not risk our escape in the night during such an event as this Game.

I thought of testing the canopy net, but the manacles on my wrists and my ankles would keep me from opening my wingspan. I was bound to the earth for these games. I knew the point of them—kill or be killed, for the entertainment of the masses who had gathered.

I saw thick blue smoke like mist along the edges of the arena; hundreds of torches lit the night; behind us, and around us, the crowds screamed with delight as they saw us. Shouts of "Burn in Hell!" "Devils will roast!" as well as cries for their warrior-heroes, and a chanting song for the ones called Chymers.

I made out some of this through the crowd's garbling song, including, "Those who bring the shadows to us! Those who run with wolf and bear! Those who speak with earthbound spirits! Chymer sisters! Chymer mothers!"

The fires burned more fiercely at the other end of the arena. Above them, in the stands, was a great pavilion rising up with two bell tents on either side of it. I could guess that the Lord and Lady of the land would be seated there, as well as any champions of the kingdom and lesser nobility.

I glanced up, hearing strange cries of birds—did the Morns patrol the skies around the arena? Above me, from the canopy of netting and the bowed rib cage of masts, many wheels and weights hung, their chains going into the floor itself—through the trapdoors, to the others in the cages beneath us.

I counted those hanging chains, and found there were at least thirty of them that went through various trapdoors beneath the ground. They were lined up in rows and hung to the side of the arena, along its main boulevard.

I also noticed several large wooden tubs, as if for bathing, placed at three intervals at either side of the arena, stopping at the halfway mark, away from the two of us.

All along the ground, there were weapons, also placed as if at measured distances from the last weapon. Some, such as pikes and tridents and flankshares were thrust in the flooring to be drawn out. Others, such as swords and daggers, seemed a spray of bright metal along the ground.

Serpent, father of my race, give me the strength, and bestow blessings upon Ewen and myself that we might defeat the mortals.

I asked the Serpent for protection and victory, though I did not believe any deity existed to hear my prayer.

I sat up, quickly looked over to Ewen, who held a long double-bladed sword, as if it had been handed to him. He stared at me as if unsure what to do. Though we had died within months of each other, and were separated in age by only a year, he always seemed much younger than I felt. My sense of protection for him was strong, and I could not watch him die in such a place. "We fight to the death," I said. "Others have survived this tournament. We shall, as well."

"The silver shoots fire through my arms," he said, though I could barely hear him for the booming cries of the stadium.

"Take up that sword," I said, pointing to another by his feet. "There are other swords along the way, and when you come to a chain, strike it with your sword. If the chain can be broken, it will keep another warrior from rising!"

"It's heavy," he said, trying to lift the sword—the silver cuffs alternately burning and freezing at our wrists and ankles. "I can only carry one!"

"Take it up!" I reached to my left, where a long pike lay, the end of it shaped as a trident. I looked over at him—he had the sword, and dragged it along the packed earth that covered the floor. "Take it up! Use both hands to fight. Do you want to go to your Extinguishing here?"

He drew the sword up with some effort.

"I know you're weak now. Clutch it and remember the battles in the wars," I said. "Remember how we cut through the Saracens and fought for the Cross and for our brothers. Remember how there was a boy named Thibaud who fought with an ax in his hand—weaker than you or I with silver cuffs!"

He swung the sword out. The strength of the fresh blood helped us both. "Do not trust the mortals here!" I shouted to him over the roar of the crowd. "Be as savage as we would in the hunt, with the power of night and the dragon wings upon our shoulders. Show no mercy!"

I pointed to the far end of the arena, through the smoke and torchlight. "To win, we reach the sacrifice. Do not look for me as we fight, but make your way toward the end of the arena, where the ring of fire burns! Weapons are all around us—if you lose your swords, grab up a spear—grab another, and another!"

Neither Kiya nor Midias had come up with us. Instead, I saw four mortals—two maidens, one youth of fifteen perhaps, and a man.

As their cages hung suspended at the other end of the long arena, shaped like an ellipse, the crowd quieted, and somewhere at the far edge, a man shouted so loud that I could hear him down where we waited for the start of this fight. "Gron the Gut-Strewer! Champion Devil-Slayer! Prince of Slaughter!"

Cheers went up, and when the clapping subsided, the announcer shouted, "Legiera, warrior of Normandy! Butcher of Demons! Killer of Twelve Devils since the first Illumination Night's Game! Woman blessed above all women!"

After the hoots and cheers and applause, yet another name was called, "Sir Rath of Jarik! The Faceless Swordsman! Nine heads has he raised! Knighted by the High Queen, Blessed by the Priests! The Dream-Light shines within him!"

For this man, the roar increased, and I covered my ears for the pain the noise caused. I scoured the crowd to make out a single face, but blue smoke and the torchlight blinded me to all but the floor of the arena.

There was no time to find the master of this spectacle or try to seek an escape route—the boy came running at me, swinging a mace over his head in one hand, and in his left, he carried a hand axe. I caught my breath watching him, this little savage, short for his age,

yet full of the bravery of men at battle—he was a man by the defini-
tion of my century, yet I could not help but see the child in him. He,
too, was scarred, and his head had been shaved. He ran as if he would
fall on all fours and leap upon me.

I crouched low, and as he neared me, I thrust the trident up,
catching his mace in its swing and flinging it off to the left.

The roar from the people watching deafened me, and the bright
light of fire caused me to keep my eyes only half-open.

The youth was undeterred by the loss of one weapon. He twirled
the ax as if it to throw it directly at my heart, but as it left his fingers,
I dropped to the ground, and on my stomach moved swiftly to the
left that the falling ax might not touch me.

Seeing this, he ran a circle around both Ewen and me—by this
time, the young maiden with braids at her hair, her breasts bare with
a torn tunic that hardly covered her thighs, came running. She had a
twin-bladed sword, curved at the ends like a scimitar. She, like the
boy, had been trained hard in this combat and went directly for Ewen.
He leapt up, but I could see in his face the fear—for with the silver
bracelets upon him, he could not fight as a vampyre. He could not
fight even as one of these maidens.

We were here to be destroyed, that was evident. The crowd wanted
to watch the public destruction of vampyres. The mortals, despite their
lack of armor and shield, despite their nakedness, had the advantage
over us. And yet, in some respects, they were sacrifices as much as who-
ever stood in the ring of fire by the pavilion.

All of us, sacrifices.

This was the Game, and its only rule was survival.

◆ 2 ◆

I saw one of the naked maidens dip her spear into a large wide tub—
and, in withdrawing it, it dripped with quicksilver. Her beautiful face
and pale flesh belied the strength of her arm—as she brought the drip-

ping spear back to her side, I saw thickly corded muscle at her shoulder. She was like some Amazon, beautiful and deadly—she ran with the swiftness of a doe, and halfway across the arena, she raised the spear and gave a battle cry that sounded like a howl. She kept running toward me, heaving the spear as she ran. Her release of it was perfection—no ordinary mortal, this woman. She was well trained in warcraft, and the spear flew fast and straight toward me. I had but a moment to escape its dart—it whizzed by my left arm, and clattered as it hit the sand-covered floor of the arena.

Ewen had his swords up, fighting off another mortal—this one, a man who had appeared from one of the traps in the floor without my noticing him. He was heavily muscled, thick of waist, his face covered in a visored helmet shaped like a boar's head. This boar-head warrior carried a net that looked as if it were spun from silver in his left hand, and in his right, a strange lance with several blades like teeth along its upper edges, ending in a curved blade at the tip, like a crescent moon.

The Boar, as I thought of this fighter, kept slinging the net toward Ewen, past Ewen's swords, trying to get it to catch him around the head. Meantime, he swung the lance downward against my friend's waist, cutting him each time he swung. Ewen had to spin, and crouch, then rise and use his blades primarily defensively against the lance.

The boy, meantime, had arisen again and was coming from behind me. I reached down for the lance that the maiden had thrown, and, drawing it up, I ran over to the tub that was opposite the one filled with quicksilver.

The water within was brownish yellow, and I dipped my fingers into it quickly, lifting them to my face. Poison of some kind. This was what Kiya had told me to do—I dipped the lance into it, washing off the last of the quicksilver, coating the lance in this poison.

As I did, the boy was right there, running toward me, his mace a whirlwind above his head—I could hear it humming as if with a sacred melody, as if a thousand locusts hummed there above his head.

I remembered another boy, younger than this one, who died when I became vampyre. I remembered his face, suddenly, and did not wish to stop this young life though he came at me with force and fury.

I heard the crowd scream with delight, as if they had waited for this moment—the boy and the vampyre, the mortal youth in his ragged cloth and the immortal youth in silver cuffs.

I watched the mace as he released its tension, and as the blade-covered ball shot toward me, I crouched low, pushing the lance upward.

The boy continued to run toward me, even after letting the mace fly, and I was sure he would run directly to the lance's blades—but instead, he dropped and slid beneath it, his foot nearly touching my knee.

I, too, dropped, as the great mace came down, its lead still in the boy's hands, and then brought the lance upward to catch the chain that held the ball to the wand. As I did so, the mace whipped the lance from my hands, and it flew across the floor.

The boy and I looked at each other for a second. He had fear in his eyes then, for, without his weapons, he lay in the shadow of a monster—I was a demon to him, and though he was nearly a man, the boy still lived there in his eyes, and he had not confronted death often.

"I do not want to kill you," I said, lifting him.

He kicked at me and tugged away, spitting at me as he went, shouting profanity and curses about the devils and their tricks. When he was several yards from me, he yelled to the audience, "I am Gron, I am the killer of the devils in three Games!" He raised his fist skyward as if to his god. "I will slaughter all these devils tonight!" He stomped the ground, and the spectators stomped their feet in response.

Those who watched this spectacle began chanting "Gron, the Champion of the Game!"

Others matched this with, "Gron the Great! Gron the Just! Gron the Young! Gron the Devil-Slayer!"

Then, the boy ran toward a fallen sword and lifted it as the crowd cheered. He raised it over his head, swinging it about. "Tonight the devils return to Hell!" he shouted.

"To Hell!" the crowd chanted back to him.

"Long live Gron! Master of the Game! Blessed of the Dream! Prince of Illuminations!" they shouted, cheering and crying out their love for him.

Ewen still fought the Boar, while the muscled maiden swung an ax at his side. I wanted to run to him to cut the maiden down, but the boy's shouting drew me back.

Gron had raised his battle cry and come running for me, his eyes wild and his hair streaming behind him. Without thinking, I tried to draw my wrist from the silver cuff—if I could but remove the cuffs, I might be able to draw my wings out. I might gain strength that had been lost. But the boy ran swiftly, and my next thought was for Ewen—the amazon had slammed her ax into his back twice, and his knees had buckled.

The Boar managed to throw the silver net over him.

Once, in my nights of power, I could run as if a wolf—or stretch my dragon wings that I could fly across this expanse easily and take down the mortals. But the silver at my ankles and wrists kept me bound to mortal ability—only fangs could descend; but they were no good if I could not reach a human throat for tearing.

As the boy came running at me, I backed up toward that tub of poison, but did not move toward any of the weapons scattered about.

I could see the smug victory on the boy's face as he ran toward me, but beyond him, I saw the Boar take Ewen down as if he were a deer in the woods, shot through with arrows.

I had but seconds as the boy's sword sang in the air as he brandished it, ready to cut off my head as he came at me.

But as he did so, I accepted a cut from his sword to my right arm—the blood burst from my skin, and the pain caused me to cry out for,

again, the quicksilver at his blade's tip weakened me—but as my
blood spattered his face, I reached forward and drew him by the
throat and was about to throw him in the tub of poison that I might
drown him in it—but, overcome with thirst, I leaned into his throat
and tore at it hungrily. His blood burst into my mouth, and I tasted
the sweetest of life from that youth though he struggled mightily
against me, his legs kicking out, his hands reaching up for my throat
as well to strangle me. I held him fast, unable to let go, unable even to
draw back for a breath or drop him that I might help Ewen—I had
not held a mortal in my hands in years, and though this one was
strong, my teeth dug in deep, and the living wine poured into me until I threw him down, an empty vessel, on the floor.

The crowd had gone silent, though the drums still beat their horrible tattoo.

Drenched in the youth's lifeblood, I felt greater strength, and
rather than dipping a weapon into the tub of poison, I leapt into it,
and soaked my body with it. I could smell its liquid death upon me,
sticking in my hair and along my flesh. Then, I got out and began
running to the other end of the arena, the drumming in my ears, the
blue smoke of incense filling my breath.

Ewen, bleeding profusely, lay there, with the muscled maiden
jabbing him now with a double-bladed sword, while the Boar had begun dragging him in the silver net along the edge of the stage, that
those who sat just above might see the Devil that had been subdued.

I leapt upon the maiden, and before she could fight me, I had torn
into her throat as well, passing the poison to her through my skin into
her bloodstream. A fire must have burned there, for she screamed as if
she were in a furnace—and I threw her down, to writhe in the pain that
had entered her body as I held her there, the poison dripping upon her.
I felt no compassion, nothing but fury, and when she had passed to the
Threshold, I lifted her and threw her toward the wall of the arena.

The Boar came at me with a trident and the ax that the maiden had dropped—he had the scars of many fights upon him, and the crowd again took up the cheers and shouts, crying out the name, "Rath! Rath! Rath!"

As they cheered, he roared within his helmet and jabbed at me. I could see Ewen from the periphery of my vision, caught in the silver net, wounded terribly, unable to move—but his eyes remained fixed on me as I fought. Had I felt the stream between us, I would have spoken into his mind to reassure him, but there was no current between us—no invisible path that connected us.

I pretended that he might hear me, and spoke within my mind in the hope that he would, *I will not let you go into the Extinguishing, my friend. I will not let these mortals send you there.*

I lifted up the trident I had dropped when the Game had begun. I swung it up against this Rath Boar-Head, catching him just beneath his left breast, jabbing as deeply as I could. Yet, the skin was rough—his flesh at his chest was like an enormous scar that had not ever healed, and it felt like bull-hide as I pressed the trident into it.

He sliced the ax down, catching me above my left knee, but I drew away before it had cut too deep. Bleeding so freely was a new experience, for when we had our full power, the healing would occur within seconds. But the silver kept my body weak, and I knew that if he got one more good hit in, I would be down, and my death would be certain.

Suddenly, I heard the banging of metal and the slamming of doors—and behind us, four more cages had popped up from below, hanging several feet up from the ground, swinging slightly from the bower of masts overhead.

A great cry and thunderous clapping came from the crowds watching.

The occupants of the cages dropped, and this distracted Rath Boar-Head. I went to the fallen maiden, and drew the double-bladed sword that Ewen had carried from under her body.

The blue smoke made it hard to see who our new adversaries might be, but soon enough, one of them had begun coming for Rath Boar-Head.

When I turned around, Rath slashed a double-bladed sword at the vampyre Midias, who held a weapon I had only seen once before, in the distant wars. It was called a Whore-Comb by some, a Fascine by others—but it was like a harpoon with many barbs upon it, each one longer than the other, until, at its tip, a long scythelike blade curved. Midias swung it about so that it might mow down any in his path.

I leapt into the fight against Rath, and as Midias plunged his Whore-Comb into Rath's chest, I came from behind, plunging the double-bladed sword just at his neck, severing his spine.

For a moment, Boar-Head stood still, while Midias and I drew back.

Then, he fell, and as soon as he did, Midias was upon him, drawing back the helmet, and using a scimitar, cut through his thick neck. He raised the helmetless head to the crowd, whose cheers and even the drumming had died. "Here is your champion! Rath who slew the devils of the first Game! Rath who survived twelve Games that he might live as a god among you! But now, I, Midias of Kalos, and the Falconer of Alkemara, have brought your god to his knees!"

"MIDIAS!" the crowds exulted. "THE DRAGON OF THE EAST! THE LORD OF THE DAMNED! GREAT MIDIAS, KILLER OF RATH OF THE BOARS!"

He grinned as they did this, and glanced over at me, a sparkle in his eye.

"They praise us, then slaughter us!" I said.

"As it ever was and ever shall be. And now, now my friend the Game is in our hands!" Midias said as he approached me. "We must reach the Sacrifice, for she holds the endgame."

I glanced down the arena to the maiden who was our sacrifice.

"We drink from her, and we are victors of this night," he said.

I felt glad for this, and knelt beside Ewen. The silver of the net was like thorns against my fingers—I went to get the pike and drew the net from him. He lay there, his wounds still weeping his blood, but it had slowed. I took his hand in mine and gripped it tight. "Take my strength," I said.

He did not seem to see me, but he gripped my fingers as well.

"Rise!" Midias shouted at me. "It is not over, fool!"

I looked over at him, but he'd already turned his back on me. Raising his Whore-Comb, he began sweeping at the air, preparing for the tiger that had come running toward him.

"The gauntlet begins!" he shouted. "More will come! Look!" He pointed to three other cages that shot up from the traps, all in a row. "Some are slaves, some are murderers, some are their saints—but all are trained for this!"

As mortals dropped to the ground, and the smoke grew thick, I said, "Ewen's losing too much blood. The silver slows our healing."

Midias glanced over at my friend. "They do not send us another vampyre until one of us is destroyed. We need aid."

"You will not kill him!" I said, snarling.

"Then we all shall extinguish here with him!" he shouted, his voice bitter with fury. "For two of us cannot defeat the many that will come! Hurry—do you see this?" And again, three more cages shot up from the blue smoke that clouded the arena. I could barely see the sacrifice, bound at the far end, for smoke and the sand that burst upward as each cage shot toward the rafterlike masts that held them suspended.

• 3 •

A T Ewen's side, I whispered to him. "My beloved, my friend, do you remember the battles with the Saracens? How we tore through them and held their heads up with shouts of victory? How we burned their city and drank their wine? You must remember this now,

Ewen. Remember your mortal courage, then remember you are of the bloodline of Merod Al Kamr. You are sacred, of a blood and breath stolen from Medhya and passed from Pythia to me, and from me to you through the Sacred Kiss. I brought you into this realm that you would rise and become my right hand. Do you understand? Do you remember these things? I will not lose my right hand, Ewen. Do you hear me?"

Ewen looked up at me, and whispered, "Let me go, Aleric. Do as Midias commands. Let me go. I would not take you into the Extinguishing. I would go there to keep you from its embrace."

"If you can speak," I said, "you can rise, Ewen. Do you think this stranger brought us mortal blood in our captivity that we might die here? The gods look over us and raise us for a reason. They do not pity us as we die. They do not hasten our deaths, but want us to fight. Fight! They raise us even in pain. Fight until the last moment is taken. Even when we are torn. And they do this because we have a place here. We are not the unnatural demons that once our mortal realm told us. You know what is within us, my best, my finest. Do you think the Serpent who is the guide of our tribe would bring us here, and bind us, if we were not meant to rise up? You have my blood in you. You are blood of my blood. You are Maz-Sherah as I am Maz-Sherah." I spoke quickly and held back the chill I felt within me. "You are more brother to me than brother. You are more love to me than love. I will not let you go to your Extinguishing." I fought against the overwhelming despair I, too, had begun to feel, yet I refused it entry. I would not go to the Extinguishing, nor would I let my friend travel to that Hell on Earth—that endless life that was no life. That conscious state that had no meaning.

I crawled to the fallen maiden. Drinking from the dead did not bring strength, but as I listened to her heartbeat, I discovered she still had a tincture of life left within her. I brought her to him, and sliced at her throat. I massaged her flesh that the blood poured into him.

Ewen drank the last moments of her earthly life. I watched a ruddiness come into his face, and the flow of his own blood onto the sand had begun to staunch.

"Now, rise, my friend," I whispered at his ear. "Rise and fight with us."

I offered him my arm and drew him up. I put my arm over his shoulder. "We are begotten of an ancient war," I said. "This is but one battle to fight."

♦ 4 ♦

MIDIAS yelled for us to prepare, and I shouted back that we would slaughter all creatures sent. Ewen had raised his weapons high, and my heart grew glad for seeing him, though he still had strength to regain. "When you have a mortal in your sights, draw them close and tear their throats," I said.

"You should be so fortunate!" Midias shouted. "They will send more than twenty at us before the dawn." He pointed to the chains and counterweights strung along the length of the arena. "Every one of them holds a warrior. What you must do is get rid of these." He flashed the silver cuff at his wrist.

"Is there a way?" I asked.

"The sacrifice. She is there with the key to remove these. Her blood is finer than that of other mortals, for she has not toiled since the end of the plagues, nor does she have any plague in her blood, nor has she tasted spoiled meat or common wine. She has slept on fur and ridden the backs of slaves for a full year. She is the reward for any who reach her. But to reach her, you must get past many warriors."

"Have you ever cut the chains?" I asked, pointing toward the many hanging chains of the cages, for there were dozens of them along the arena's wide boulevard.

"The—" He realized what I meant. "Impossible."

"Do you see?" I asked, pointing with my sword to a trapdoor a few feet from us. "There is a bolt from the door to the chain that draws it upward."

"And you think we can break these? Bust them with swords? All of them? The bolts are iron and strong."

"No," I said. "Bolts may be iron. Locks may be metal. But the doors are made of wood, and if we cut through the planking we weaken the traps."

"They will still rise," he said, not understanding. "Even if you break the door, the cages still rise."

"But when the cages above open, and the mortals fall . . ." I said.

"They keep heading downward . . ." He grinned at this, his great jaw of spiked teeth gleaming "Kiya told me you had piss in you, and she was right." He laughed, not taking his eyes from the line of warriors who had come to attack. "We have but seconds now. I do not know how to fight them and break the doors and still stand."

"The doors are in straight lines and follow together like the paths in the Forest that run alongside the roads," I said, pointing to the cages that hung suspended above us, spaced at various intervals. "You and I fight, and Ewen will hack at the wooden doors. We guard him as we go. We move as soldiers in battle—two in front, and one behind."

He grunted his assent as several mortals dropped from their cages.

"Keep watch," I told my friend. "If one of the mortals breaks through us, you will not have time. And we will fight while you reach the sacrifice. Get the key from her and do not drink, for our freedom is more important than the temptation of blood."

Other mortals rose, grabbing the weapons nearest them. These warriors were thick as tree trunks and carried shields studded with curved blades; they wore helmets as if they were knights, and though their tunics were short, they had leg shields and leather arm coverings. At least three of them wore visored helmets with what looked like fins jutting out from them, with a wide mouth of a visor so that, from a distance, they seemed to be bronze fish standing with tridents and nets. Still two others, near the quicksilver tubs, raised scimitars and daggers—these were youths with heavy muscles, their loincloths drawn tight, their skin heavily oiled. They dipped their blades in the silver and swung them so swiftly they blurred and seemed to be whips more than scimitars. The roars from the crowd increased, and the names of these heroes of the Game were called as if they were naming saints and martyrs and the gods themselves.

From the thick blue smoke, two horse-drawn chariots thundered up from a ramplike trap that had opened. These were the Essedar, the horse-warriors. Each chariot had drivers in full armor and helms for protection, but the women who raised their crossbows from behind the drivers were dressed almost as queens of some hellish country. They wore gold and silk garments, with false sleeves that their arms might have free movement. Their hair was drawn beneath double-coned hennins that gave them the effect of demon's horns as they leaned over the side of the chariot for better aim. The only armor they wore that could be seen was an unusual thin brow-and-nose guard coming off the hennin's coronet, further adding to the effect that these were otherworldly fighters. The arrows sang in the air as the Essedar leaned to the outer edges of their chariots and fired upon us, one after the other. It looked like a rain of lances, and all the three of us could do was outrun, outjump, outdistance ourselves from the falling arrows.

Still more fighters came, and while Midias and I hacked our way through the many, Ewen broke through the wooden trapdoors so that as more cages arose, when the floors dropped beneath the mortal warriors, they often fell back into the holding cellar rather than upon the ground.

The Game had begun to make me feel alive as I had not in the years of the well. Even in the midst of grabbing the driver of one of the Essedar chariots and flinging him to the earth, I thought of our benefactor who had brought us fresh mortal blood for several nights before we had been drawn to this Game. If Ewen and I had not had that sustaining blood, we might not have been able to slaughter the mortals who came at us.

Midias tore away many a mortal life, but we also sustained further injury—for the arrows sometimes hit, and the quicksilver burned at the wound. I had taken three ax cuts, a slice to my hand, and deep cuts to my thigh. I had numerous burns from the whippings of a huge mortal with a shaved head and a shield nearly as tall as he himself. The gauntlet we had to cross blurred, for it seemed one mortal after another came up from the traps below, though Ewen's efforts kept still many others from arising to fight us.

At each turn of the fight, at each ax cut, each sword thrust into flesh, the crowds roar had changed as they seemed to be cheering us—the demons—onward. They had stopped shouting the names of their mortal champions. Instead, the names Falconer the Slaughterer and Midias the Bloody and Ewen Tormentor were called out. Many lamps and torches were lit so that the arena's edge become brighter. This illumination highlighted the rim of the arena in a way I hadn't noticed before. I began to realize in all this that we fought in an arena shaped like a disk—the Disk itself. This Game was a Game of the believers of Taranis-Hir. Even those of us who defended our existences were playing for the pleasure of the Myrrydanai themselves. The Disk that had hung from the mortals' necks as we'd slaughtered them was the very Disk in which we fought.

I glanced through that blue smoke as we three slaughtered our ways toward the sacrifice. There, in the pavilion, I saw the great Queen of this land, and her King, though their faces were made vague by distance. And all around them, priests in white robes.

Blood was upon all of us, and I tasted its mud on my tongue;

Midias was soaked from his scalp to his feet in it. Sweat poured from me, and it nearly made me feel mortal again. I thought that one thing I had not felt or considered since I had come to vampyrism:

I felt the glory of being alive.

• 5 •

A beast had dropped from one cage behind me. I looked back, bringing my sword up in case any warrior should come out of the blue smoke. It was a large tiger, and yet another beast was there, as well: a wolf like none I had seen. This one was black, and the size of a man, though it crouched and watched rather than leapt upon anyone. Neither it nor the tiger seemed interested in the Game, but they stood on guard, not far from where they'd dropped.

Midias ran toward a warrior who had dropped into an open trap, but had managed to cling to the edges of the open doorway. The warrior had drawn a trident and net with him, and circled Midias, who sliced the Whore-Comb through the air. Ewen brought a scimitar down against a helmeted man, but the man dodged him, and Ewen spun about, crouching and grabbing a short sword that he jabbed into the man's gut as he came up.

The beasts moved slowly—the tiger toward Midias, but the wolf retreated toward the far end of the arena, as if it were wounded.

As if the moment had frozen in time, I heard an explosion off in the dark beyond the torchlight, and the blue smoke of the incense and the flash of light that occurred forced me to take in the scene before me—Midias with his weapon swung, his arms outstretched with it, his cloak falling off his shoulders as his thick dark hair fell along his back; Ewen, bounding toward Midias to stop the beast; the tiger leaping with its powerful grace toward Midias.

Farther down through the light and smoke, the maiden sacrifice, who stood with her breasts bared and her yellow hair braided, her hands behind her back; the vague crowd beyond the lights, screaming as if they did not wish this outcome.

Above us, the spiderweb of nets and masts and pulleys and ropes and chains and counterweights.

The sacrifice stops the Game.

I raced to the ring of fire and leapt through to its center. I rolled toward the maiden's feet, grabbing them, then her legs that I might draw myself upward again. Her face was tense with fear and shame. She was not beautiful by nature's hand, but the tears in her eyes reminded me of life itself, of the humility and suffering of the mortal, caught in the silver restraints of the world of men.

Behind me, the wolf slowed, dropping to its haunches. It watched me with a fierce intelligence.

I glanced back at the maiden as I touched her shoulders with my hands. She had been put there as my prize. She shivered like a tame fawn, suddenly seeing the spear of its keeper. I was meant to drink from her and take her key and raise the victory howl for my brothers and sisters of the Blood of Medhya, the children of the Dark Madonna and the Priests of Blood and Flesh and Shadow.

She looked into my eyes as if I were a god who had come to take her into oblivion.

"Where is this key?" I asked. "Quick!"

She opened her mouth, and there on her tongue, lay a small turnkey.

I drew it from her, and pressed it along the ridge of my left cuff, finding the hole that was tinier than any lock I had ever before seen devised. Turning it, the silver bracelet fell to the earth. Then, the other, and the ones at my ankle. Even as they fell, I felt the relief and the surge of power.

In her despair, the maiden turned her head to the side, offering me her throat. I heard the cries of the crowd—they were not pleading for her life, but viciously commanding me to drain her that they might watch and enjoy the vampyric bloodfeast.

I felt my lips ache for the salt upon her throat and imagined ripping the skin and digging into her flesh that I might burst her life into my mouth.

As I leaned forward to this, I saw the pavilion more clearly behind her, through the ring of fire.

The smoke of incense had been blown by a chilly breeze, and it was as if the smoke had parted that I might better view her face.

I saw the Queen of this Game, wrapped in the furs of bears and wolves.

It was Alienora—now called Enora by her people—and yet it was not she.

Her fair red hair was drawn back, though ringlets fell along her neck; she wore a coronet of gold that encircled a low mitre. She wore a triumphant smile. I knew this smile was not for me, nor was it for the maiden sacrifice, nor for any other in the arena.

Her smile was for the Game itself, and her power over it. The spectators represented her will, and it was their bloodthirsty cry that pleased her.

She was at the high throne of the Game itself. Beside her, her consort, my half brother Corentin Falmouth. All around them, the white-robed priests—the Myrrydanai in disguise. They, too, chanted for the sacrifice to be slaughtered.

I drew back from the maiden's throat.

I turned to the throng that had gathered closest to the ring of fire, beyond the netting and the masts and the cages that protected them from those of the arena. They shouted for me to tear into the girl, to suck from her blossom, to drink her like ale from a pitcher.

I had once before grown weary of mortals who desired only destruction. Though my nature was to drink the blood of the living, I did not want be the slave to this mindless mass of human life. I would drink a hundred of them before I touched this sacrificial offering.

"I will not take her to Death!" I shouted, my voice hoarse yet strong. I raised my left hand, turning it into a fist as if I were beating at the sky. "I will not give you that pleasure! You have proven yourselves and your kingdom worthy of the name 'monster'! You have outdone even those of us who drink the blood of innocents! You have turned slaughter into a game which no one can win. The winged devils you fear slaughter for survival, not for entertainment!"

For a moment, I felt another presence there. It was as if in these shouts to the bloodthirsty crowds around the arena, I had begun pushing back a doorway that I myself had shut and locked. I had begun feeling something for even my prey—for this maiden who had been presented as just a sacrifice to the winner of the Game. Drink for the vampyre, and glory for the crowd to watch one final act of slaughter, but in this, not the slaughter of a vampyre or a warrior, but of a girl who had reached her blossoming, and been chained here for the sole purpose of her defilement as entertainment for the world at large. I wondered at these humans who would rather tear the maiden to whom nature had brought beauty and the awakening of life itself, than to admire and love her for those qualities of youth that so quickly passed.

It was the Serpent—called by some the *wisdom* of our tribe, by others, its darkness.

I felt the presence of a great stream again, despite the silver at my wrists and ankles. I felt, for lack of a better word, *divinity*. At that moment. I felt that this was not simply an Arena of Vampyres. This was not simply a game. It was the Game, and this field of battle was the crossroads where earthly life and earthly death touched, and at its center, the Great Serpent that separated the worlds.

The stream flowed here strong and wide. Its currents connected all who were vampyre.

Yet, how could this be? How in this torchlight, this land now owned by the Myrrydanai who were slaves to the dark goddess herself, could the stream exist here?

And there in the sense of the stream, I heard Merod's voice, in my blood, *"Do not abandon hope here, Falconer. I did not bring you to your destiny to watch you die in a wolf's maw. You have power, still, though you do not understand it."*

Why then? I wanted to ask *To what am I Maz-Sherah, Priest? To what purpose do I exist when the world has begun its unmaking?*

The stream itself lessened, but I had felt it again. I had felt it despite my imprisonment, and knew that what good there was in creatures such as myself and my tribal brothers and sisters, existed even here, in exile, in slavery, in the edge of survival itself. We were not yet destroyed, and the stream could be tapped into here, even here with its silver bracelets and silver-tipped lances. The Myrrydanai had not destroyed it, and the fire we had felt within it had not yet blocked its currents.

I felt Kiya within it, below in that holding cage; I felt others of our kind, though not many.

I glanced outward, toward Ewen—he, too, had felt the stream between us, that vampyre consciousness that recognized our brethren and connected us to each other in our day's sleep and nocturnal hunts. He had fallen, and had begun crawling toward me. I rushed to him. Using the key, I unlocked his cuffs.

Then, the stream ebbed slightly, and became a thin current, and then, it stopped again.

Gone now, but we had a moment of the stream passing through us, connecting us.

* 6 *

THE crowd remained silent, watching me. Midias, who had made quick work of the tiger that had attacked him, came over to me and spat at the ground in front of me. "You fool!" he said. "You fool. Give me the key. Give it!"

When he had dropped his silver cuffs, he said, "The Game is all we have before the Scorpion."

Then he went toward the ring of fire.

"Midias!" I shouted.

He continued, his dragon wings erupting from his muscled shoulders as he went. He glanced back before stepping inside the ring where the maiden had remained. "It is not over until she is drained!"

He grabbed her in his arms, and his wings spread wide as they both rose into the air. Her head fell backward, her braids undone as her hair flowed freely downward. His wings beat slowly that he might hover, just above the ring of fire, and give a show of bleeding the maiden for the throngs of people, for the nobles in their pavilion.

"No!" I cried out, and felt my wings take up the wind that had come down from the north, dispersing the smoke, changing the direction of the torch-fires that were strung along the arena's walls.

I barely heard the shouts from the seats, as I grabbed Midias's wing, and tore it back. He swung around, nearly dropping the maiden, who shrieked and began beating at his face. He had already bitten along her shoulder, and blood dripped down her back. He dropped her, and I dove beneath him to save her from the fall but could not. She hit the earth, and grabbed at her sides as if her ribs had been broken. Midias came after me, and we fought in the air. Like flying wolves, we went at each other, tooth and claw. He tore my shoulder between his teeth, and white-hot pain went through me. But I kept at his wings, because they were any vampyre's vulnerability. Finally, I cracked one of them backward at the tip, and it was enough for him to drop, crouching just outside the ring of fire. I landed beside him and drew him up by the scalp. My full fury unleashed, I threw him across the arena floor. When he hit the wall, he did not rise, but lay there, watching me.

I went to him and leaned over to whisper in his ear. "We are not their entertainment. You are the son of the Great Serpent. You are a descendant of the Priests of Blood and of the Nahhashim, and of the stolen immortality of Medhya. It is the breath of the gods within you that brings you eternal life. Better to extinguish than take the life of one who is the slave of these people. Those who watch us now would gladly see a boy of fourteen rip our innards and spill them on the sand. And you would give them this pleasure."

"You are stupid," he snarled. "Stupid. She is dead. They"—he pointed upward, toward the walls around us—"*they* have ordered her death. Whether tonight at the Game, or tomorrow night at the burnings. She was lucky that you reached her, for a death at our lips is better than the tongues of fire that will find her in the Illumination Nights."

"Is this true?" I felt as if the wind were knocked out of me.

I offered my hand, which he took, grasping up to my forearm in a grip of trust. I pointed to Ewen, who lay in a heap. "Go help him. Now."

When I returned to the sacrifice, she wrapped her arms around my feet. "Please save me. Please save me," she wept against my ankles. "They will kill me. They will kill me, whether you drink from me or not. Please, drink from me, and if I die with your stain upon me, perhaps I will come back from the dead as you once did."

I crouched down, and said, "Is there no escape for you?"

"None," she said, speaking so quickly that I did not catch all that she told me. "My uncle . . . executed . . . His son sentenced me to death . . . our whole family. My mother . . . my sisters . . . burned as witches, but they practiced no such sorcery." As she spilled the litany of her crimes, I remembered my own mother, tied up with kindling, set ablaze before a crowd that might also cheer this maiden's horrific death.

"What would you do if you were free?"

"I would pluck the eyes from everyone here and cut out their hearts," she said, with nearly a growl in her throat.

"What is your name?" I asked.

"Jehan," she said.

"Jehan, do you swear you cannot escape this fate?"

She nodded.

Then I whispered in her ear, glancing at the spectators, many of whom had gone to the edge of the wall and clung to the thick netting that kept them safe from us. "If I brought you into the realm in which I live, of immortality, you would need to drink blood to survive. And you would never see the sun, nor those you love again. And these people, all around you, would seek to put you in this arena to watch your blood spilled again for their fun." There was a flurry of movement along the pavilion benches, as Enora herself stood up and came down to an area as close as she could to the arena's edge.

"I don't care," she said. "I hate them. I have hated them since I was a child. Since everything changed. Since the plagues. Since I watched my sisters burning, crying out to God for mercy. Crying out to the White Robes for help. Pleading for their lives from the unholy Lady of this land."

"If I take your life here," I said. "I would do it so that there would be no pain. Death would be a brief sleep. But if I brought the breath of immortality to you . . ."

"Give it to me," she demanded, pleading. "Give it to me. Please. I want to be like you."

"Is there a tomb for your family? For you must be found and brought from it soon after you return from the Threshold between life and death."

She nodded. "It is tended by the White Robes, for my uncle was once trusted by Lady Enora herself." She told me the family name of this tomb, and I had known that name well. "Sensterre," she said, the name of a man I had once known who had nearly been like a father to me before he turned against me in my youth.

The name of that spirit that had spoken to the ashling.

Kenan, the huntsman, who had loved my mother once.

Had loved me, once, almost as a second son.

"I knew your uncle," I told her.

"Yes," she said, sadly. "He trusted his own bastard, Corentin, and sought to destroy you. But he repented, and turned against Enora's court. He tried to free you a year ago from the well. They caught him. They tortured him over many months. They tried to force him to confess that he was in league with the Devil, but he would not. And when at last they had flayed the skin from his back and chest, and were pressing him against the block to take his head from him, he shouted out to the crowd that vengeance would come to them, riding on the wings of the Devil himself. By that, he meant you, Aleric, Falconer of the barony. But I want those wings of the Devil, as well. I want to be one of you that I might exact vengeance as he would wish me to do." Her eyes lit as if on fire, and her voice thrilled with the words she spoke. "Make me as you," she said. "For I am dead, and I would rise again from the dead to drive this evil from my home."

◆ 7 ◆

THE spectators had begun shouting curses upon us, but when I lifted Jehan into my arms, they cheered and admonished me to end the Game by drinking from her.

Ewen, leaning against Midias for support, had come closer to us. I signaled for both of them to gather.

"We will bleed this one, all of us," I said. I could see Midias's ire rising again, and I held my hand up as a signal of calm. "But we will do so that she does not suffer. We will give them a show as none they have seen. When you feel the last moments of her life in your mouths, draw back from her. Spread your wings over us that no one may see."

We raised Jehan into our embrace, bringing her up as if she were levitating between us. I told her to know that the prickling of our teeth at her veins would only give her a slight but swift pain. We held her aloft, careful of her broken leg for I did not wish to add to her suffering. Midias brought his mouth to her left forearm, and Ewen, to her right.

I took her throat. My sharpest fangs, as they emerged, sliced like the thinnest of razors into her skin. Her head fell backward as I lapped at the blood, and she closed her eyes as if wandering into that sleep mortals fear. We drank her while the people who watched us went silent again, as if they had never seen three devils take a maiden like this. I felt as if they had collectively held their breath while her life spilled down our throats.

When I felt that last taste of blood, before the hand of death had taken her, I whispered to my companions, "Now."

We brought her back to the ground. Midias's wings opened, as did Ewen's, and they became a dark cloak that covered the two of us.

I leaned over Jehan, feeling her last puffs of life on my face. I pressed my lips to hers, forcing them open wider that my breath could enter her lungs.

I felt the fire of the Sacred Kiss as it moved from me—an entity created between us, a third individual that only existed there, in that moment, the creature that she would become a few days after her death, a bridge between the one who could not die and the one who would turn back from death's threshold.

It only took a few moments. When it was done, her soul had fled its cage as she took in her last breath.

We lifted her for the crowd to see, for this was their prize, their goal, their hunger:

Another corpse, a pale maiden, a bloodletting, a victory of the winged devils in the Game.

Many rushed to the nets to get a closer glimpse, and some piled atop each other. They sighed and wept and cheered and roared and stomped their feet and praised the name of the Falconer and of the winged devils. Some of the women pressed garlands of flowers through the netting, as if to show affection to us. They whistled, too, and shrieked their joy.

We paraded the sacrifice to all sides of the arena, but lastly before the nobility. They, too, had come to the edge of the nets and the wall to see us.

I glanced up at Alienora, who no longer was Alienora, and she looked at me as if she had never seen me before.

Beside her, the thickened Corentin stood, dressed in the foppery of the highborn.

We laid Jehan's body there, gently, and I kept my hand beneath her head as I brought it to the dirt-covered floor.

I left my friends there, kissing them both on the cheek, as was right for champions. I lifted their arms for the crowd to show their adoration for the devils who had won the Game that night.

To Midias, I said, "The three of us now." I nodded toward the masts and nets above and around us.

"I have tried," Midias said. "Many of us have. Do you think in all these years stronger vampyres than you or I have not attempted what you are planning? Even the swords cannot cut that net, and then there are the Morns. They are up there, in the sky."

"Are they so strong?" I asked.

"They don't need strength." He laughed bitterly. "There are nearly one hundred of them now, and they swarm on their victims like hornets on a mouse. Do you hear them? Above this barbarous shouting? Do you hear them?"

I glanced up into the night, and thought perhaps I had heard a high-pitched shriek, as if someone were being tortured in the heavens.

"They love it when one of us escapes," he said. "They swarm and bring us down. In the sky, the Morns. On earth, the wolves. This is a place of sorcery greater than ours."

Still, I felt it was worth trying, and looked up and down the arena as the people stomped their feet and shouted for us, exulting in the death of the sacrificial maiden, in the blood spilled in the arena of their own kind. My revulsion for the mortal world reached its heights that night, for they had no care for their fallen heroes or their maidens. I looked down the arena, to those open trapdoors, and wondered if there might be a way to slip down them. But in looking, I saw movement along one of the quicksilver buckets.

I saw the wolf that had dropped from its cage well before I reached the sacrifice of the Game.

It had waited, as if patient for the end of the night. It began moving toward us, and then I saw there were other wolves, moving toward Ewen and Midias, as well. We drew up what weapons we found, and each readied himself for these to attack.

They moved at a trot and then faster, until they seemed to bound across the arena floor. I had drawn a spear out of a fallen warrior's gut, and held it at the ready. The three of us drew apart, each to take a wolf, each to fight one more adversary.

You are the last fighter, wolf, I thought as it came toward me. *Come get me. Come.*

◆ 8 ◆

THE running wolf changed course, slightly. It bounded toward the wall edge of the stage, just beneath the stands. I watched as it moved slowly, too cautiously, toward the large tub of quicksilver. How was this? How could a wolf know to dip its paws into the liquid silver, and yet it did.

Then, it reared upon its haunches. For a moment I thought it stood up, and as I raced toward it, I saw the wolf itself seem to dissipate as if into mist, or my eyesight failed me in the smoke and torch-fires—for it had become a woman—a phantasmic woman whose face seemed to blur with that of a dog and whose body was covered in wolf's fur, her scalp hooded with the muzzle and ears of the creature.

She raised her hands, and they dripped with the liquid silver.

I did not understand this sorcery, but she drew from the folds of her wolf's fur a crossbow, and as she moved toward me, her hands dripping silver, she shot it as quickly. Her aim was true, and the arrow shot into my stomach. I dropped to my knees, gasping in pain. I briefly turned, hoping Midias would be there, or Ewen, with a scimitar, but they had already been covered in silver nets, thrown by similarly strange women in ceremonial robes, who had come through traps that we had not yet seen.

No one wins the Game.

The arrow had barbs along it, and was made of carved bone. Instinctively, I reached for it, to draw it from my body, but the barbs stung my fingers—tipped with something more than mere silver.

I turned my palms upward to see the small barbs—shark's teeth, I supposed—sticking into the flesh of my hands. I felt an infusion in my bloodstream.

The pain subsided quickly, as a strange, disorienting feeling overcame me. My breath became weak, and I was only barely aware that the wolf-woman had a slender but strong line attached to the bone arrow. With some strength, she began tugging at it, dragging me slowly across the floor.

Within my body, the hooked barbs of the arrow had caught on to a lower rib, and though it tore at me, I went, like a fish, caught.

I recognized what mysterious poison her arrow had brought to my blood—it was the juice of that graveyard flower, what the vampyres called the Flesh of Medhya, a deadly poison to mortals—the vampyric doorway between this world and what lay beyond the Veil. It was the same juice that I had tasted—but only a drop—in order to make my blood the blood of life that Ewen and I might survive off each other, though we grew weak with the mixture. But the dose that had coated the arrow—and the barbs—infused me with a feeling of light-headedness, and my fear grew that I would move toward the Veil, causing a further tear in its fabric. This drug was not to be abused, nor was it meant to become an escape from this world. Merod Al Kamr had used it sparingly, as had I. But this wolf-woman had doused her arrow with it.

Soon, I grew less aware of the incense and the crowd's roar. I saw the face of the wolf-woman above me, and she seemed familiar though I could not remember how I might have seen her before.

When she spoke, I knew: I had seen her in that Glass of Second Sight, when Merod has first given me the flower to bite for its nectar, when I had seen my beloved Alienora give birth among the anchoresses of the caves.

This was an anchoress, the one who had been there at the birth of my child.

Do not think of your son, Falconer. Do not think of what has been lost.

This hag's voice came into my mind, and she smiled as she saw recognition in my eyes. *"I have given you the juice of a thousand of the blood flowers,"* she said, though her lips did not move. *"You will open the Veil for us that the Lord of Shadow comes, and his Lady of Darkness."*

For a moment, I saw her as a wolf again, a great beast whose paws pressed against my chest.

The blue smoke covered the wolf's jaws as they opened, coming toward my throat, though the flower's juice had made me feel so wonderful, free of pain and anguish.

The wolf whispered to me, "You will be a slave to her. You will be a serpent beneath her heel. Your flesh will open. You will be a doorway between this world and the next."

The wolf's voice seemed to grow distant as if many leagues

away. I felt my soul move away from my body into a marsh-mist of white.

I knew the Veil, for I had torn it before.

I saw a great explosion of fire to my left, and within it, my mother stood, her form made up of leaping flames as she lifted her arm to reach toward me. As if in a dream, I reached for her, and her body turned to crumbling ash. To the right of me, coming through the fire, my brother Frey, his body torn by the weapons of war, his face half-hanging from his skull. He stood there, glaring at me, as if I had done some evil to him, and he had not yet forgiven me. But he, too, evaporated into a smoky column as the fire died down, and all became mist, though the smell of burning embers remained.

I saw there, in that mist, Merod Al Kamr, the Priest of Blood, whom I had brought into my flesh through his death, through devouring, to fulfill the great prophecy of Medhya, the Dark Madonna, the Lady of Darkness, the Mother of Vampyres, the Destroyer of Vampyres.

Merod, his shaved head tattooed with those picture-words I had seen come alive upon him once; his tunic wrapped in an ancient style; his great clawlike wings, leathery and beating slowly against an unfelt wind; his hands outstretched to me; his bloodred eyes half-lidded as if he, too, were drugged by the heavy potency of the flower.

In his hands, what seemed at first, a human face, a mask of skin.

His lips moved, but I could hear nothing but the voice of the wolf-woman beyond this tear in the Veil. "You are the doorway, Maz-Sherah. Tear the Veil that they may cross."

◆ 9 ◆

I had the sensation of being dragged, then raised, but my mind had begun spinning to darkness. When I awoke, through the haze, I looked up at the man who stood above me.

Was he a man at all? He seemed more machine than mortal.

His helm shone in the flickering candlelight, upon it, the face of that basilisk known to many as a cockatrice—that bastard offspring of serpent and bird, though this seemed almost as a gryphon for the fierce aspect of it. Upon the visor was etched small writing of some occult origin that seemed Arabic in nature; the place whence he might see was a slatted opening, too thin for even a finger to penetrate it; where his nostrils might inhale, a slightly raised curvature of metal; where mouth might exist, a slender slit. It was like seeing an entombed king arise in the raiments of a rich barrow rather than a man hiding within it.

To look upon a man so attired would not have raised within me what I felt. It was terror as he watched me, as if he were some other being—neither mortal nor vampyre, neither god nor monster. Perhaps the flower's drug had done this to me—weakened me to such an extent that I, a slaughterer of mortals, the Maz-Sherah of my tribe, would feel horror for this man who looked, in his metal, like a living statue, or worse, a silver cocoon wrapped around some terrible emptiness.

The air around him was thick, as if his presence lay heavy upon it, an impenetrable aura. To say that one feels dread is not enough—when one is a vampyre and may drink the blood of mortals, the awe of terror is not enough. What it felt like to be in his presence was as of some alien creature, fallen to earth, and the shine of his metal made him seem a marriage of spirit and machine. He stank of an immortality I could not fathom. Yet, despite the fear I felt—and the revulsion toward him, for well I remembered the fate to which he had brought Merod Al Kamr and Alkemara itself—he had a warm, vibrant, and terrible charisma. I understood then why Pythia might give herself to him and betray her father and her sisters and the kingdom of the vampyres. I understood how he could lure many vampyres to their own destructions, for he was hypnotic though I could not see his face. He had a secret magnetism to him that lay beneath the bronze and silver.

I was in his thrall.

I felt this power, even through the gauze gloves upon his hands as he touched my throat, as if feeling for life. It was like a spider crawling across my Adam's apple, light as a feather beneath my chin, as if about to sting. Had he suffered from the plagues? I wondered, for the wrapping of hands was common among the diseased. Could an immortal suffer as any mortal might, but without cure?

Silver had been interlaced with the bronze, and gave the effect—as the helmet covered his throat—of golden fire to his collar and shoulders. Upon his shoulders, the talons of an eagle clasped as a holding pin for the helmet. He wore a red silk robe over a camlet—the robe had to have been brought from the Saracens, for I knew none other who had such fine cloth.

He drew close to me as if reading my eyes, sniffing at me for some odor. I, too, sniffed at him—I did not smell mortality upon him, yet he was not of my tribe. I had none of the hunger for his blood that I might feel with a mortal man.

His gloved hands explored my arms and shoulders, as if feeling for breaks and tenderness. He brought his hands down along my ribs, feeling the wounds that had not healed, pressing his fingers there, though I felt no pain. Then, he pressed down on my stomach and chest, as if ensuring that my lungs would exhale air. He returned to study my face, and through the visorlike slits where his eyes would be, I saw piercing deep eyes that seemed like round spheres of black surrounded by a rim of sky blue. Even beneath the mask, his face was covered in a gauzelike *guimp* so that all I could see beneath the helmet were his eyes and the curve of his lips, as if his entire body, beneath armor, were covered in a great bandage.

He nodded to me, as if acknowledging my wakeful state. "Do not fight, little falcon," he whispered. "Your blood is too thick with the Sang-Fleur, blood-drinker. Were you not told? A bite of one flower may strengthen your blood, but this much—that wolf-bitch and her sisters took the entire harvest to make this. They have too much wolf in them, I think."

Watching him, my curiosity grew. I noticed the Arabic writing at the throat of the helmet, and I wondered if he ever removed it—or if life was a territory of war for him, and his armor, preparation for constant battle.

I tried to speak, but when I moved my lips, he touched them lightly with his fingers. "Shh, little falcon," he whispered. "Save your strength. You have lost much blood. Speak not, and rest. Wait a little while until we are done here. Do not be afraid of me, my boy. I am here to care for you. I am here that you may fight again. I have wanted to draw you from the well for many years, but have stayed my hand. I watched you in Alkemara with your companions. I have watched you many years before. I know who you are. And you per-haps know me?"

And I did know him. I had sensed his presence in Alkemara. Merod had spoken of him.

"Show me your face," I gasped, fighting for breath.

"You would not like it," he said.

"Show me your face, Artephius," I said.

Artephius. Alchemist. Architect of the Inverted and Buried Kingdom of Alkemara. Architect of the destruction of the city of the Priest of Blood. Seducer of Pythia, stealer of the secrets of the immortal world, the man who had lived many lifetimes and whose sole purpose had seemed to be to destroy god and man.

Even in my drugged state, I wanted to tear him apart with my bare hands.

I sensed a lurking horror in his presence; I sensed a terrible love of the world from him, as well.

He nodded in answer to my request. "When you are ready to see my face, I will show it to you. To you alone, little falcon," he said. He brought his visored face close to mine and peered at me as if searching my eyes for something.

I saw the same strips of gauze that were on his hands, about his eyes. His eyes burned with red blood pulsing behind their darkness.

"You are so beautiful," he whispered as he studied my features, smelling my skin, his fingers parting my lips as he felt my teeth and gums. "Your teeth, sharp and perfect. You have the breath of Pythia within you. I can smell her on you. I can smell . . . your bloodline."

· CHAPTER 7 ·

· 1 ·

IT was my need to see the woman I once knew as Alienora, when I had been in the tomb of the Priest of Blood, to go into a different state of consciousness using the flower of the Serpent's Venom to see through the Glass, which is Second Sight, into the mists of the Veil itself. But it was that very act that began the rip in the Veil that brought the creatures—those whispering shadows that rode in with plagues upon their backs, seeking me, seeking what I loved most, breathing inhumanity into the maiden I loved and had lost. But the Veil had torn further. More of the Myrrydanai had come, and when I returned to the Baron's castle in my homeland, I was too late—Alienora had given herself, body and soul, to the shadows.

The great staff of power, the Nahhashim, had been stolen from me before my imprisonment.

Destiny brings us to our crossroads, and so this was mine—and I did not then know how the Veil could mend, or how Medhya, the Mother of Darkness, would find us with her hounds, these shadows.

One thing I knew: Artephius, the Alchemist, the Architect, the Immortal, had engineered much of this. When I thought of those I loved, I wanted to reach up and tear his throat out.

But I had gone into the Veil again, I had been sent there by the drug of the flower, polluting my bloodstream. Not the tincture that I had tasted for Ewen's sake that we might drink in the well and live. No, this was a dose so great that I felt as if I must be dying there, looking up at the immortal who had destroyed so much.

◆ 2 ◆

IN the years of my captivity beneath the earth, I had thought of him. I knew he was close, for Merod's voice within visions mentioned him. *Artephius. Artefeo. Al-Togheri.* All the names of this man who had crossed the world's seas, its deserts, its great cities and desolate places. He may have been a thousand years old, as old as Pythia herself.

He was called the Alchemist, for he dealt in immortality and precious metals. His genius was engineering devices of torment and science. I feared him more than any other being on Earth, even more than I feared the Dark Madonna, who would happily tear my flesh from my bones and suck the blood from my marrow.

I wondered that he did not cut off my head, then, for if I truly were the Maz-Sherah, Artephius would want me extinguished above all others.

"That Chymer nearly destroyed him," the alchemist said, glancing to his right. He barked orders to servants unseen. "They are greedy for their shadow priests—*you,* get the cloth. *There,* in the bowl." He shouted several words in a foreign language. In my drugged state, I could not focus enough to understand the meaning—yet it sounded as if no mortal had ever spoken this tongue before.

He brought a cool, damp cloth to my brow, wiping my forehead clean of sweat. "You have been asleep for many hours," he said. His ministrations to me filled me with repulsion. He treated me as if I were some helpless child laid out before him. As if he would do something terrible to me, after treating me sweetly. "Your skin is dry. You need blood."

Then, I watched as he drew a small curved blade up. It glinted in the candlelight. Quickly, he passed it through the flame of one of the hanging candles. Then, he called for the servant who stood nearby holding a pitcher; the servant moved closer.

The servant was a man of twenty or so, wearing an open brown blouse. "Jean," he said to the servant, "do not keep that look of terror. You will not die from this. Do you understand?" I noticed Jean's hair was cut as the hunters often styled theirs—just over the ears and slightly down the back of the neck. His cheeks were flush pink as if he had warmed himself by the hearth, and his eyes were wide with fear, like a rabbit caught in a trap. He reminded me somewhat of Ewen, when he had been mortal, and my consciousness had become so dimmed that I called to him as if he were my beloved friend. "Jean, come, have I not cut you before?"

The servant nodded, keeping his eyes on the alchemist as if too terrified to look at my face.

"There," Artephius said, reaching over to touch the youth's shoulder. "Maidens have given more blood in a month than you will give tonight." His hand slid down Jean's arm, and came to rest at his wrist.

Artephius tore at the sleeve of his blouse, drawing it back from his forearm; he brought the blade swiftly across Jean's wrist; the pitcher fell from the servant's other hand to the floor. I heard the smash of its clay, and the splash of water.

"Drink this," the man said, pressing the servant's wrist against my teeth. "Drink it now or it will staunch."

I pressed my lips against the young man's wrist, feeling his pulse beat rapidly, then, as I took too much, slowly, ever slowly that drumbeat toward mortal death. Yet, I did not drink so much as to kill him.

"Take all of him," Artephius growled. "All of him. You must drain him to the dregs."

I saw the look in Jean's eyes—he had gone from fear to that drugged place, that rapping slowly at the Threshold between life and death, the pleasure of those last moments of surrender. I could not take him there, I could not make this young man lose life simply to satisfy me. He had done me no wrong, and I had drunk enough from him.

I drew my teeth from his wrist, closing my mouth.

When Artephius let go of his wrist, the young man fell to the floor.

"You should have finished him off," the alchemist said. He glanced down at the youth. "I suppose I will bleed him while he sleeps. And others." He ran his hands along my face. "You have the fever of the Veil still within you."

I tasted the blood, and the memories of my life returned—my childhood with my mother and brothers and sisters in the fields, and the work in the Baron's castle, the battles, and when my memory brought the Pythoness to my lips, bringing vampyrism into my body through her breath, I went into the dark embrace of sleep.

As I went, I heard Artephius call orders to another servant, "Bring the surgeons and you, and you, any young prisoners. Young as you can find them. The blood needs to be vital, and strong, so no sicklings, none with disease. I want seven bowlsful of blood in him, and seven bowls out of him."

• 3 •

I had crossed the Veil again. This panicked me, for I feared tearing it further. It was like breaking through the membrane of birth to go there, and within it, all was like mist and smoke, and anything I saw was like a dream within a dream.

I could feel the steam of it, and through the mist that rose at all sides, my mind and my eyes created the creatures that were there, for none were as they appeared to me. Yet I saw the phantasms of my age—the mermaids who seemed as crawling sea monsters, the tentacled god whose single great eye burned against sulfurous flesh, and there among the mist and the beasts and the shadows, I saw that face of Medhya called Datbathani, the Serpent Goddess, and the golden mask of the Disk dream was upon her face.

In her hand, she carried a curved dagger of sacrifice.

"Why do you threaten our world?" I asked her. "Why do you bring plagues and terrors?"

She spoke with a voice that held seduction and glamour within it. "Maz-Sherah," she said. "I am not the Dark Mother you fear. Medhya sleeps while you cross the Veil. The Great Serpent is with you even now as you are tormented. You are to find the mask I have lost, and bring it, for your existence—and the existence of your children—depend upon this."

"I don't understand," I said. I reached toward her, though snakes wrapped about her waist, clothing her nakedness. The vipers at her throat struck at my fingers as I reached toward her face to draw the mask from her that I might see her. My hand nearly touched the gold mask, but the vipers stung me with their bites. Their venom became flames running along my fingertips so that when I drew my hand back I saw what the sorcerers called the Hand of Glory there—a murderer's hand, lit at each tip, a diabolical candle for invoking demons and the dead.

"How can I have children?" I asked, as I looked at my burning hand.

She nodded. "Two came from the maiden. In your loins, the serpent of life lives. The Maz-Sherah has the seed of the tribe within him. You create a bloodline of the Maz-Sherah."

"But in the Glass," I said. "In the Veil, I saw only one. A boy. And she . . . sacrificed my child to the bogs. To . . ."

"To Medhya," she said. The masked goddess looked down at me, and brought her hand to my burning palm. She intertwined her fingers with mine. "What seemed a sacrifice was a baptism. What seemed one child, was two, for from the Maz-Sherah, twins shall be born. One of fire and one of blood, one to tear the Veil and one to mend it." The fire of my hand spread to hers, and soon ran along her arm and up to her shoulder. I watched as her entire body began burning, its snakes writhing and dropping from her, and in the last, the gold mask turned molten and red like lava and began pouring from her face, leaving blackened ash. Her words came to me as her body exploded outward with a great force, a fireball explosion that consumed all around me, except my own body. I stepped through the fire, as she said, "The mask was stolen, Maz-Sherah, and taken far across the seas. It is a mask of unleashing, and you must find it to fulfill your destiny."

I heard the voice of Artephius intrude upon this drugged vision of fire. His words drew me back into the windowless chamber where he had ministered fresh blood to me to wash away the effects of the flower's nectar.

He said, "This creature is going to his destruction. Quick, the blood, bring the blood. His blood boils beneath his skin. The blood! The blood!"

◆ 4 ◆

I felt it, as well. A terrible burning within me, and I remembered all that Kiya had once taught me about the Extinguishing. It was a state of awareness, yet with no ability, no movement, unending thirst, and endless life in every particle of being, yet it was its own Hell. I slipped back and forth through the Veil and saw many terrible and wondrous things, but the goddess was not there, nor was the Serpent, and I felt a madness overtake me, as I wondered if my consciousness would be held between the worlds if I went to my Extinguishing here, upon the surgeon's table.

In the night, I felt fresh blood fuse my thoughts into coherent form. I drew back from the visions and the chaos. Above me, the alchemist's helmeted face, and the gauze of his fingers as he held my lips apart, pouring blood down my throat.

Through the night, I watched Artephius perform as if he were an expert surgeon, with several barbers surrounding, taking his orders of where to cut at my ankles and under my arms to drain the blood. All the while he spoke to me, though I did not remain lucid through the hours of this. "We need to take the poisoned blood from your body, and replace it with this." He flicked his hand toward the servants as if swatting at flies. "More blood, Marie. Yes, fill the bowl."

Another servant—a maiden with her hair wrapped in a cloth— brought up a large wooden bowl. "You are to drink from this. It is fresh and has not yet thickened. As you drink, we will bleed another. Do you understand?"

I nodded. I heard the moans of a youth at some distance, and knew that another bowl was being filled with blood for this transfusion.

He instructed an unseen servant to raise my head, and the maiden brought the bowl to my lips. At my feet, barbers set about to cut ridges at my ankle and calf to bleed me.

"Drink it at a draught," Artephius said. "We must be quick as you drain." He turned to the three surgeons behind him as they ministered to my legs. "He is not like you. The physic you use with others will not work on this creature. Dig the lancet in deep, and hold it there. The devil's wounds will heal quickly, so you may need to constantly open the vein again each time it closes. Are you surgeons or leeches? Do it like this." I felt a deep gouge in the calf of my leg as he said this, then an unpleasantness as he drew the lancet back and forth.

The pains of the razors lessened as they cut at my flesh—these surgeons did not mind treating me a bit roughly. I am certain they wondered at the need to keep a devil alive at all.

More bowls were brought, more cuts were made. I sensed the

loss of blood even as I took more in, fresh from young slaves or servants who were being cut nearby.

My last memory of the night, after many bowls were drunk, was the alchemist saying to me, "Dawn approaches. A coffin has been prepared for you. Your bracelets must remain, for even I do not trust you, my friend. Soon enough, I will show you my inventions, and you will need no restraint."

• 5 •

EARLY the following night, servants came with the bowls of blood. The alchemist stood by, his gloved fingertips spattered red as he tipped a bowl up to my mouth as if I were a baby, nursing.

I felt fevers overcome me. The Veil seemed all around me, reaching for me, and I reached for it.

In it, many visions came to me:

I saw the earth changed, with greater and greater upheavals of land and sea; I saw vast continents breaking off into islands; I saw mountains on fire, with rolling clouds of ash choking the inhabitants of the Earth; I saw the Alkemars, those throwbacks of vampyrism, half-maiden, half-eel, with their lamprey jaws and their crocodilian tails, swimming the newly formed rivers; I saw the elemental spirits of forest and fire take physical form as a race of beings whose aim was to steal the children of the mortal realm; I saw the legendary creatures of old, those minotaurs and centaurs and satyrs, brought not by the gods but by alchemists and architects of blood and flesh who brought together the essences of man and beast into single beings; I watched as those nameless energies, which many think of as chance and luck and misfortune and dread and horror and lethargy, were born into flesh, and rose to destroy nations and to lift those who would bring about mass extinction of entire races of mortals on a scale well beyond any battle I had witnessed in the Crusades. I saw dragons made of silver soaring across the skies, such as I would not see again for many centuries. From their snouts, fire shot out across an already scorched land. From their wombs they dropped their off-spring upon the cities of the world, which burst into great billowing clouds that vibrated against the earth such that every living creature burst into flame and turned to ash. I saw the skins of men and of vampyres hanging from the blackened trees of a forest; skins flayed so perfectly that it was as if one might step into them and wear them as costumes. It was as if some charging bull carried me upon its back, through the layers of visions, running swiftly forward.

But as the membrane of this Otherworld broke and parted, a web within a web within a web, I finally came to that desolate hall of the dead. I stood now on solid ground. A marble floor beneath my feet. All around me, the statues of the gods and goddesses, their forms and features made in the image of mortals. Here were the gods of the Canaanites, and there the Hurrites, and there the Egyptians, and as I moved through this hall, walking with the sound of echoing foot-steps all around me from unseen watchers, I began to see the pattern of the sculptures here. The faces of the gods changed, and the wings or antlers or beards or headdresses or the sacred instruments they held. I observed that they all were the same gods dressed to please their mortal worshippers. There was the mother goddess with her baby on her lap; there was the harsh, judging father with his flowing beard; there the eternal youth with bow and sword and the antlers of the stag; and there was the eternal maiden with her heavy breasts and crescent moon upon her brow; there was the king god with his braided beard and feathered wings; and there an ox-god; and here a wolf-goddess suckling her twins.

When I came to the end of that hall of the dead, two great statues stood, blocking entrance to an arched doorway. The doorway had a legend written in a language unknown to me. Yet, as I watched it, trying to decipher its strange forks and arrows, it wriggled and turned like snakes until it was in my own language. It said, WITHIN, DEATH. WITHOUT, TERROR.

I drew back from the threshold of the doorway. Instead, I turned my attention to the statues on either side of it.

Both were seated upon thrones. These statues were carved from bone and festooned with garlands of gold and scarlet. Their legs were thick and bare, and the bone had been carved into a shining ivory; upon their toes, amber rings; upon their muscled arms, the vine of that flower called the Serpent's Venom, the Flesh of Medhya, or the Veil itself.

I climbed the statue of the goddess, stepping onto her lap. I reached the veils that covered her face. I drew back her veil to see the face that had brought creation to my kind, and hated us for having stolen her immortal blood. But the more I unraveled this veil, the more veil there seemed to be, until when I had drawn it back completely, the world was her veil, and she, the darkness at its center. Yet, I did not feel this was Medhya. This was some unknown goddess to me.

And from this darkness, I saw another—the one I often saw in my visions:

Pythia, her skin luminescent, her eyes black as night, her golden hair wound about her shoulders in serpentine braids, her breasts heavy as if with milk, her hips, wide, and entwined about them, the serpents of the earth, forming a gown of iridescent green and black, constantly moving and re-forming to hide her pale nakedness. As I watched, the serpents emerged from her vaginal opening, born from her womb, writhing as they spilled to the ground, circling her hips as they rose to her throat.

"Why does Medhya wish to kill her children?" I asked Pythia.

Pythia nodded, as if understanding my question. She held up her hand, and in its palm, a razor's cut from which poured the blackest of blood. She pressed her hand to my lips and I tasted the pure blood of the goddess. And within it, I was swept into a vision of that kingdom of Myrryd, where once Medhya ruled as the immortal queen. Only, as a dream might be, I did not feel this was Myrryd at all, but another kingdom, magnificent and foreign, its pyramids like ziggurats with thousands of steps to the flat peaks. And there, priests tore the heart from a bronze-skinned maiden.

From this vision, I awoke.

Six times did I dream of this, and five times did I climb the statue and see Pythia, as if through the dark water of a bog.

But once, when I entered the Veil, I went to the other statue, which was male. Against his throne, his enormous dark wings were carefully carved; upon his hands, curved talons. His thighs were thickly muscled, and at his feet, the skulls of men. In his left hand, he held an orb of blackest stone, yet it had a translucence like crystal; in his right hand, he carried a sword, about which two serpents were entwined; and upon his face, as if I had not noticed it before, the gold mask of the Gorgon, the mask of Datbathani. This god was the Great Serpent, the one who brought knowledge to vampyres and protected the mortal world from the crossing of the Veil.

When I drew back the gold mask, the face beneath had no features—not eye, not nose, not lips. Instead, four words were written upon it: ALSO, I AM HERE.

I stared at the words, trying to comprehend their meaning.

Here? I thought. *Here, at the threshold between life and death; between the mortal-sculpted statues of the gods and the realm of their beings? Or are you there, behind the gold mask of the Gorgon? Or there in the kingdom held in your right hand, or the black orb in your left?*

But the words began to melt as I watched them, and I no longer stood upon the lap of a great statue but instead was drawn back through the membrane of the Veil into waking.

◆ 6 ◆

As I awoke that night, I said the words in my mind over and over again, "Also, I am here." I did not want to forget them, nor even the words above the doorway. "Within, Death. Without, Terror." I felt as if this were a riddle that I could not understand.

Artephius, his helmet-mask gleaming in candlelight, held a sphere in his hand. "Are you up yet, Falconer?"

I recognized the sphere—it was the same one that had kept Merod Al Kamr within an inch of the Extinguishing as he lay in his crystal tomb. It contained a bit of quicksilver in a glass tube. The tube had tiny barbs on its side, barely more than slight raisings of glass, but these were to ensure that it would hook into the flesh and the heart and remain there, keeping the vampyre still, unable to fight. The end of the tube was a blade, more slender than any mortals had made, like a needle, but the kind that had not been seen in that age. Within the tube and the needle, just enough quicksilver would be there to slow my heart until it nearly stopped completely.

"Why do you do this?" I asked, my voice barely loud enough to hear.

He leaned in close to me, and whispered in my ear, "There is a greater field of war than the ones you fight, little falcon. You are important to me, but my battle is with another who rises to meet me in the West. Merod Al Kamr is still within you. In your blood, in your flesh—as he once was in a sepulcher of crystal beneath the Temple of Lemesharra. You see him there, when the Serpent's Venom from the Sang-Fleur presses you through the Veil. You are tearing the Veil yourself, with each breath you take."

With every ounce of my being, I snarled and snapped at his visor, imagining I could tear through it as a dog gnaws through bone to get to the marrow. I tried to rise, for I wished to draw back the visor that I might at last see the face of the man who had stolen immortality and destroyed Alkemara. I managed to push myself up from the table, and my hands went to his helmet. I whispered, "Show yourself to me, Alchemist."

He pressed the sphere down at my chest, positioning it in such a way that I knew he had done many surgeries and knew the precise location of the heart.

"Accept your fate," he said. "You were once mortal, Falconer. But you have become—what? A messiah of the damned? Is that what you dreamed of as a boy as you grew up in the hovel in the fields? Is that what you desired when you trained the Baron's falcons, or . . . made love to his daughter? You need no longer hope. You are a devil to this world. The Age of Man reaches its end. The Age of the Veil is upon us. Your children will grow under the shadows of Medhya. The ancient sorceries grow within Enora herself. Her flesh will carry Medhya's spirit. The blood of mortals will again run as in the last great Age of the Dark Mother. You and your tribes will die out, extinguished, and in your ashes, you will know the end of mortal life has come at last."

I felt the burning sensation that spread out in lightning-bolt jabs of pain along my chest and arms, all radiating from the sphere and its blade.

◆ 7 ◆

BY day, I was sealed into a coffin within a sepulcher, surrounded by other such coffins. For two more nights, I was brought out again, chained, the sphere removed from my heart when I was thrown into the cage. A new night of the Game would begin.

Foremost in my mind: *my children*. In my visions, the masked goddess had told me of their fates.

And Artephius, in his madness, knew of them.

Had there been twins? Had Alienora given birth to more than one child that night, in that vision when I saw her among the anchoresses?

Enora. My beloved once. My enemy. My end.

Twin children, alive.

My children.

Born mortal, from love.

Born to the end of times.

One of fire and one of blood, one to tear the Veil and one to mend it.

These thoughts brought a strange and terrible hope to me as I returned to fight another night in the arena.

BOOK TWO

THE LADY OF SERPENTS

"... Dreadful was the din
Of hissing through the hall, thick swarming now
With complicated monsters, head and tail—
Scorpion, and asp, and amphisbaena dire,
Cerastes horned, hydrus, and ellops drear,
And dipsas (not so thick swarmed once the soil
Bedropped with the blood of the Gorgon, or the isle
Ophiusa); but still greatest he in the midst,
Now dragon grown, larger than whom the sun
Engendered in the Pythian vale ..."

—John Milton, *Paradise Lost*, Book 10

I

THE RED SCORPION

CHAPTER 8

· 1 ·

FOR two more nights, the arena was my battleground. Each night, the sphere was drawn from my heart that I might fight; at each dawn, it was thrust into me to keep me weak. I struggled against the silver bonds and the iron chains, but I had no more strength than a mortal. I could not will the expansion of my wings from my body, nor could I wield a heavy sword and ax any better than I had as a youth before the war. Yet my muscles and bones had strengthened with fresh blood. I had once been a warrior in battle. I took to it well, and knew that my performances in the arena would ensure my existence until I saw a means of escape.

Ewen fought beside me, and we spoke briefly when a foe had fallen. He had kept his courage, and we fought like brothers in war, reveling in the slaughter of those mortals foolish enough to believe they could defeat us. The nights were bloody, yet none as terrible as the first. I was pitted against mortals and beasts and vampyres whom I had never before seen. All of them would gladly have raised my head upon their blades to the roar of the crowd.

Sometimes, I failed in the fight, but Ewen came to my rescue, his muscles growing stronger from the infusions of blood they had given him. Midias, too, rose, was cut down, and yet rose again to fight the next night. Quickly, we had become accustomed to these nightly games, which occurred during a feast time of Taranis-Hir.

There were no sacrificial maidens these two nights, merely a call of championship at the end—or of defeat. Each night I watched the nets and the pavilion, to see the city's ruler and to look for those two children who were mine and yet unknown to me. Yet the torchlight remained as blinding, and the stench of death overwhelmed my senses. I saw mostly outlines of humans in the stands and beneath the great tents. The silver cuffs did not come off, and I had to fight as a mortal. Fresh blood and renewed strength came to all of us—Kiya rose beside me to fight one night, then the next, she and I were pitted against each other.

At the end of the third night's Game, I raised my fists, a champion, having laid low many mortals as horns sounded, and the crowd rose, cheering as they had on my first night.

A trapdoor near the pavilions opened.

A lone figure strode through the blue smoke and fiery light of the arena. As she approached me, I saw the shadows of Myrrydanai around her, encircling her as if they were her aura.

In her left hand, the Nahhashim staff.

In her right, a short sword that looked as if it were made of pure gold but with a hilt made of black stone.

About her shoulders, the leather straps held wolf pelts as a long ceremonial robe. Beneath this, a midnight blue robe.

Her tunic had been wrapped and corseted with leather and silver threads so that it was tight against her body to the thigh, then free as the white tunic reached the ground. Along her arms were bracelets of silver, studded with amber and ruby.

She wore a dark veil over her head, and it came down across her brow as if shielding her from light.

Alienora stood before me. I could no longer even think of her by that name. She had become this other creature—this woman called Enora.

"On your knees," she said, her voice as cold as stone.

I could not look at her face.

I knelt, looking only at the dirt that covered the planked floor beneath me. She did not speak for the crowd to hear, but only for me.

"You are the champion of the games, but this does not buy your freedom," she said. "What would you ask, as a slave of this city? What is your desire? Whores? Blood? Mortals to rip apart in your tomb? These are what the devils ask when they win the Game."

I looked up at her, seeing the pale white paint on her face, with the streaks of red and blue, as if she were preparing for war. *War goddess.* That is what she was becoming. A tribal warrior queen, wearing the pelts of wild animals and painted as the ancient Queen Taranis herself.

"You remember nothing of our past," I said.

"Tell me your desire, slave," she said. "Or you shall have no reward."

"The shadows use you," I said. "The alchemist uses you. They will discard you when their sorceries are complete, Alienora."

"Do not call me by that name," she said. "As you once died, so that name has died. I am Enora, and you will bow to my staff. You will bow to the sacred sword of Taranis." She held the Nahhashim staff just above my head, and raised the sword. I saw strange shapes moving upon it, as if it contained some life of its own. Yet she still did not understand the power of the Nahhashim staff—it had not been unlocked by the Myrrydanai sorceries or by Artephius and his magick. It held power, but none could wield it.

None but me, I thought. I could lunge for it, and grab it. It was so close to me. It called to me, and I felt the need for it. I began to reach out, slowly, carefully, that she might not notice.

"I want my children," I said.

Her eyes narrowed, and her lips curled. She brought the gold sword down to my shoulder, pressing the flat of its blade against my skin. It had been heated, that sword, and burned and blistered where it touched. *"You have no children."*

I looked back at the ground.

"You are dead even as you kneel before me. Yet, once I cared for you. I sought out those places where the powers of the gods might reside," she said. "To save you. But you are one of the legions of the damned, and the boy I loved died in distant wars."

"I want my children," I repeated.

"You may find them among the dead. I bled them over a sacred pool, sacrifices to one greater than all mortals. Ask for whores or blood, but do not ask for the dead. Take your pleasures before you feel the embrace of the Red Scorpion, Falconer."

I felt a blow to my head—I glanced up to see her bring the Nah-hashim staff down on me with great force. As it hit me, I looked at her and saw another face superimposed on her own. It was as if a ghost peered out from within that painted face, through the eyes, watching me.

A shadow of the Myrrydanai was there, within her.

She shouted to the crowd, her voice resonant and deep, the voice of a queen. With each sentence she uttered, they responded with cheers. "You have had your games!" she said. "This devil has proven himself worthy! Tomorrow night we will have the final burnings! Praise the Disk! Praise the White Robes! Long live Taranis-Hir and the Illumination Nights! Yet one more entertainment with the champion, Falconer!"

She brought the staff down against my skull—I felt a crack as it hit. Then I heard yet other trapdoors open around us as if I were to fight again as my reward for becoming champion of the Game.

I looked up and saw twelve wolves coming from beneath the trapdoors. I remembered the shapeshifting wolf-woman and wondered what was planned. They gathered around me with Enora standing among them as if they were her beloved pets. "Those who wish for no reward, receive punishment," she said.

A chain from above lowered, and upon it, a grappling hook.

I saw a man in helmet and tunic as well as a brown fur vest drawn over his thick figure. He reminded me of a bear loping across the arena. In his hand, two long whips, wound about his arms, as well as a length of thick rope.

From beneath a trapdoor, a cage drew up.

• 2 •

EWEN lay in a heap in the cage, and when the floor dropped from it, and he fell, he did not rise from the ground.

I stood up to go to him, but the wolves surrounded me, growling.

"The Master of the Whip is here to teach you humility, as all champions must learn this," Enora said. She raised her sword to me that I did not leave the circle of wolves to help Ewen.

The Master of the Whip strode to where the hook hung down, and knotted the rope among its curved prongs. Then he crouched and with his mallet and metal pegs, hammered these into the dirt-covered flooring. He wrapped the second length of rope to these pegs, drawing them tight to ensure that they would not come off. He tested the rope on the hook by pulling down hard on the rope, which did not budge, after which he went to Ewen and dragged him to the rope, securing his wrists to it and drawing him upward to hang by his wrists, with his feet solidly on the ground. He bound Ewen's legs at the ankles to the pegs on either side of him so that Ewen could not kick his legs out or swing away.

Ewen's head had been shaved, and there were a myriad of scars upon his body indicating that he had already begun the tortures that would lead, eventually, to his becoming a Morn. When he saw me, he began crying out to me, "Aleric! Aleric!"

I could not stand to watch him like this, nor did I understand the sadism of these torturers. "He has done nothing to you!" I shouted to Enora, who kept her blade near my throat. "Do this to me! Do this to me! Do not hurt him! Do not! I will give you anything you wish!" As I shouted at her, I did not know if the watchful crowd cheered or was silent. All I thought of was my friend's pain. All I thought of was how I had brought him to this. I had selfishly brought him into this existence. I began to sob as I cried out, and my words became garbled.

Enora's face was set in stone. The wolves growled as I began moving. Yet I could not stop myself if I tried. Ewen began bleating as the first lash of the whip met his back. I could barely see as I pushed away Enora's blade, singeing my fingers in its heat.

I did not care about the wolves at my heels. I walked through them, toward him. Soon two wolves had jumped upon my back, tearing at my flesh. I struggled against them, but when a third joined, they dropped me to the dirt. I could not keep myself from calling his name over and over again. I reached out as if I could touch his hand, but he was so far away. I saw his face as the whip hit him again, and again.

I watched him as skin tore from his back and shoulders, as his tears turned to blood.

I raised myself upon my elbows, and turned back to Enora. "Why do you do this?" I shouted.

Enora came to me, crouching as she shooed the wolves back. "It pleases me to watch you suffer, Devil. Do you wish him peace? You may take his place, champion. You may stop this now."

"Yes," I moaned. *"Yes. Now."*

After the count of a hundred lashes, with the crowd proudly shouting each number, Ewen was cut down from the grappling hook and the pegs, and I was drawn up in his stead. He crawled away into the dirt, unable to watch what was to be done to me.

It is good you do not watch, I wanted to tell him. *Do not fear for me. Rest. I will come to you. I will rescue you, Ewen. Calyx will help us. Merod would not abandon us here. I am still the Maz-Sherah. I will not let you go to your Extinguishing. I will not let you become a Morn.* I thought all of this, hoping he might feel the stream from me, and know I did not wish this fate upon him.

After I was secured by the ropes, a special silver torque was attached at my throat. A thin but strong chain ran from this to Enora herself, who stood among her wolves. If she pulled on the slender chain, the torque tightened that I might feel her displeasure.

I looked up at the quarter moon above us and silently prayed for the help of the Serpent that I might endure this for the sake of the others of my tribe whom I wished to deliver from this land.

And for the sake of my children.

At the first crack of the whip, a searing pain went through my back, and I felt a strip of skin tear off. Then, another, and another. All the while, Enora tugged at the chain, and the torque tightened so that breathing became difficult. I closed my eyes that I might not give satisfaction to the Baroness or the crowd that watched this display.

Why? I asked, as if asking Merod. *Why did you bring us here? Why did Ewen and I survive in the well to come to this? To what purpose are we brought?*

I heard no answer, nor did I escape into some vision of the Veil where I might see the gods, the creatures of another world, and not feel the torments of this one.

As the whip slashed at my skin, I began to pray to extinguish; even then, I could not. A rain of whips fell upon me; I had to remain there, accept it, feel every nerve in my body burn while nothing healed, for the silver weakened those powers.

With each slash at my flesh, I thought of my vengeance upon this place of my birth. I thought of my mother burning for the entertainment of the Baron's family. I saw her face in the flames and remembered how I had struggled to get to her. How I had failed to save her from that horrible death, that terrible judgment brought against her. I thought of Yset, a Morn, pressing down upon me, her milky eyes betraying no intelligence. Her brain had been cut, her blood had been changed by the sorceries of the alchemist, her body had been tortured that the flesh itself had changed its quality and hue. All the Morns had once been as Ewen and I were. All of them had come here to fight Enora and the shadows. All of them had been taken captive and been held by the machinery of the dungeon, with its diabolical engineer sifting through their blood as if eternal life itself were there for the taking.

The wolves who guarded Enora and watched my humiliation—these were the shapeshifting Chymer women. How I would enjoy tearing their throats out. How I would enjoy taking Enora and bleeding her to the edge of death before throwing her carcass over the city walls.

Where are you Merod? Where is your Maz-Sherah? Why do you not bring me strength, for I have taken you into my body and you course through my blood, yet you are silent as our tribe is destroyed. Where is that great war of vampyres to come? The world grows cold here, and yet the Great Serpent does not bring warmth to me.

After a while, the lashes at my back began to numb, and I felt as if I had always felt them there, always been whipped, always had this pain.

When the two hours had passed, I was drawn to the dirt, and laid at Enora's feet.

She drew the chain taut between us and brought her face close to mine. "Now, you may have your reward, devil. You have brought me pleasure tonight. I will send pleasures to you before dawn comes."

I glanced over at Ewen, though I could barely see him. He lay in a heap as if dead.

Around me, the Chymer wolves gathered, sniffing the blood at my back.

• 3 •

GUARDS came with their cudgels and swords. They chained and blindfolded me, dragging me along the dirt, down into the cellars beneath the arena, through narrow passageways into the bowels of the city where water dripped from the stone ceiling, and where the smell of sewage and burning metal filled the air. All the while, the physical pain seemed as nothing now.

I felt a deeper pain than flesh.

My guards brought the reward that the Baroness had deemed worthy of one who was champion. I saw my winnings when the blindfold was drawn from my face.

Three whores, cloaks covering their forms, entered the small chamber where I had been tied to a chair. Above me, a great gaping round hole in the domed roof, through which people watched and spat down upon me, still calling me their champion though my blood soaked the stones beneath my back.

I lay there in pain, my wounds very slowly healing, faster perhaps than mortal wounds might, but slow for my kind.

The first wench dropped the cloth that covered her, revealing a pleasing form as she danced to music played in the doorway of my cell by a boy with pipes and an old man who beat the drum to her swayings. She writhed and moved, her hips bucking the air as she came toward me. I felt no pleasure from this, though she brought her body close to mine. Then, the second whore joined her. One whore took the position of a man and began licking and fondling the other, who kept her gaze upon me. I noticed that they had marks of plague upon them, many covered with tattoos and jewels—but I saw their shame and their disease. I did not even want to drink their blood, for I felt these women had the worst lot of this city.

The third whore kept the hood of her cloak drawn close to her face. As the pipe and drum continued the hypnotic tune that seemed an old one I had heard as a boy, this third wench came toward me, and when she was close enough, she whispered in my ear. "There is a way out."

She drew the hood down.

It was Calyx, the ashling, the veiled one.

Though she held deformity and marks upon her face, the fire beneath her skin glowed a yellow-red, and her face seemed to change and re-form as if it were molten. Her hair fell across half of her face, hiding her left eye and cheek, while the other half grew beautiful. Her cloak dropped from her shoulders as she moved between the two other women and began her slow, strange dance. As her shoulders moved, her hands gracefully open with her palms toward me, moving faster and faster until it seemed as if she had four arms moving in an elegant, fluid motion. Her dance seemed obscene and sacred, as if she had learned it from watching the dance of creation itself. What had seemed deformity in her limbs now seemed like the movements of an expert contortionist as she twisted her body around, her hips falling above her head, her legs, bent at the knees, her toes pointed toward her breasts.

She was more than human. Whatever the plagues had brought into her body, the fire beneath her skin gave her a glow and a smoldering quality that I had never seen on a mortal. As the boy with the pipes began playing faster, and the drumbeat quickened, so Calyx turned and twisted for my view in rhythm with the sound until she began whirling before me, spinning so fast I could see her—frozen—within the cyclone of movement.

As the blur of motion continued, she looked directly at me, and I saw something terrible in her aspect.

The words came to me:

Plague Maiden.

She was the plague maiden. Beneath her skin, she carried some power, brought to her by the plagues.

Raised by the Forest women, this veiled one had second sight, and the plagues had brought something more to her.

She was becoming a force of nature itself.

An elemental.

Within her form, a new plague existed. I could sense it there, the luminous light beneath her skin. As she danced, I saw that windlike movement, spoken of among the Forest women, called the invocation—for this was no whore dance, this was a ritual performed before me. This was a dance of creation, and she invoked forces of the natural world into her body, through her body. The extent of her power was unknown to me, and given her secrecy, she herself might not understand it.

To know of the elementals of the Forest was to know the madness of the wilds. The Briary Maidens were such creatures—products of the marsh and bog mists that lingered at the edge of brambles and thickets, they foretold doom to those who had wandered off the forest paths. There were others—the nameless energies felt in the loamy earth, among the ferns and briars and bogs of the forest. They did not often enter cities or villages, for their power lessened. The elementals were of fire, earth, air, and water, although there may have been others.

Watching her dance, I saw her nature manifest in the movement, for she looked—for just a moment—like a whirling column of dust and fire. Within that fire, I saw my own mother's face as the flames consumed her; I saw the bowl of fire in Hedammu, where I had met my fate with the Pythoness who continued to haunt my dreams; and

I saw Calyx, her face neither deformed nor marked, but perfect and whole, watching me as if I were not a vampyre or made of flesh at all, but a sword waiting to be drawn from the sheath and used to destroy.

As the other women danced beside her, their cloaks and clothes abandoned to the floor, they moved ever closer to me. Their breasts pressed at my lips, and their bodies writhed upon me as I lay there. I took no pleasure from them, but could only watch as they performed as strange payment from the Baroness for my suffering.

Calyx pressed herself close to me that she might whisper, "I will come to you. *You must help us.*"

"My children," I said, barely able to speak above a whisper for I derived no pleasure from the women who pressed themselves against me. The fire along my back had not abated, nor had my soul's sorrow forgotten Ewen's face—the marks and scars upon him. The fate to which we both would be consigned.

"Safe. For now. But time runs out," she whispered, and this was the last she spoke before leaving.

"Free my friend," I whispered. "You . . . must."

But the pain overcame me, and I could no longer speak.

• 4 •

AT dawn, as I closed my eyes, I felt that gentle tugging of the stream, its current growing stronger. It seemed to flow outward from me, and within it, I reached for Ewen's mind, though I did not find it. Yet I felt others there, around me. I counted nearly four vampyres among those imprisoned in the castle, although I could not be sure, for none of them seemed to be able to reach back through the stream to me. Still, I felt them, and I sensed Ewen, as well, sleeping in my vicinity. I began dreaming of Pythia, that Pythoness, a priestess of Alkemara, treacherous daughter of Merod. I saw her as when she had taken my soul hostage and pressed her lips to mine that the breath of eternity might pass between us.

And yet, even in sleep, I felt some other presence, as if the Myrry-danai hovered over my coffin, or Alienora herself in her new guise as Enora, the Baroness of Taranis-Hir. Again, it was as if a fly had touched a strand of a web, sending its vibration along the silken thread.

It was destiny itself, through a child.

· CHAPTER 9 ·

I flew as if in a dream, but could feel this was no dream. Some entity of some kind directed my vision, my movement. *Is it you, Merod? I asked the emptiness. Do you draw me upward from my body like a raven flying over Taranis-Hir? Or is it the pain of torment that pushes me to the Veil's edge to travel in the mind while the vampyric flesh heals from the night's wounds?*

Or does Calyx herself, in her hypnotic dance, in her plague-soaked flesh, send me into this dream, guide me along the white towers and the canals? What powers did that maiden possess, brought to her by birth, or by the Forest gods, or by the plague itself?

I saw all of Taranis-Hir beneath me. The walled city had been built with an eye toward both beauty and function. Its towers were tall and magnificent, and its high walls hid well its inhabitants from outsiders. Although it contained engineering marvels that its architect had brought from the East, few knew the nature of its mechanics. It had been built as a fortification during those fearful first years of the plague to keep out the diseased and those with the mark of the Akkadite upon them; then, the Alchemist Artephius had elaborated its towers into a grander, nearly Turkish design, with great pinnacles at their tops.

Within the city, nearly at its center, were the original *motte* and bailey of the old barony castle, and around these, the donjon—which was the Keep—of the House of White-Horse. Unlike other cities of its day, it had not been built to house a large population but was ornamented with towers and walls in a series of concentric circles to honor the shape of the Disk. The donjon had been built atop the sloping hill that had housed the original hillfort to which the de Whithors family had laid claim a generation earlier. The old castle remained, but had been overwhelmed by the new as an old oak is taken over by a thick overgrowth, a captive of the conquering vine. Four gardens ran alongside the donjon's edge, two that were full of flowers and ponds, one that was more a series of hedges for walking, and one that was not truly a garden at all, but was called the Tomb Garden for its mausoleums and monuments to the dead of this royal household and its families.

Around the House of White-Horse, another wall. Beyond this, land had been cleared, both from the tremblings of the earth and from labor, and marshes had been drained, canals dug. The winding streets between the towers and among the merchants' rows arched like bridges over the swampy land beneath. The canals that stretched outward from the walls also ran beneath them, with arched *contreforts* buttressing the structure. Beneath the city streets, the canals moved as did the drum towers above them, in circles within circles until each flowed toward the other. The towers resembled many that I had seen in the distant wars for the Holy Land, for the architects of this city had known of ancient places and ways that none in Christendom had yet heard.

Though the Disk was represented through the circles that defined the shape of the walled city, the cross of Christendom still rose above the places of worship. The Disk, I would soon learn, had come to be seen as a sign of a great virgin saint, prophesied in these territories for centuries, though not precisely as she was seen in shadows in the Plague Dream. Yet Rome did not quarrel with the pilgrims who came every season for the Illumination Nights or for healing, and the bishops of the French and the English chose not to speak out against what others might consider a heresy, for they, too, had dreamed of the Disk and had seen the Virgin of Shadows. They, too, had watched their loved ones and their cities and villages die away from the plagues sent to take the sinners of the world into purgatory. Kings of other lands believed this Baroness was an ally, and that her white-robed priests would rid much of the countryside of its heresies and dissidents, leaving the whole of Brittany open to conquest—for though England often laid claim to this land, Normandy and Anjou and Maine, and the western and southern parts of Brittany itself, had made plans over the years to bring this small but powerful barony into their fold, for they each saw the power of this living saint—even while they suspected sorcery. A new language arose in the barony, a mingling of the English and the French and an even older tongue that was spoken in whispers by the priests of the land.

I heard her voice in my mind as I saw all this. Calyx. So it was she who had sent me this vision. She whispered, "So long as the kingdoms of the world had frozen harbors where ships could not sail; so long as the winters had come on the tail of August and lasted until nearly midsummer; so long as the threat of plague and apocalypse cloud the minds of all who had been touched by it—the barony is safe from invasion, though early in the plague years, some tried to lay siege, but most died of fevers and madness."

Why do you show me these things? I asked her. *Why do you send me here?*

Yet the voice did not return, and there I was, looking down from above.

But my vision was guided toward a rounded tower, and I moved swiftly, a raven headed for a slender window covered from the icy wind by planks and thick tapestries, yet I moved through them all, and saw that I was in a bedroom.

The paneled bed was closed, and still I moved into it and saw a girl of twelve or so sleeping.

I saw my own face within hers, as I saw Alienora's.

I knew who this was.

My daughter.

And then, I was drawn from the vision, sucked back into my tomb in the Barrow-Depths of Taranis-Hir.

◆ CHAPTER 10 ◆

◆ 1 ◆

I tried each night to find the course of the stream that I might sense Ewen in the room, or if Kiya was near. But it was as if the stream barely existed. I felt a very slight pull along what had once been its current.

◆ 2 ◆

OTHERS of this castle came to view me in the night, and so the guard often left the lid off my tomb—the silver restraints were enough to keep me from even lifting my head. I had begun to believe that I was displayed there for novelty and for no other reason. One evening, just after sunset, several young men and ladies dressed in elegant finery and gemstones and furs came before my coffin. As I watched them watch me, I picked up from their words that they were nobility who had traveled from the south and the west, some of them speaking English, others French, and still others the Spanish tongue. These were lords and ladies, princes and princesses, who had heard of the

winged demons held here by the great power of Enora and her council. They praised her often; they spoke of her greatness and whispered
of the Apocalypse that was upon mankind; I heard news of the kings
who had fallen to the plague; of the snows that had covered the roads;
of the lands that were torn by wars brought by inheritors; of attacks
along the coastline where "the ice was thin," though I did not understand the meaning at that moment.

Then, the priests and monks and nuns arrived, all of them clutching their crosses and their beads, kissing bony relics stolen from the
graves of saints as they hailed Latin curses upon me. Because they
mentioned others in the room, I was sure that Ewen still lay not far
from me; and I hoped that Kiya might also be there.

Priests spoke of Hell letting loose its demons, and the old monks
spoke of my mother, who had been burned for witchcraft and the
murder of an unbaptized child. Several of the nuns, who had come
from Toulouse, murmured among themselves about the penance
needed to free the Earth of devils. One young monk, while others did
not look, reached for my loins beneath my rags, as if reassuring himself that demons truly had terrifying generative organs.

Late one night, just hours before morning, a visitor arrived alone,
wrapped in hood and cloak, and in her arms, great bladders full of
fresh blood for me.

⋆ 3 ⋆

SHE smelled of wolf-thistle and mosswort, two herbs I had only
known of in the Great Forest, among the women who followed the
Old Ways. I could not see her face, but she seemed to be able to look
through the cloths that covered her features as she leaned over my
face. I knew who this was before I saw her. The whore who had
danced for me. The changeling of the Forest.

Calyx.

She removed the silver torque from about my neck.

I felt relief flood through my throat as she did so, as if she'd dis-lodged a piece of meat from my gullet, allowing me to breathe. I found myself able to speak, though my voice was weak and hoarse. "Thank you. I do not need this blood. Please give it to others who are here tonight, though I cannot see them."

She nodded, and I heard her move about the room. When she re-turned several minutes later, she said, "You must remain here."

"Why do you help us?"

"Shh," she said. "Do not speak so much."

"Are there others like me here?"

She nodded.

"A youth?"

Again, she nodded.

"A lady?"

She nodded. "And others."

"How many?"

"Six."

"Help us tonight."

"The guard will change soon. I must leave."

I repeated my first question. "Why do you help us?"

"You need to end this," she said. "It is not of our making. I call to our goddess and hear no answer to my prayer. Many have forgotten the world before the plagues came. Before the Alchemist raised up this city. Before the shadows whispered. Some do not believe the world has changed at all, but that this is how it has always been and shall al-ways be—forever and ever."

"Will you free us?"

She nodded. "It is not safe. The Morns wander the skies. The Chymer wolves hunt the forest floor. But soon."

"When?"

A tapping echo of footsteps came down the long hallway outside the chamber. Calyx covered her face again and leaned to whisper at my ear, "Tomorrow night, at twilight. There is a vampire you have made in the arena. She is arisen, and knows our sorrows."

She replaced the torque around my neck and left the room. I heard the sound of skittering and mewling of cats as they followed their mistress out through the door.

"Ewen," I gasped, with barely a voice left. I had not felt his presence since the night of the final Game.

• 4 •

IT was nearly dawn when I heard muffled voices beyond the black ceiling of my coffin.

Two children approached my coffin, its lid removed by a servant who bore a torch that they might see better.

"She would throw me in the furnaces were she to find out what I've done," the elderly servant said, his voice crackling as if he was in need of drink. He had an accent as of one of the fields—a dialect I recognized, having been raised in the mud and marshes myself.

The one, the boy, had hair so golden it looked as if he had been touched by the sun itself; the girl had long, dark red ringlets, tangled against each other as if she had just come from bed. At first they said nothing. Their servant, a tall thin man with a curved spine who spoke in whispers too soft for me to hear, seemed to want them to leave this place quickly.

"We will go when we're ready," the girl said, in a voice well beyond her years.

"Look at the silver at his throat," the boy said, pointing. He reached down and touched the torque at my neck, then let his small fingers graze my throat and chin. He parted my lips, and gasped. "I had heard they were longer."

"Like a wolf's," she said.

"They are small. Like a dog's," he said, chuckling. "Why are people afraid of these creatures?" He slapped my left cheek, then my right. "They are feeble devils."

The servant reached for the boy, drawing him back. The boy tugged away from the man, scolding him. "I will have you whipped if you touch me again, Constantine," he said to the old man. "You and your wench, both. Stripped and whipped and left at the post without food or water."

The boy took the torch from the servant and brought its flame down to light the coffin. "He wears rags. I heard he was a prince of devils. He is simply a . . . a beggar demon." He laughed as he said this. He stepped away from me, and I heard him say at some distance. "Come away from there, Lyan. They may carry plague."

The girl peered over the coffin's rim. Her eyes were dark as walnuts. She had a sprinkling of freckles on her cheeks and across the bridge of her nose. She looked the way that Alienora must have as a little girl. My heart beat faster as I watched her, despite the pain from the sphere pressed at my breast. "Do you really think this is him, Taran?"

The boy snarled, "Don't believe the lies you hear from slaves. These beasts are like the Morns before the torments. They brought the first plagues from Hell on their wings."

"Where are his wings?"

"They hide them when asleep," Taran said, as if he knew everything about demons that there was to know.

"She told me they are helpless when bound like this," Lyan whispered. "But do you see how he watches?"

Taran returned to my coffin, leaning into it. I saw Alienora in his face, as well.

When I looked at the shape of his nose and the turn of his lip and chin, I saw a reflection of my face, and that of my own mother. I saw a bit of my mother in the girl's face as well.

"The Devil watches but can do nothing," Taran said.

Something was wrong with the boy's left eye—it seemed to be bloodred as if someone had hit him hard there once, and damaged it. He also had scars at his throat, faint but still visible. The hair that fell over his right eye could not hide another small tattoo along the line of his scalp—like the strange markings I had seen at Enora's neck.

I remembered the vision I'd once had, in the tomb of Merod Al Kamr, as I went through the Veil to see through the Glass that showed what might come to pass:

Alienora seeking the goddess of the accursed bog, holding our baby in her arms, striking it with a blade that its blood would pour into the dark waters. Seeking those shadows and Medhya herself, the Dark Madonna, in the deepest and most corrupt of waters.

She had not killed him.

She had spilled his blood, and marked him.

But my son was alive.

And a daughter.

Twins.

"He is beautiful," Lyan said. "So are the others."

"Devils use beauty to fool little girls like you," Taran said, smugness in his voice. "But I can see through him. We should set them all on fire. All of them. Devils. Devils in our city."

"Don't you dare," Lyan said, pushing him back from my coffin. "They are special."

"So special they shall suffer the Red Scorpion," the boy said.

"Quiet," she whispered. "I never want to think of that."

"Did you see it? You did. You peeked, Lyan. You looked. That is what they do. They skin them and stab them. That is how Morns are made," he said.

The girl who was my daughter looked down at me, a deep sorrow in her eyes. "He does not seem too terrible now. Look. His face—he seems like any one of us, Taran. He does not seem a devil."

"It is the trick they play. They look like us to deceive us. Remember how he rose in the Game? How he slaughtered Gron the Devil-Slayer? How he drank the blood of the maiden? That is what devils do. Do not start feeling sorry for the princes of Hell as you do the rabbit poachers. He has no family to protect. He is just a blood-drinker bringing plague to us. It is his kind that killed many in the world, Lyan. Do not forget that. He would like nothing more than to tear your throat open and suck your blood until you were dry."

The servant called to them from the doorway. It was late, he told them, and others would notice they were not in their beds. The boy groused about having to sleep, and the girl said that she might not sleep at all from fear that "those demons might rise and find us," but eventually, I heard their footsteps grow faint.

The coffin lid closed; sealed; I stared up into blackness.

• 5 •

I lay there, barely able to comprehend what I had just heard.

My children.

A son, a daughter.

Taran.

Lyan.

In the day's sleep, I imagined how Calyx and her confederates would come break the silver at my throat and heart and wrists. How we would raise Kiya and Ewen and Midias and all others who were trapped in these dungeons.

How I would take my children from this place before I brought the end of this kingdom, the end of Enora's sorceries, and the end of Artephius and his Red Scorpion tortures.

I could no longer despair. I had seen my children. Calyx had been the angel who had brought Ewen and me strength in the well of our captivity. She had the magick of the Forest in her blood, as I had the power of vampyres within my own.

I slept well and long, and when I awoke at twilight, I waited for signs of her arrival.

Yet, when my coffin was opened, it was not her face I saw, but Artephius. "Tonight, my friend," he said.

• 6 •

I was dragged out again by soldiers who carried me down a long and twisting flight of stairs. I glanced back along a stairway and thought I saw someone watching. Was it Calyx? Was it the vampyre I had made in the arena the night of my first Game? Who stood there in shadow, watching? When would Calyx come with help? I had no power on my own. I was less than mortal. If I could have but torn off the silver that shackled me, I would have torn these guards apart with my bare hands. *Where are you, Calyx?* I asked. *Where is the help I need to escape?*

Artephius waited in a chamber at the end of a long corridor. "Tonight, I am afraid, falcon, you will feel the embrace of the Red Scorpion."

◆ CHAPTER 11 ◆

◆ 1 ◆

HE drew the quicksilver sphere from my heart and the torque from my throat. The bindings at my wrists and ankles remained. He continued, "You must prepare yourself for this, for you offer a great gift to us. We do not want you weak. That display, last night in the arena. I do not like this kind of unnecessary damage. Your blood is important to me, and oh, when I saw it spill upon the arena floor . . . it pained me. You must drink." He motioned to the guards, who brought in a young woman of no more than nineteen. She was dressed in a filthy tunic, and her hair was a tangled bird's nest. "She will do. Drink well from her." He took the maiden's hand, and, though she struggled against him, brought her to me.

"I am not thirsty," I said. I glanced about the room. It held several books and papers. *His study*. I had never seen many books before at that point, although I had heard of the manuscripts of the monks and the grimoire of sorcerers. These were his grimoires. His wisdom was locked in their pages. Upon a pedestal at the center of the room was a thick book with a raised pale leather binding and silver cords tying it shut.

"Is that your magick?" I said, nodding toward the book.

He glanced at it. "You have an interest in alchemy?"

I did not answer his question. I looked at the maiden beside me. "Take her away. I will not drink."

"You need blood. You are weak."

I held up my wrists, bound in silver. "Remove these and I will not have such weakness."

"It is your blood that must be strong, not your body."

"Show me your face, and I will drink from her," I said.

The maiden whimpered as she heard this and rushed to the door. A guard caught her arm and drew her back into the chamber.

"My face is of no interest to you," Artephius said.

"I want to see the face of the man who will destroy me."

He came close to me.

I looked at the visored helmet. "All I know of you is this metal mask."

"I will give you this, if you drink from her."

I nodded.

Quickly, he dismissed the guards, who took the maiden from his room. The door was shut and locked.

He reached up to his visor and drew it back from the jaw of the helmet.

I gasped as I saw the face of the great alchemist who had overthrown Alkemara and engineered the tomb of Merod himself.

His face beneath was nothing more than skull wrapped in thin strips of cloth as if these would suffice for flesh itself. His eyes existed within this skull, and skeins of yellow hair were tamped down amid the thin cloth that had been pasted in some way to the brown-gray skull. His lipless mouth parted, and said, "Immortality without youth. This is what I have from the secrets stolen from Alkemara. This is what Pythia brought to me with her love, falcon. Look upon me and know what you would be without the glamour of your tribe!" He shut his visor, and laughed at the look upon my face. "We have an hour here before I must take you on your night's journey. I do not hate you, falcon. Far from it. I understand you. You have fear and greatness in you. You are a creature I have wished to study like this for many years. I would share much more with you if I could, my boy. Tonight, I will tell you what you long to know."

And then, he told me how he had come to immortality.

• 2 •

"I was born, little falcon, in a country distant from this, in a civilization that flourished with wisdom and knowledge long before these barbarian kingdoms grew, before your ancestors were raped and slaughtered by the Romans; before even Rome itself had risen; and in the fertile valley in which I'd been born, we were masters of the world. I was the son of a temple priestess, and by the time I was nine years old, I was sent to the priests of a god who I knew even at that age was a lie, for I had seen the tricks and sleight of hand my mother and the other priestesses performed to show the miracles of the deities. Yet, I was smart enough to say nothing of this when the elder priests tested me on matters of divinity and the sacred arts of the land. My mother had prepared me for these tests, for she herself had escaped a life that would have been drudgery. Most of the people of our land could not escape this fate, and many were servants to the royal family. Few had power on their own, as my great-great-aunt had once been a queen of this land, but when her husband discovered her infidelity, she was buried alive—as were many of my relatives. But the ones who had gone into hiding never spoke of their shame outside of the family hearthfire, and even then in whispers. But I was from royal blood, and my mother and I both intended to be as close to the luxuries of the wealthy as we could.

"In my youth, devotion to the gods as priest or priestess was the chosen field, and many were lucky enough to be born to this work. It was our job to follow the rituals laid down by the gods day and night. We worked in temples more magnificent than these dark and gloomy castles, and a thousand times more beautiful than any cathedral in Christendom.

"As I mentioned, I was tested by the priests of a particular god. My mother bribed the leader of a band of grave robbers to sneak me into a particular tomb that was among those of the great kings of my land. In this tomb, the robbers had kept much of their treasure, and upon the walls, for many leagues, was written the history of the god. It was wondrous to me—I had taken to my studies and could read the picture-words that had been carved there, nearly three hundred or more years before my birth. I spent the whole night with a torch in my hand, reading of the land of the dead. This god was Lord of the Dead, and his many secrets were written throughout the maze of rooms.

"But when I finally came to the room in which the king and his family and household rested, I was even more enthralled. I knew then that I wanted to be a particular kind of priest.

"For in that room were jars filled with organs, carefully salted and wrapped, while in the tomb of the king and his wife and his servants and even the cats and jackals—the bodies had been wrapped in cloth and treated for preservation. I unraveled one of the younger servants, and saw how, despite its being hundreds of years old, I could see the face of a boy, who was not unlike me.

"In the morning, when I went to my tests, the priests asked me a thousand questions. It was said that the children whom the god most loved would tell of the hidden knowledge, but the priests received more than they had bargained for in me. I could recite much of what I had read the previous night, and even more than that, I knew the death-blossom they stuffed the bodies with, and the shape of the jars for the various organs of the body. I knew the stars in the heavens that traced the doorway into the realm of the upper gods, as well as the places of the earth where the underworld passage began, for these, too, had been marked along the walls of that tomb; and I spoke prophecies that only this priesthood would know, for even the grave robbers in the tomb had not been taught to read the picture-words.

"And so, I began my apprenticeship. I worked primarily on the knowledge of the last days of the royal family, how to prepare for this, how to clean the bodies, what to lay in store for them on the long journey to the afterworld, and how to draw the brain through the nose, and how to keep the heart fresh and thick even when salting it. I grew up to become a priest of my land, and found that I had a knack for invention, as well, for I began working with the architects on the designs of my king's tomb, and I devised ways that no grave robbers should ever enter, nor should the treasures be found. I advanced beyond my station and soon lived in the palace itself, among those priests and advisors most trusted by the king. From those who watched the skies, I learned not only of the influence of the stars upon our lives, but also how to measure direction and distance. From the engineers, I learned more about buildings and construction. These are ignorant times, falcon, and have been for centuries—for in those days, our explorers traveled the world and knew much of what has yet to be rediscovered by these countries of the West. Our explorers went beyond the sea itself, and those who survived it returned with riches beyond compare—not simply gold, but dyes, and animals, and plants, many of which we had never seen before. It was a magnificent life for a young man who had not arrived into this world with any great prospect of success, and I can tell you, I blessed my mother many times over for her foresight in teaching me to read the pictures and to understand their meaning.

"The king's wife lay near death one dry season, and I was asked to come speak to her of the Lord of the Dead to prepare her for his hand. Yet when I met her, I knew she was not near death at all—she suffered from melancholy and wished death. We fell in love, or I did, but because I understood that my death, and the deaths of my sisters and my mother would accompany my own should I be discovered in the arms of the queen, I sent for poisoners to learn of their arts. I would murder the king and his children, and my beloved would become ruler in his place, as had happened more than once before. Those were my plans—remember, I was not much older than you were when your life was taken. I did not understand the world or the consequences of such terrible decisions.

"Yet, I was thwarted in all this by my beloved herself. She decided to alert the king, and both of us were arrested. Soon enough, in the very tomb I had designed, we were to be imprisoned.

"Worse, we were not to be murdered in the tomb, but sealed in. We were left to thirst and hunger until the last days took us. I truly loved her, my friend. I loved her as no other. We spoke of the gods, though I did not believe in their existence even then. Yet I swore to her I would bring her out of that place. I swore to her that we would escape and live in exile, together, until the end of time itself. And she believed me. I suppose I believed those words, as well. I told her that if I could find the key room from which I could find our way out— for it was built into every great tomb after an engineer was accidentally trapped in his own creation and found years later when the king was being buried—I would return to her and rescue her.

"By the time I found this key room—a small chamber, barely big enough for one man, and I saw the route upward and out into daylight, I was so thirsty, I thought that if I just went out to get some water, and returned to her with food and water, she would recover and then we could escape. I should have turned around, and gone to find her to bring her to that room, but I suppose I cared more for my own thirst than for her life. When I emerged into daylight, I crawled along the tomb valley and fell from exhaustion.

"When I awoke, it was nearly evening. A laborer from the tombs had already begun pouring honeyed water down my throat. Terrified for my beloved, I returned to the tombs when I had strength that night—and found she had already sought her own death. Before she died, she had tried to drink her own blood for its moisture, and then had dipped the blade in too deep and too often to recover from the wounds.

"I suppose I went mad, and began wandering the Earth. I lived as a beggar, and many took pity upon me. A teacher on an Aegean island took me in. He was in exile there, and worked with the king of the land to make arenas and temples with certain secret passageways and unusual entrances. Like me, he had often invented devices and had developed a style of architecture based completely on the constellations and their relationships to one another. I spent twenty years working with him, always as his apprentice, for I did not hunger for a better position. It was during this sojourn that I learned from him of that essence of immortality that exists all around us, yet few harness its power.

"He taught me about the Veil, of which you know. He called it a caul, and he said its membrane was all around us, and yet we could only experience it through an alteration in our minds. He taught me about the brain, and would use a dead man's brain to show me its aspects. He taught me where death resides in the mortal brain, and where eternal life exists in the immortal—for, yes, he had captured several of the vampyres that had once plagued his island. When he died—murdered by one of his many enemies—I continued his work and research. But I wanted to find the source of these blood-drinking creatures rather than just use the preserved remains of the ones he had captured, years before I met him. He had no wife or children, and willed his wealth to me, which was vast for its time. He had told me to seek out the temple at a city called Pergamos, and so, when I was able to hire a ship and sailors, I set out for this place. I crossed mountains to get there, but when I found this city, I was shocked at how primitive it seemed to me.

"It was as if I were stepping back in time, for all the buildings were clay huts and there was no king, no ruler of the city. Instead, it was overrun with vipers, which were treated as if they were little gods. Parents allowed their children to be bitten many times by the serpents, and despite the resulting deaths or the years of illness suffered, no one seemed to care and felt it was all in the hands of fate.

"There, it was said, was a woman who spoke with the snakes and prophesied from them. She was rumored to be a basilisk—a queen of some realm who could kill with a glance, and who was more serpent than woman. She came to the caverns of the temple after dark, and it was said she escorted some to the land of the dead, and others returned to tell the tale of her prophecies. I sought her out at midnight, for I felt that only one of these beings could bring the secrets of immortality to me.

"She was Pythoness of a city that had been built upon a serpent's nest.

"For, you see, there is a secret knowledge that brings the mortal into immortality without the death you suffered. Without the bestial nature that brings fangs into your mouth when your prey is near. Without the need for blood. Without the wings of a flying lizard upon your back. Your kind came into being a thousand years or more before even my birth, and I am more than a thousand years old. But I discovered a source of your immortality, and with the aid of the Pythoness, who loved me as a creature obsessed, I spent nearly five hundred years developing my own immortality, bringing it along, that I might perfect it one day.

"It was only through the goddess who seeks your destruction that I attained the knowledge necessary. It was she—your Medhya—who whispered in my ear as I drank that poisoned flower of the Veil, and felt the claws of her shadows as they drew themselves to me. You know of this other world where the gods exist, and of this world, falcon. But do you know of the many worlds that exist, most of which are unknown to any who have lived the short life span that is the mortal's fate? Do you know that stream you feel between those of your tribe. It is simply one membrane—one caul—that is stretched between you and all who are immortal. It crosses the membranes of mortals, and of animals, and of plants. The source of each of these is the one, and from these origins, all are connected.

"Yes, I know of your stream as well. I feel it when it is strong, and I sense the nearness of your tribe. It is weak now, barely a trickle, but it exists, still.

"I have gone farther into the stream, falcon. I can control it. I can direct it. It is a strand I may pull, or a current I may dam at one end to create a pool at another.

"I have learned how to shape those changes, little falcon. I have learned the art of creation and destruction, using the caul of the Veil."

• 3 •

"AND yet you use this knowledge to destroy life itself," I said.

"And you do not?" he asked. "You, who drink the life of maidens and boys and old men? It is not life I destroy, falcon. You are blinded by your own desires. I seek the knowledge of the gods themselves. You are immortal. I know the prophecy of the Maz-Sherah, little falcon. I read the words of blood centuries ago—Pythia herself possessed them, for she had followed her father's instructions on where he had heard the whispering grasses whose tips of grain had brought him the knowledge of the great prophecies of the messiah to come. It was she who dug up the scrolls from the earth and bound them." He pointed at the ancient grimoire on the pedestal. "She passed them to me, and I read of Medhya's curse upon her robber-priests. But there were other scrolls taken by the priests of Myrryd—hidden in high mountains, buried beneath the earth. I used the stream to seek them out, for the origins of your race may be found by following the skeins of the thinnest threads. And through the knowledge of the Myrrydanai . . ." He grew silent for a moment, as if afraid to reveal some secret knowledge not meant for me. Then, he said, "Time meant nothing to me, and lifetimes passed as I realized that I could be a catalyst."

"To bring about Medhya?"

"To bring immortality to all mortals," he said.

"And beneath your ideals," I said. "Thousands die."

"Mortals always die by the thousands. By the millions. What are these lives to creating immortality? Isn't that what you ask each time you drink mortal blood?" he said, and then called to the guards to return to us.

I drank from the maiden he had provided until she fainted, then I stopped. "I will not kill her for my pleasure, as you and your Baroness do." I held her body against mine until a soldier took her from me and bound my wrists together again.

With Artephius walking ahead of the guard, I was dragged along the narrow damp corridors into other rooms, passing soldiers and forges, and as I went I looked for a sign of Calyx, of the maiden I had killed in the arena. Yet none but the guards were there, and these looked upon me as if I were lower than a beast of the field to them.

Finally, we came to a long low room, with hooks hanging from its ceilings as if it were a great butcher's shop. Chairs and wheels and tubs all lined the walls. Pincers had been thrown to the floor, and blood stained half a wall. I was brought before a victim in a chair, his head hanging downward as if he would fall had he not been bound to it.

It was then that I felt the torments of Hell written upon my soul.

The device itself was a large wheel that radiated from a flat block of wood set up that the victim might lie upon it. As the wheel turned— powered by the victim's own bloodstream as it shot into the long blown-glass tubes that I'd once seen make the human wine cellar of the

Priest of Blood's own tomb—the victim was drawn up from the block, by the feet, and a series of pulleys and smaller wheels turned and raised him until he hung suspended, head earthward. The tubes, situated at the throat, the thigh, and beneath both armpits, helped keep struggle to a minimum. Too much movement caused the glass to break—and this, in and of itself, would shoot the blood out rapidly. Thus, the vampyre would lose his entire supply, and just as mortals need their blood, so do vampyres. The Extinguishing would be swift if the victim lost all blood, and the pile of flesh might be tossed to the side of the room once the blood was cleaned up from the stones of the floor.

To additionally hold the vampyre still, quicksilver was painted upon him, from head to toe. His head was shaved for this purpose, and all garments removed.

The pumping bloodstream of the victim moved the mechanisms as the tubes of blood filled and emptied, and a strong, constant, but thin stream of blood flowed along the cups at the wheel's edges before returning into a large curved-glass bowl.

The creature who lay upon the block of wood, prostrated in wretched sleep after nights of this torture, moaned as I approached him.

When I whispered his name, he opened his eyes.

"Ewen," I repeated.

A metal band had been laid over his teeth so that his jaw was locked and he could not speak or bite. Because all of these things were of silver of some kind, I could not touch it without the burning sensations and the spark of a shock that repulsed me strongly enough to stop my attempts after the third try.

I saw within his eyes the formation of tears. I imagined how ridiculous this would seem to mortals—that a vampyre might weep. But we were no less vulnerable to sorrow and despair than the most wretched of humankind. We did not lose these things when we returned from death's threshold.

I longed to draw him up in my arms, to pull those tubes from him, to knock the sphere at his heart away from it. But I was certain that this would simply increase his suffering and that I would send him to the Extinguishing myself.

I turned back to Artephius. "Stop this now. What good is this torture? What does it bring you? You will not find your flesh by stealing the blood of my tribe."

He said nothing to me, and the guards dragged me farther back into another room. The room was nearly boiling hot, and a man of thick muscles worked the bellows at the fire, while a young servant brought irons to the hearth, laying them across the coals. Yet another worker—a smith of some kind—hammered at his forge as he shaped a piece of metal.

The guards laid me upon my stomach on the round table at the center of the room. Hands tore at the clothes I wore, already rags upon my body.

The forger reached for the branding iron at the hearth, and raised it, looking at the red end of it. "This for the chest, I think," he said.

"Yes," Artephius said. "Be quick."

The forger shot the Alchemist a harsh glance. He came over to me and turned me to my side and drew apart the remnants of my shirt. "Here goes," he said, and pressed the brand beneath my throat. The searing pain caught me by surprise, but I held my breath as he kept the brand there. I smelled my own flesh burn.

He drew it back, tossing the iron into a bucket of water. Steam hissed as it rose from the bucket. Another brand was pulled from the coals—this seemed smaller. It was pressed at my right thigh and held for a full minute before being released.

I was pulled to my feet again.

"Upon your chest, the mark of the Disk," Artephius said. "And upon your thigh, the mark of my ownership of you. It is the shape of the letter Aleph, and through this letter, the figure of a scorpion. For this is what you face today, as many of your tribe have faced it. As I watched your friend Kiya face it for seven nights over a period of four years. Seven nights is all she will need to become a Morn, Aleric. Some of you take ten or twelve. But her seventh night comes swiftly. She will soon patrol the city towers, hearing only my voice and the voices of the Myrrydanai priests. Your friend Ewen will be harder to break. In his blood, I have culled an essence that is strong. You bestowed upon him that Sacred Kiss of life. He has drunk your blood, which has special properties, for yes, in our nightly transfusions, I took much of it. He has faced the Scorpion once, and now sits in the chair of distillation. But your blood is different from the blood of your brethren, falcon. Your blood is finer. You will be hard to break, as well. But break you will, as all of your tribe have done before you."

I spat at his face, struggling against my bonds.

I felt a blow to the back of my head, and I passed out from the pain of it.

When I came to, I had been set in a corridor of mirrors.

Alone.

• 4 •

NEITHER my hands nor feet were bound together, though the silver remained upon them to weaken me.

Why was I here? Why had Artephius brought me to a mirror?

"We are invisible to the mirror," I said aloud, thinking I could be heard. It was the silver behind the glass of the mirror—it did not reflect us. That is what I had been told.

Yet, when I looked at the mirror before me, I began to see a blur of movement upon it. Was this a preparation for torture? Was this alchemy?

The mirror silver moved as a whirling maelstrom, and the shine of it proved too much for my eyes. Yet soon enough the liquid calmed upon the glass. I saw what those of my tribe see in mirrors, and understood why we were not meant to look upon them. I saw myself, not as the young man with the pale beauty of youth and of the vampyre. Instead, I saw that terrible being beneath my flesh—the corpse of the soldier who had died years before in a tower of Hedammu at the hands of Pythia, drinking from me. My yellowed skull thrust through a dark leather of torn skin. Shattered and twisted bones thrust out from the fine tunic and breeches with which I had been dressed that night. I looked upon my dead self, unburied, shiny black beetles rippling what skin was left to it, and the maggots of time ever turning white and brown making a new skin of their slick forms as they ate away at what gristle remained, attaching bone to socket, skull to spine.

Was this enough to drive a vampyre mad? To remember one's death, to see the true self that remained beneath that glamour of our tribe, that immortal beauty that was the cosmetic of the grave over the rotting corpse? Was I there, in that roiling quicksilver, or was I here, this flesh I could look upon, at my hands and arms, and say, "No, this is truth. The mirror is a lie."

Behind me, as if entering that hall with me, I saw all of those from whom I had drunk and killed in my thirst. There, see? The first maiden bound to me in my grave at my vampyric birth, to the servants of the Alchemist who had given up their lifeblood that I might be revived for the torments and games of this madman. They numbered in the hundreds, though I did not recall drinking from so many, and had lost count of the pretty young things I had taken to death's threshold. I saw their wounds, unhealed, at throats and arms and shoulders, where my teeth had torn their seals of flesh.

I felt that stinging of silver as I beheld this in the mirror. Perhaps the legends were true that mortals did not see the vampyre in the looking glass, but I had discovered that secret of silver itself—of its reflective qualities. It showed us to ourselves as we truly were. As the monsters we had become—not the succubus and incubus of men's dreams, but the undead, resurrected in the flesh, a mockery of eternal life.

The quicksilver in the glass moved again, and the faces washed away. The layers of my own skull and leathered skin and bone tore back, as if eroding from me.

Someone else was there, in the mirror, staring back at me. Neither corpse nor my own visage, but the Priest of Blood, Merod Al Kamr.

His face was twisted in fury, and he sneered at me as he pointed at me as if delivering a curse. "You have waited too long! Do not believe the lies of the mirror, Falconer. Do not give in to these despairs sent to you and your brethren. Death is the illusion, and the rotting corpse is the lie. You are the truth. Reflections and shadows are half-truth at best. Why have you not heard me? I have come to you in visions, and you have ignored me." He stood there as he had the last time I had seen him—his head shaved, his eyes like translucent black orbs pulsing with bright red blood behind them. A blue robe had been wrapped about his thighs and draped to his feet. His chest bore the tattoos of the history of the vampyres and the Priests of Medhya. His wings, grander than any vampyre's I had seen, spread out long and glorious as if a billowing cloak behind him.

"How do you come . . . here?" I asked.

"I am within you, Maz-Sherah," he said, and the fury of his face subsided as he spoke. "For as you devoured me, so I reside within you. But there are ceremonies you must perform. The winter approaches too swiftly, and the Alchemist knows you have few nights left to gather the sacred objects of these ceremonies."

As he said this, the mirror dissolved, and I saw again that vision that had haunted me from the moment I first raised Merod from his tomb in Alkemara:

Merod, with the Nahhashim staff in his hand.

Behind him, an altar of stone.

A maiden lay upon the altar, raised from her elbows, looking at me, her face covered with a terrible gold mask. Upon the mask, the face of Datbathani, serpents entwined about her hair. The Serpent Goddess, called the Lady of Serpents by our tribe.

"Immortality is not a gift," Merod said. "It is a sacred obligation, even unto the prey. A sacrifice must be made. An atonement with the goddess of our tribe. We cannot avoid the wars to come when we will return to fight those who wish to destroy us. Those who wish to darken the Earth have already made their way to the altar stone. The signs are here, Maz-Sherah. The omens of the Great Crossing have come. You were born to this. Your destiny is to take your place here. Take up the Nahhashim staff. Find the sword of fire. Bring the mask from the land to which my daughter fled, far across the seas, beyond the Earth's edge. There are those of our tribes there, older vampyres than even those of the Medhyic line. The elemental maiden may not be trusted, yet you need her. Above all, we are nothing, Falconer, but the gates that must close against the Dark Madonna, Medhya, who must never enter this world in flesh or blood. She is the madness of destruction, and only you may perform the ceremonies that will unleash a power strong enough to stop her. Strong enough to wage war upon her followers and her hounds and shadows. You were not born to live a life as other men. Nor did you return from death to be as other vampyres. You are the hope of immortal and mortal." Then he cautioned me, raising his hand. "You will be tortured here. You will undergo those torments that others have passed through. You must fight with your will to survive this. You must find the Gorgon Mask, in the land to the west, beyond the edge of the sea. You will know it when you feel the stream grow strong. You must find Pythia there and take the mask from her. You must regain the staff, and find the sword. All of it. All, for you have languished in your prisons too long, Maz-Sherah. The ceremonies of the tribe must be performed."

"What are these ceremonies of which you speak? How will I know their ritual?"

"These sacred objects will inform you," he said. "You must have them. At solstice time, the Veil is weakest. You must overcome these bonds, Maz-Sherah. You must fight silver itself, for you have no other choice. Heal the Veil within the full moon's length. Heal the Veil and keep Medhya from entering the world of men."

The altar dissolved, as well as the maiden in the mask, and Merod himself, became the liquid silver beneath the mirror's surface.

Again, I saw my dead self staring back at me. The bone and rotting meat of the dead. The lies of the mirror. The truth of who I had once been, and turned away. I walked down the corridor, avoiding the other mirrors as well.

A door at the far end of the corridor opened. A guard at the doorway ushered me into the next room. Here again were the grappling hooks hung from the low ceiling and the stench of rotting flesh and drying blood. Men wearing the masks of torturers stood here, working the machinery of torment on many heretics whose moans and screams echoed throughout the long chamber. I felt the stinging at my wrists of the silver. *Merod, you must help me. How do I overcome the silver? How do I fight without the strength? How do I unfurl my wings if I am held back by this metal?*

I saw the Red Scorpion—its chair made of bone and leather. Its claws of shiny metal, and the wheels and gears behind it spinning slowly as if it would begin its mechanical dance before I was even placed in it. At its peak, there was a halolike band of silver to be bound at the vampyre's scalp. Guards strapped me into the chair, tying my wrists and legs against the machine.

When the claws of the Red Scorpion snapped into place, covering my face with their pincer tips poised at my eyes and my nostrils,

Artephius leaned into me, and whispered, "You are monsters. Yet, within you, are the secrets of youth and life. Your body and blood will bring eternal life to the Baroness herself. Your essence will bring flesh to my bones. For it was to this that you were made Maz-Sherah." He drew back from me. Glancing at the torturers, he said, "I take no pleasure in his torment. Draw out the essence. Flay him. Then, return him to me before morning comes that I might heal his wounds."

I watched him go, escorted by his guards through an arched doorway.

Then, I heard the whirring noise like a thousand flies swarming; the clunk and clank of chains as they groaned; the needle-sharp prongs that slowly began to thrust into my body, tiny tubes of glass extracting my blood, and pushing the Sang-Fleur juice into me so that I experienced the delirium of the Veil, yet knew that in a moment, my skin would be torn from my face, my eyes punctured, my nostrils explored up to the bone plate that protected my brain from the intrusive spiny fingers of the Red Scorpion and Artephius's explorations of my body and blood.

I heard a series of snaps, like the jaws of some creature coming down upon its prey. The mechanical claws moved toward my face, their pincers sharp as knives as they neared my eyes.

I felt the tugs of the pincers as the machine began to cut the skin from my chest, as glass tubes with sharpened tips thrust into me to extract blood. The grinding of wheels and gears grew louder and louder until I heard nothing else but the infernal machine.

It was then I gave up all hope.

Two thin lancets poised at my eyes slowly moved, inch by inch, toward their targets as I felt the brush of other pincers at my lips.

I could not focus on the guards or Artephius as they watched.

The end of my existence would begin here, in this Red Scorpion, with blood spattered on the walls, and my sight destroyed by these knives and pincers, and my skin flayed.

It is over, I thought. *It is over.*

And then, the machine stopped a hairbreadth short of the lancets piercing my eyes.

· CHAPTER 12 ·

· 1 ·

IN the moments of a sudden reprieve from some torture—when hope, the last casualty of the mind, dies—the swiftness of the change is incalculable. And yet, it all went slowly, as if each moment froze when the machinery of the torturer stopped.

The gears and turning wheels and metallic scrape and slide of it went suddenly silent. Perhaps this had happened in a second, or within the hour of a second, but it stopped. I heard the shouts of the guard, and then the machinery was drawn carefully back from my face.

The maiden Jehan, whom I had brought into vampyrism, was there and an elderly man dressed in the tunic and leggings of a servant of the castle.

With them, Calyx, drawing a knife out from a fallen guard.

The servant came to me, carefully drawing the lancets and pincers back from my face. I did not know him by face, yet he drew me out from the Red Scorpion chair. Calyx brought me to a table and, using a vise and knife, managed to cut the silver from my wrists and ankles.

"Your wings," she said.

Before she had finished speaking, I brought them from my shoulder blades.

"Do you think you can fly faster than the Morns? Hide your wings now," she said.

◆ 2 ◆

CONSTANTINE and Jehan left by the chamber door; none had entered since Artephius and his guards had abandoned the room.

I desired to free the others who lay upon the torturer's tables at some distance from us, but I would risk too much by doing so.

I wanted to find Ewen and free him.

As if seeing such plans in my eyes, Calyx said, "In moments, the guards will return. The Red Scorpion is efficient and quick, Aleric. They return for the glass bowls full of vampyre blood, for Artephius needs them for his work."

I followed her out into the corridor, and there she drew me up and up stairs and down hallways and through the narrowest of passages. Ten minutes had passed, though it seemed like hours to me as I ran with her along the warren of passageways she knew by heart through the Barrow-Depths of the city. We emerged onto a street through the grates of a culvert near the foundries and furnaces that roared with life. We passed many beggars and whores as they plied their trades along the midnight-dark streets, the mist of their breath clouding the icy air. It was then that suddenly bells began ringing from towers, and shouts from the criers of escaped devils in the city walls.

She drew me into an alleyway just as guards ran by us, searching for the traitors and devils.

I felt the shadows whisper within me. The Myrrydanai had been awakened and sought me, as well. Soon, the Morns would come.

Calyx, who knew every secret way and avenue of Taranis-Hir drew me along, winding farther and farther away from the gates. "They will look for you there, first. The skies, and the gates. We will go to the one place they would not seek you."

After nearly an hour, she had brought me into my daughter's bedchamber.

Here we whispered, for the panels to my daughter's bed were closed shut.

"She sleeps," Calyx said. "If you wish to wake her . . ."

"I want to see her," I said.

"If she cries out . . ." Calyx did not finish her thought.

"I will risk that." I went to the dark panels around the large bed, and drew one of them back slightly. I peered in at my daughter as she slept. Her face was rounded, and her hair a tangle over half her face. She breathed lightly. I reached over to her and drew back her hair that I might see her again.

Then, I heard the door to the chamber open.

I drew back, shutting the panel, baring my fangs for a fight.

The servant called Constantine, who had helped me escape the Red Scorpion, stood there. "You bring him *here*? To Lyan's room? Endangering all of us?"

"The soldiers cover the streets. Where is Jehan? Where is she? She was to meet us at the foundries," Calyx said.

"She did not . . . she did not make it," Constantine said, sadness in his voice. He glanced over at me. His tone became sharp. "You must leave. You endanger your own daughter by being here. You do not understand what hunts you. Enora has called the Chymers to track the Forest for your scent. The Morns patrol the boundaries beyond the walls. You must leave right now. Do you care about your daughter? Do you care that your son lives? Then you must go, for if the Morns follow your scent here . . . I have watched them slaughter any who were near their prey. They do not discriminate when they are on the hunt."

• 3 •

W E left Constantine at the door to my daughter's room. As I had wanted to free Ewen, so I wanted to gather up my children and take them with me. But the risk to their lives was too great. "I watch over them," Constantine said. "The boy is too much his mother's son. But Lyan has good in her. I will lay down my life rather than see harm come to them."

Down more stairs Calyx and I went, across the buttresses and arches between towers we crawled like ants.

I saw Morns flying along the black smoke of the furnaces, their eyes to the earth, watching. As they dove toward us, we ducked into a narrow passage.

The Morns did not enter the towers themselves. Still, we heard the shouts of soldiers as they came running up a stairway, their echoing footsteps following us as Calyx led me through an intricate series of corridors that were strangely empty, as if few mortals wished to live within these royal chambers.

Where the smoke was thickest as it came up from the foundries, Calyx led me again out onto the parapet that led between two of the white towers.

The shrieks of the Morns were all around us. "The smoke blinds them," Calyx whispered as she drew me again through a doorway and beneath a tapestry, then down a secret corridor. "The Morns may be outrun, as well. I have seen the knight Per Ambler race his dark stallion out along the rim of the quarries to escape them. They cannot fly low in the Forest, for they are stupid creatures with poor sight. The Myrrydanai fear the elementals of the deep Forest beyond the bogs, so few venture there from Taranis-Hir. Once we reach the deep woods, we are nearly safe, for even the Chymer wolf-bitches will not go far. The bog sorcery of these creatures weakens where the spirits of marsh and briar seek refuge."

Then, she went out across the curved rim of a tower, and the smoke cleared here, though the Morns' cries were in another area of the citadel.

"Quickly," she said, as we crawled along the upper rim of a tower. She wrapped her arms about my waist. "Upward. Fly now. If a stallion can outrace them, than surely a devil with wings can outfly lesser demons."

◆ 4 ◆

M Y wings emerged from my shoulder blades, as I focused my energy on bringing them to full span. They wavered and folded against each other, then sprang outward. My wings flapped slowly, but powerfully, and though a guard rushing toward the top of the tower brought his sword against my ankle, cutting, we rose above him, heading upward into the foundry smoke.

I glanced back and saw a dozen soldiers with drawn swords running along the towers, lighting torches as they went. Archers out along the watchtowers drew back their bows, and a shower of arrows seemed to fly across the darkening sky.

For the first time, through black smoke belched up from the courtyard below, I saw the enormity of this castle that Enora and the Alchemist had built. It had a shining white wall that stretched to the horizon, and along it were bowmen and guards and enormous vats that might be used to rain fiery oil down upon any who attacked. I heard the whizzing of arrows as the bowmen aimed for us again and again. I was struck twice in the thighs, but pushed my wings to go higher and higher, and I held Calyx beneath me, keeping her safe from attack. My breathing grew heavy through this, but I managed to rise above even the arrows.

And then I heard the shrieks of the Morns as they saw us.

I glanced back to see them. They all seemed like a flock of ravens across the smoky sky, racing toward us. I beat my wings against the icy wind, fighting it to push farther and farther toward the Forest.

I felt that old strength in me again as a Morn began nipping at my heels. Calyx screamed from fear, and I clutched her closer as I sought the power within me—that ability of our tribe to move so swiftly as to seem a blur of movement on earth or in the sky.

"Beneath the trees!" Calyx shouted to me, reminding me of the Morns' weakness of sight.

As I dropped down along the edge of the Forest, far from the castle, they followed. Still, they slowed down as they came at us. As I swooped and shifted among the branches and those narrow ways between oak and ash, their grasping at me lessened. I heard them shriek at some distance as I was able to navigate the forest though the sharp briars tore at my skin. More than once I narrowly missed crashing into a tree or slamming my head against a thick branch.

Soon, I outdistanced them, but a new danger followed us through the woods.

We heard the howling along the wooded paths.

"Get to the cliffs, get to them now!" Calyx said as she clung to me, close enough that we were were nearly one being as her arms were wrapped tight around me and her face close to mine.

The shapeshifting wolf-women had picked up my scent, and soon they howled and yipped as they chased us. I flew along low to the ground, feeling the hot breath of their muzzles nearby, hearing their panting and heaves as they ran. I glanced back so briefly I was afraid I would hit a tree if I did not immediately look forward again. The silver-backed wolves were many, and yet, I knew they were those women I had seen in the vision in the old stone chambers of the anchoresses once known to me as Magdalens. Their eyes were human, and even their snaps and growls sounded like voices shouting and yelling at us as we flew.

I rose higher, but as I came up toward the forest canopy, I saw Morns patrolling the skies, flying above the trees to wait for us. I dipped down again, and Calyx whispered against my ear how many leagues we needed to go, and where the golden tree was, and where the cliffs began.

As the branches of the Forest parted, I saw what seemed a sheer cliff face of gray rock rise up suddenly from the earth—only a shattering of the earth could have created such a tall and rocky cliff from a deep forest floor—I had to turn to the north and swiftly fly upward to avoid a rocky death.

Below us, the wolves jumped and howled, unable to follow us up the cliff. The Morns, as well, seemed to have dropped back, and when I rested on a ledge for just a moment, I saw their flock return to the now-distant city, whose towers could barely be seen.

"Because the Nahhashim staff's power does not extend beyond Enora's grasp of it, they also grow weak at this distance," Calyx said. "It has kept my people safe here, for many would be burned at the Illumination Nights if those wolves or demons could reach us."

"But you," I said, catching my breath. "You live in the castle."

"Not anymore," she said. "I could live there as long as I was a whore and an ashling. As long as many feared the plague beneath my skin. But now, they know I am an Akkadite. They know, and they would burn me if I ever returned."

Calyx pointed up toward the Akkadite Cliffs. There, at the top, leaning over the edge of the rocks, was a great oak tree, painted gold. "You come from a line of Druids, Aleric. Your grandfather was one, though he left the arts when the Baron took the lands before your birth. But this golden tree is one of the oldest, and even the trembling of the earth could not shake its roots. It is our beacon in dark times.

Beyond it, the caverns of the skull. The home of those who follow the Old Ways and keep sacred the path of the briars and the trees."

As she spoke, I felt a tug of weakness within me and sensed that my wings had begun to shrivel, though I did not understand it until I saw a faint pink-purple light along the western hills.

Dawn approached, and I needed to find a place to rest. We had flown nearly a hundred leagues from Taranis-Hir, deep into the last of the Forest.

Far below, the wolves kept up their howls and yips, but they too moved back into the Forest to return to that stone dwelling, to return to their forms as Chymer women.

I felt blistering along my scalp and neck as the sun touched me, and smoke came from my wings as I carried Calyx toward the skull-shaped caves where the exiles and outcasts of Taranis-Hir had survived during the years of the Disk and its terrible dream.

◆ 5 ◆

I slept deep in the caves, covered with fresh dirt brought by Forest women, some of whom I recognized as friends of my mother's. The burning of my skin would heal by nightfall, and I fell asleep there, feeling as if somehow all would be well.

Calyx awakened me and brought me blood to drink. "Many contribute to your health," she said. "For you are the only hope we have."

After I drank from the sheep's bladder, she led me out among the trees. I scanned the night, but did not feel a threat from the skies.

"They will return. Soon. Taranis-Hir leaves the Akkadites alone, for many of us carry plagues within us that they fear in the unleashing. Yet, with you here, Enora may not care about plagues. Artephius and the shadow priests value you above all others," she said. She put her hand over mine. "Your burns have healed."

"My strength returns," I said. "Thanks to you."

"Your friends need your help," she said. "Your children, as well.

There is a knight of Normandy who has challenged Enora's authority here. He does not like her sorcery, and the dream did not convince him of the supremacy of the White Robes. His name is Per Ambler, and he raises money for armies along the borders of the Anjou and in Paris, though he must do this in secret. We bring the Forest magick to our fight, as well, though we have many elderly folk and some too young, and others who sustain wounds that cannot heal. You may help your friends and your children and us. I have spoken to a spirit of the dead man called Kenan Sensterre."

"I saw this in a vision," I said. "You went to the Chymers so that they might raise his spirit. Why did you not raise it yourself, for you know the ways of sorcery."

Her eyes narrowed to slits as she looked at me. "Those who practice the sorceries of bog and bone become allies of Taranis-Hir. It was enough that I called for the dead through those vile wolf-bitches. I would not do it myself. Only the spirits of life are called here. Only the elementals may be invoked, or the goddess herself."

"I understand," I said. "Tell me, when I saw you in the Sight, did you sense me there?"

She hesitated before answering. She said, "I did not sense you, Falconer. But I did sense someone, though I had grown afraid it was a White Robe priest, his skin shed, following me as a shadow."

"Can you tell me why you called Kenan Sensterre from the dead?"

"To find you. To help you escape. That is all. For I know you are not just the Maz-Sherah of your race, Falconer. You are the only one who can end the rule of the Disk, and the White Robes. The world is unmaking, and the Earth burns and freezes. The elementals weep, and the lamentation of the hidden spirits is deafening to those of us who speak with them. Your night in the Game was coming, your time to face the torment of the Red Scorpion. I wanted you strong. I wanted you to know I would help, and others would, too. Kenan Sensterre knew where the old well was because once you had led him to it.

Once, you had drawn up some ancient of your tribe, when you were but a boy. I needed to find you."

I could not help myself. I leaned over to her and embraced her, though she drew back slightly as if still with some slight fear of winged devils. "You are no plague maiden," I said. "You are a light in the dark. The strength you brought me helped in the arena. My friend Ewen and I would have extinguished that night without it, for we were as weak as the dying when you came to us in the well."

• 6 •

AFTER we had spoken more of these things, Calyx returned to Kenan Sensterre and what else he had in his possession, stolen from the Alchemist himself. "He passed this to Constantine, who is a loyal servant but not to Enora. To your children, Lyan and Taran. And to the Akkadite cause, as well. Here," she said. She reached into her ragged cloak and brought out a piece of paper, folded many times.

I unfolded it and spread it out between us.

It was an ancient map of the Earth, with more lands and seas upon it than I had seen before.

"Here we are," she said, pointing to Brittany. "There is Britain. Here, see?" She moved her finger across the great ocean and there was an enormous land. "Beyond the edge of the Earth, beyond the seas, to the south and west, there is this."

Marked upon the landmass was the word AZTLANTEUM.

Scrawled beneath it was another word, IXTAR.

"I have heard the legends of Aztlanteum," I said. "That it is a paradise of gold and of magick. But these are tales from those who have never been beyond the Earth's edge."

She turned the map over to show me the writing on the back. "Can you read this?" I shook my head.

She read aloud from the Alchemist's scrawl, speaking of a constellation like a spiderweb, and of boats that crossed from the land of the

Saracens to Aztlanteum, of a route from Africa, following the flights of certain birds. And at the end of this fanciful writing, were the words, "She has the Gorgon Mask." When she showed me these last words, she said, "These have been written more recently than the others. Do you know of this mask?"

I nodded. "Yes."

"As do we. The spirit of the dead man told me that we must gather it with the Nahhashim staff and a sword that burns. Do you know what this means?"

I nodded, though I dreaded that with which I was burned. "There are ceremonies of the priests of the tribe of vampyres from which I was resurrected. I am the one to perform these rituals. Yet I do not understand what I am to do, though I am shown visions of things. I saw the mask when I became a vampyre. I saw it again when the Disk dream came. I saw it many times in visions, though I do not understand its power."

"It is one full moon until the solstice, Aleric. At the solstice, the Myrrydanai are at their weakest, and it is then we must strike. It is then that these ceremonies must be done."

"Yes," I said. "Yes. We must. But first, we must go back and rescue others. My companion, Ewen, is more than brother to me, and Kiya . . . Midias . . . others. And I've seen my children. They live. I must take them from her. From Taranis-Hir."

She lowered her voice as if not wishing to be overheard by anyone. "You will be captured. Your kind are captured easily, and though you escaped them once, you do not know what the Nahhashim staff's power may do if it is Enora herself who hunts you. There is no time for your friends. For your children. I have been given the omens of this, as have you. Tonight, we call the Briary Maidens, for the mists on the marshes below have risen as the snow and ice cover the land. Tomorrow night, when you are rested, you must go and find this mask, for it may be the one from the Disk dream that we were not meant to see."

"If I leave this soon," I said. "My friends will die."

"If you do not leave soon," she said, sorrow in her voice, "all will die. The solstice is our chance, Falconer. It is but a short time, yet if you find this mask, and return with it, you may save many."

* 7 *

"TELL me of the Briary Maidens," I said. "For they are but legend to me."

"They take the form of light and marsh gas," she said. "And they play tricks and are deceitful. Yet they have much knowledge, and you must speak to them before your journey."

I followed her out through the tunnels of the caves as they came to a narrow slant of an opening, and what seemed like a doorway of evergreen covered the rock face as we emerged into the frosty air.

I sat with Calyx and several women on flat rocks arranged as if in a ceremonial way.

We were bundled in heavy cloths, and even so, I felt chilled to the bone by icy air.

Before a priestess of the Forest called the Briary Maidens into being, I was warned, "They will test you. You are unnatural to them, and not meant to exist in their Forest. You must show them respect, or they will depart too quickly."

A gas formed on the edge of the briars clinging to fallen trees that lay in a circle before us. It shimmered green and blue as if it were the lights of the northern sky. As a woman named Morla played her panpipes, the colored gases shifted and formed into corporeal bodies, though as shiny and thin as a bubble blown from a tube.

After several minutes, I could see the outlines of the Briary Maidens, one brighter than the next as the lights within their souls came up, like a candle just lit.

These energies, as the Forest women called them, moved in a slow dance that seemed to be more of ritual than of music—circling around the brambles that grew wild there. Their hands seemed touched by a spirit fire, for small translucent flames grew from their fingers as they moved, and motes of flame danced from one to the other. Likewise, their hair seemed like waterfalls flowing from them, and when I looked at their feet, I saw none at all, for their spirit matter dissolved into air as it neared the ground. They melted in and out of each other's bodies as they moved, such that I could not count how many there were of these spirits.

"They are ready," one of the women said.

The Briary Maidens, these wraiths whose bodies were not entirely solid, nor were they liquid, stopped their dance and stood before me, shoulder to shoulder as if they were one solid being.

"Dear maidens of the mists," I said, remembering the respect that all spirits required. "I come with a question."

"Blood-drinker," they all spoke at once, their voices low and sad, as if they had just buried the dead that night. "You are not welcome among the living. Yet our sisters tell us that you come for the good of all. Do you enjoy murdering the mortals of the world?"

"Good maidens, I hunt when I must. It is the curse put upon me. I do not hunt your woods, though when I was a child, I came here often to hunt the stag and the wild bird."

"Do not treat us as you would young mortals, Falconer. We are not like the maidens you would kill for their blood. We have no blood to offer you, and no fear of your kind. Why do you come to us?"

"I seek to end these terrible times."

"Why does a blood-drinker care what happens to the mortal realm? Are you not a butcher of men and a devourer of children?"

"I am here to save mortals."

"Why would a blood-drinker do this?"

"Does not the wolf kill the lamb that it might live? Is not the wolf of nature?"

"It is the nature of life to devour life," they said in unison.

"Does not the turnip, when drawn from the earth, scream as only other turnips might hear? And yet the wild pig must still eat the turnip that she may give milk to her young."

"It is the nature of life to be indifferent to the suffering of that which it cannot understand."

"If nature has made me a blood-drinker, am I not like the wolf and the wild boar? Am I not like mortal man himself who kills the pig and the wolf for food and warmth? And do not men war with each other, spilling their sacred blood upon the earth. Do you revile all men for this?"

"It is the nature of man to seek the face of Death," they said. "For it is the path that all of the mortal realm must travel."

"And did nature not make me a blood-drinker?"

"Blood-drinkers are not of nature. They are unnatural, for they have refused Death's Hand and returned to life."

I sighed, frustrated with this roundabout talk. I glanced at Calyx, who nodded toward me as if I were doing well. "When the vampyre called Pythia breathed this life-in-death into my mouth, had I the choice of nature? I had grown to believe life was treachery and madness. I watched my mother, Armaela of the Fields, burn for a crime that was a crime of nature, and not one that she had committed. I watched my brother cut down by men who simply wished him dead. And I cut down men in my mortal life for the same reason. In war, we piled the bodies high and praised Heaven if we held their severed heads in our hands. And yet, when I was forced to flee from that Threshold that marks the territory of death from life, and return to this life—was I worse than I had been when I sent hundreds of men to their deaths? Was I worse than the Baron and the priests and the monks who sent my mother to the flames? Have blood-drinkers ever slaughtered and destroyed on such a grand scale as the woman called

Enora, who wakes the dead with her Chymers? Have blood-drinkers killed the innocent children of the village with plagues of bog-flies? Or the animals of the field, dying in agony? No, I and my kind have not done these things. And further, in my mortal life, my nature was dark and greedy. I desired much and did nothing to alleviate the suffering of others. In my immortal life, though I have killed a handful to survive and slake my thirst, I am here to war with those who have destroyed much of the Great Forest, and will destroy more of it. Those who have invoked the ancient spirits of the bogs who slept for thousands of years and those who bring miasma and plague across the land. Children have been sacrificed, their blood spilled. The dead are called to speak, for the living cannot. Nature herself has felt the irons and cuffs of the intruders from the tear in the Veil. This is the Great Crossing that must never occur. And I am here to fight it."

"We cannot trust a blood-drinker, no matter how pretty his words," they said.

Calyx stepped forward, into their circle. Though their forms shimmered like gas, they did not step back from her. "You have known me since my birth."

"You are the changeling child," they said, and for a moment I was certain they bowed their heads to her as if she were royalty. "We are the ones who found you and guided Mere Morwenna to the rocks that cradled you by the Meringon springs. We warmed you with the fire of our hands and brought you the she-wolf that you might suckle at her teat. And when Mere Morwenna lifted you, we kissed you that you might be blessed in life."

"I am that child, a woman now," she said. "And I have known Falconer since his youth. In mortal life, he had no sacredness about him. But as a blood-drinker, he has a flame within his soul, and it grows daily."

"We love you as one of our own," they said, "our dear child. But our prophecies are for mortals to hear, not for blood-drinkers, no matter how well-spoken."

"And you?" I asked, interrupting them. "Are you natural, you maidens of marsh gas?"

Calyx shot me a look of anger, as if I had now gone too far.

The Briary Maidens watched me curiously, as if wondering at the audacity of my question.

Calyx raised her arms to them, wanting to calm them.

As I watched their faces, they melted into each other, moving together, becoming one being. I felt an intense heat, as if she—the one they had all become—had grown in fury and would begin to burn with anger at my words.

She had several faces within the light of one, and all their lips, as she spoke, overlapped with all their mouths; and the eyes seemed several as they formed closely together, many spirits within one.

A green-yellow corona of fire burst along her arms and up around her head, a halo of flames.

She stretched her arms toward me, her index finger pointed at me as if cursing or accusing. "Do not conjure those of the briar and bramble to your aid and insult them, blood-drinker!" Her voice was like thunder, and I felt vibrations from it in my bones. "You do not speak to some marsh gas from the woods! We are the elements of air and fire, water and earth, and before us, you bow down!" As she said this, I felt a thumping in my chest as if my heart would burst. I clutched at it. Calyx entreated them to forgive me, but I felt my knees buckling, and I fell to the earth.

On my knees, I fell forward, prostrate, feeling the lightning heat of their presence upon me.

Even with my eyes shut, I saw the green corona of fiery light that surround their being.

I heard Calyx speak in a language that even my vampyric mind could not translate, so old was it.

After several minutes, I felt the strength to rise again. I remained on my knees before them—they had separated into several maidens of green-yellow light again.

"The changeling has spoken on your behalf," they said. "And we forgive you your trespass."

"I must save my children," I said.

"Twins," they responded. "You may only save one."

"Why?"

"Do not question us. Only one of your children may be saved, though you will not know which until the last battle has been fought."

"I must save my friends."

"If they are blood-drinkers, they are doomed," the sisters said. "For they are not meant to be."

"Is there no way to avert the Great Crossing?"

"Nature is under the weight of the Veil, and we cannot know the outcome of this age," they said. "But you have had dreams of the very thing that may protect many who have dreamed of the dark."

"Is it the mask?" I asked.

"It is a mask of a terrible goddess. A goddess of vipers and pythons. A goddess of slaughter."

"Where might I find this mask?"

"The mask was taken by those in the low boats, thousands of years ago, and rests in the mountains of a land that has been forgotten, but will be found again, as mortals forget and remember and discover and forget again. As even this terrible age may one day be forgotten, as other ages have been lost in mists."

"Where may I find these mountains?"

"To the west," they said. "Beyond the world itself. Beyond the place where mortals believe the seas bind the Earth."

"To the west, beyond even the islands?" I asked.

"Beyond all islands you know of," they said. "It is a land of legend."

"Aztlanteum some have called it. Ketzal, others have named it. Brasileum to some. A land of much burning and yet much beauty. An ancient kingdom thrives there, though it, too, has been touched by the tearing of the Veil."

"The mask is there in Aztlanteum, but the one who wears it will not give it up easily. It is a mask that always seeks a face."

"How will I know it?"

"You will know it, Falconer, for you have seen it in visions. But you must make haste. The solstice comes, and with it, the mother of your tribe seeks entry."

"What is the power of the mask?" I asked. "What does it hold?"

"It holds what you need," they said. "We have not beheld it, for it was forged in a dark and lonely place where blood-drinkers alone knew of its magick. You must leave soon, before dawn, for each night that you do not have the Gorgon Mask, the Earth suffers and all its creatures. So many will die. We weep now for the spirits that will pass before their time."

"How can I travel the seas, beyond all islands, to this land? For in daylight, I must sleep, and I cannot sleep in the sea itself."

"Islands have arisen," they said. "Mountains of fire have burst from the sea itself, beyond its frozen edges. But you must fly swiftly, for it is a great sea you must cross. Though the Veil's rip has brought up the fire mountains from beneath the deep sea, you cannot depend that they will be there for your daily rest. We do not know if you will survive this journey, but the perishing of a blood-drinker is of no concern to us."

As they spoke this, the lights of their bodies faded, and the mist seemed to pour from the circle back down the side of the cliff itself.

I turned to Calyx. "I will do this. Now. Give me the map. I will follow it to Aztlanteum."

"If you fly with the stars, you can outrace the sun," she said, embracing me and thanking me for the undertaking to which I had been born.

We both knew that even if I found Aztlanteum, returning might well destroy me.

II

IXTAR

◆ CHAPTER 13 ◆

◆ 1 ◆

THAT night, departing the Akkadite Cliffs, I flew hundreds of miles to the south, far past Taranis-Hir and its guardians.

I slept along the western coast of Ireland and when I awoke, I fed upon a woman who I found wandering the shoreline. I did not kill her, but laid her body to rest within a cove that she might recover from her wounds.

That night I stood upon a volcanic hill—one of several that had erupted from the Atlantic Ocean. The water was frozen solid along the shore for a mile or two into the ocean, and the gray ash of the island of volcanoes had formed ridges in the ice. An icy mist blew off the ocean, exposing here and there the wrecks of ships caught in the grip of the winter that had come after the earth had torn itself. Beneath the sheen of ice, there were those who had frozen there, trapped as if in a diamond, staring up from their graves, while the fires still burned along the volcanic ridges, candles to light my way. I slept at dawn beneath the deck of one of the long ships that a curl of ice held.

The frozen bodies of men who dressed as the Normans did, their helms heavy and decorated, their armor loose upon them. The frozen night had come to them at once, and some sat at their watches, still, without thaw. Still others, belowdecks, had warmed and rotted, and I lay that dawn amid the stench of the dead. That night I opened the map to be sure of my direction, which would be southerly. I went to the prow of the boat to check the stars as to find the twelve stars that had been set on the map. I found a constellation in the sky called Arachne, which formed a web of stars leading to my destination. I remembered the birds that crossed this great ocean, and the tales of Arabs and Egyptians who had traveled these seas many years before the Romans had ever built their city. *If you fly with the stars, you can outrace the sun,* I thought, remembering Calyx's words.

I folded the map, and thrust it into my bag, in which two bladders of blood had been stored, mingled with gambrel root to keep it from clotting. I drank a bit from it—it had turned sour already, but it was enough to bring strength to me. Not as fresh as the woman I had drunk from earlier, but enough to sustain me on the journey.

I ran across the frozen sea, following the volcanic lights, then soared up into the darkness, pushing myself harder than ever before, for I would not have rest for more than twenty hours. When the volcanic ridges I had left were a distant memory behind me, I saw below the churning of the water again. The night warmed as I went, but not from the sun—as I crossed the ocean, I felt winter fall behind me, like a cloak that had blown away. The frozen ocean left off, a roiling curve of ice with the rush of water beneath it. I did not glance to the water much, for I kept my eyes on the horizon and the stars to ensure I would not lose my way. But now and then, I heard strange noises and looked down. Beneath the ocean, strange green and yellow lights emerged, while mists flowed up from the spots—as if volcanoes burned eternally beneath the water. I saw great behemoths—whales and other sea creatures that I had never known before, as well as a great tentacled squid, its skin luminous beneath the surface of the waves, as it shad-owed me, flying beneath the sea as I flew above it.

If the sunlight caught me in midflight, I would fall, burning, to the ice and water. By the twelfth hour, I had grown exhausted, and by the fourteenth, I felt that twinge of sleep, of the need to escape into some hidden place. And yet, I continued on, the need to find land like a new thirst within me.

I felt the stream, stronger than it had ever been, like a burning lamp on the edge of the horizon. There were others like me there. Other vampyres. Pythia would be there, and I felt the movements of many as they sought to slake their thirsts, as they flew into the night themselves, hunting. And they could feel me, as well. They were there, across this new continent.

I did not reach the source of the stream, but could feel the strength of the ones who held its strand. As night came to its close, after the long hours of flying, there below me was the smallest of rock islands. Upon it, I found shelter in its narrow cove, and there I slept that morning while the sun passed overhead.

The following night, I reached an inlet sea, and its many islands. I kept the course of the constellation that formed a web; at its center, a spider, which was my destination. I flew toward the crescent of land beyond the many islands and found a cave along a high mountain ridge. I slept there, deep within the crevices. I checked the map, and where I had gone off course, corrected this, following the pathways outlined crossing a peninsula. The land was not mired in the long winter I had left, but was temperate and reminded me of summer, though it was nearly the end of November.

I found a village along a slender freshwater stream, and took my fill of a man who had stepped out in the night to pass water. His blood was sweet. I had perfected the art of leaving them without killing, though I had no moral compass for this—yet, I had begun to consider the purpose within the universe of the vampyre. I did not believe we were meant to be merely assassins of men or butchers of maidens, though both came as easily to us as it did to a lion who finds the savanna rich with gazelle. I thought of what the Priest of Blood had told me, and those words of Mere Morwenna. We were guardians, and as immortals, we were meant to protect those from whom we drank as well as to take their blood gift carefully. I found I could drink some of the victim's blood, and allow the mortal to go free, weakened, perhaps, but able to survive the bite and any infection it might bring.

With just enough blood to take wing in the night, I flew across the beauty of jungles and mountains, and saw the canals and avenues of a civilization as it cut across this continent, like I had never before witnessed—and yet my awe had just begun, for these were the highways of these peoples, and the villages and temples at their centers were impressive enough. As I moved westward, the stream grew overpowering, and I began to wonder if this civilization did not teem with vampyres. Somewhere, here in this land of mountains and jungles and desert, my kind flourished.

◆ 2 ◆

AS I followed the lines upon the earth below, and moved with the stream itself as if I could nearly touch the vampyres who might be tugging at the current of it, I came upon a vast city rivaling in some respects the fallen kingdom of Alkemara.

I came over a mountain range, flying low to the trees. I began to feel that waning of spirit that accompanied the distant sun as it sped along the eastern sky.

And there, in a valley plateau, an enormous marsh surrounded what looked from the mountains like a great white island. I say it was white because it had luminous qualities in the dark that gave off an eerie light. Perhaps this was marsh light, or reflections off many of the structures and temples that reflected the moon overhead. Within

the city, great avenues and boulevards cut across a circular series of
canals dug from deep trenches with no apparent source of water beyond the marsh itself.

I saw the great city of Aztlanteum for the first time. In the moonlight, flocks of white birds flew across the marshes and seemed like
spirits migrating toward the Otherworld. As my eyes adjusted, I saw
that the city was not white at all, but built of dark stone, some of
which reflected the marsh mist so that it seemed bright and nearly as
white as the caelum stone of Taranis-Hir. But the temples here were
plated with obsidian and crystal, and the effect was dazzling. The
temples were stone giants, and rivaled the legends of the Great Pyramid of Egypt. A great procession of men and women, dressed in
colorful feathers and brightly dyed robes, stood upon the thousand
or so steps of the tallest of the temples as if celebrating some great
event.

I smelled blood, as well, freshly spilled blood, and the sound of
strange music echoing along the marshes.

This was Aztlanteum, a kingdom lost to those of Europe and
Africa, upon a continent unknown to those of my lifetime.

• 3 •

IN the modern world of the twenty-first century, it is hard to imagine what this great kingdom in the valley resembled, for its power
was lost well before those of Europe arrived at its shore. It had magnificent structures that seemed to nearly touch the stars. The stone,
which was gray in sunlight, shone with a strange blue-white light beneath the moon, or so it seemed to my eyes, for I saw its phosphores-
cent glow in the darkness.

It was nearly as if Alkemara, that ancient city, had a sister in this,
although this seemed grander, for it had not been buried, neither was
it broken and ravaged by cataclysm.

When I found my resting place for the day, as I crawled down along a narrow tunnel that had once been, perhaps, some wild animal's den, I closed my eyes thinking of what I had seen—for even a glimpse of that city overpowered me.

I did not think mortal man capable of the extent of it, of the colors, of the canals between the temples and great buildings, of the observatory that rose nearly to the heavens, of what looked like islandlike acreages of crops, and a terraced tower upon which grew trees and flowers of such variety as I had never before seen—the hanging gardens were like a shock, for the land around this kingdom had gone dry as a bone.

Yet, with some source of water inside this land, it was a heaven filled with milk and honey.

Even as I dreamed of it, I felt a heavy disturbance in the stream—as if my kind were here, many of them, and they had power beyond imagining.

It was as if, somewhere in the stream, a great god of vampyres moved here.

I had reached the land of the Ketsali, on the continent called by the Forest women, Aztlanteum, the White Island, though it was in the center of a mountain valley. On the map, stolen from Artephius, it had simply been called Ketzatzlantea.

And all I could think of was:

The Serpent.

The Great Serpent lives here, exists here.

This was one of the birthplaces of my kind, though this was not the realm of Medhya or her two sister aspects.

This was not the world of the Dark Madonna, but of the Serpent himself.

As I thought about the great city, its shape even reminded me of a serpent, coiled upon itself, for it was set up in avenues of circles. Though broad boulevards cut through the circles, still the circles held their integrity. It was the domain of serpents, and yet it teemed with men and women.

And the stream was nearly smothering here, for it infused the very air I breathed. It was as if there was a magnetic pull to those of my kind. There was no Disk dream here—the Myrrydanai could not reach it.

A surge of power existed here.

I remembered Merod's words at the mirror. *There are those of our tribes, older vampyres than even those of the Medhyic line.*

• 4 •

I awoke with the thirst but ignored it while I climbed along a ledge of the mountain and looked again at the glorious citadel. In the night, the stone of its temples and the banners flying along the villages within it, as well as the many islet-farms that seemed bound together along the canals, all were vivid, though the bright fires that lit the broad boulevards blinded me a bit with their number. Thousands of people moved along the streets and many slender boats and barges traveled the canals as I watched—I had never seen a place so busy in the dead of night. Not a horse was in sight, and as I watched, I saw vampyres take flight from the temples themselves—a flock of them moving as one off to some distant mountain for their hunting.

I spread my wings and swooped down across the valley, gliding over the bright canals and streets, looking down at the men, many of them half-naked but wearing cloaks, while the women went bare-breasted. They carried baskets full of food and goods upon their backs, and slender barges moved along the canals, packed with flowers and animals being taken to some end point of the city. If any looked up to see me, I did not hear them cry out—but if they were used to vampyres in this place, they might not even think me strange. I landed upon the flat roof of some kind of public house, raised above a pyramid. The stone I clutched had jaguars and rabbits engraved in it. It was a pumicelike stone, and I looked to the mountains around the city and saw that they were, to a one, volcanic. One of them, far to the west, had the yellow-red spume of lava along its edge and the gray ash that was swept farther to the west by the wind.

Below me, long-leafed plants sprouted and flourished along the street gutters, and dogs roamed the alleys. The pull of the stream was nearly excruciating, and I felt as if I had come upon the source of all my kind. Somehow, this civilization tolerated us.

Somehow, we lived here alongside mortals, and all thrived.

Then, it was as if the stream thickened, and I could nearly feel the touch of a vampyre.

The stream itself seemed to wrap itself about my throat, tightening like a viper until I could barely breathe from its heaviness.

Then, it released.

At that moment, someone touched my back, just at the center of my spine. I swiftly turned, and there standing above me, hands on his hips, was a vampyre whose eyes shone a glassy blue. He was a striking figure. His skin had none of the pallor of the undead, but was swarthy and even rosy in its complexion. His forehead was high, the line of his nose bent slightly as if broken, and his thick black hair hung down past his shoulders. Upon his face, small white gems had been embedded about his eyebrows, and one at his nose, with two smooth rounded obsidian disks piercing his earlobes. His chest was bare, but here gold studs and small rubies pierced the flesh at his nipples and navel. He wore a kind of wrapped cloth at his waist and loins. He wore no sandals or shoes upon his feet. Even with this humble appearance, I knew he was a warlord of some kind. He had a look to his face that seemed cruel and judging. When he spoke, it was in my language. "We felt your arrival two nights past," he said. "You must come with me, for this is a time of war in these mountains, and it is not safe."

He pointed along the ridge of volcanoes where steady plumes of gray smoke billowed up. As I followed the line of his finger, I saw the

fires of encampments along the rims of the mountains. "We have been
besieged since the night of a thousand falling stars, many years ago,"
he said. "When the pestilence swept across the seas and burned the
mountains that protect us."

• 5 •

I followed him in flight to the place he called the Palace of the Lords
of Death. To its highest level we flew, and as he landed, he turned
back to smile at me as I touched the stone floor. The palace within was
unlit, which was better for our seeing. It was thick with gold and jade,
and adorned with crystal skulls and beautiful men and women carved
in obsidian. Great stone bowls full of fresh blood awaited me. I was instructed to drink, for it had been brought for me alone. I could not resist, and drank my fill. The hall was packed with other vampyres, many
who looked so different from my tribe that I was not sure that they
truly had ever been men. Several seemed to have the winged arms of
bats, and their faces likewise seemed ratlike and not human at all, while
their thighs and legs resumed a human semblance. Some of the women
were heavy with child, which shocked me, for I did not expect our kind
to be fertile, though we felt the full pleasures of the flesh among ourselves. Still others held spears and bows, and upon their heads, long
blue and red feathers woven into helmets of sorts. Most of them were
naked, but some wore breeches, and others loincloths, while others
were in full tunic and cloak, though with dyes and materials I had never
seen. Some were dark of skin, and some pale as winter snow.

Arched doorways led out to other corridors that seemed all black
stone. I saw the shadows of others there, and guessed that there were
nearly a hundred vampyres gathered here. But along with them, tall
mortal men wearing the ceremonial robes of priests—the servants of
these vampyres rather than priests of the tribe. They sat in the darkness
as if in prayer, no doubt hearing the rustling of movement and our
voices, but not seeing us all around them.

My host flew without wings to a throne raised several steps from the floor. It was as if he had taken a great leap beside me, and in a blur of motion was upon the chair, looking down at me. He clapped his hands, as if dismissing or calling someone, yet no one stirred. The claps were for me, a signal to approach him here. He adopted the pose of the rogue prince—his legs bent and heels raised as he pressed his toes to the stone, as if he were restless and might take off at any moment.

This vampyre was one of the most intriguing creatures of our kind I had ever beheld. He had more than the usual beauty of our race—his face, swarthy as dusk yet incandescent, his eyes shining as if with the moon's deep light. There was an intelligence behind them and yet a sense of play and childishness as well. His luxurious hair, too long by the standards of Europe, almost feminine in the way it fell about his shoulders. The jewels and gold piercing his skin, the shine of jade and ruby and pearl thrust into flesh. And yet, he had that threatening presence as Saracen might—as if he were at the ready, always, for battle.

He leaned back against the carved jaguars of his throne, and shouted words in the native tongue to those assembled around us as I stepped forward toward him. Behind the throne, I saw several statues of gods with the heads of animals and birds and serpents while their bodies were of men and women. "My brother Aquil and his armies of the south rage against us, and those warring tribes along the coast burn the villages of the mortals who trade with us," he said. "My brother Kulcan brings his nation in the north to the border of this land, and my people are slaughtered. My granddaughter, Pacala, raises her city in the jungles that when my brothers are done with me, she will bring her mortal army to their lands to steal their wealth. There is no peace among us, nor has there been since the Great Crossing was felt from the Veil. My children are ripped from their flesh. The mortals think we have abandoned them. It is a time of unrest. You come as an enemy to us?"

"No," I said, but grew fearful as I watched the assembly of vampyres move closer in, forming a half circle that I might not escape through the great entry at the terrace to this palace.

"You come to us in need. You *seek*. And yet, we have enemies who come to burn our city and its inhabitants. They are greedy and frightened. They see the signs in the sky and hear the tearing of the Veil. How shall we trust you?"

"I have no weapon. No army," I said. "I am but one who has crossed the sea and the edge of the Earth to come to this country."

He smirked. "Yes. We've watched you." He held up his hands, palm outward, to the gathering of vampyres. He spoke words to them. By his expression, I could tell he tried to allay their fears. Several of the vampyres snarled and snapped and shouted what must have been the obscenities of their language. The vampyre on the throne shook his head, and laughed, pointing at me as he spoke to them. Then, he returned his gaze to me. "I am Nezahual, son of Ixtar. I rule this land. We do not take kindly to intruders."

"I am Aleric, Falconer," I said.

"You are not of the line of Ixtar," he said. "You are not one of the tribes. From whom were you born."

"From the Sacred Kiss of the Pythoness, Pythia, daughter of Merod Al Kamr."

"So," he said, as if he were about to spit on the floor. "The breath itself, entering your lungs at death. The bloodline of Medhya."

I nodded.

"You were born mortal," he said. He paused for a moment, his eyes gleaming in the darkness.

My eyes narrowed, watching him. I did not understand. "All are born mortal."

"I have never been mortal." He grinned. His teeth were like obsidian itself, and each fang was painted gold. "You are half-breed. From death to undeath. I never died, Aleric, Falconer. I never reached the Threshold. Nor did any who are here." He raised his right arm and spread his hand out. "The children of our kingdom are not undead."

"It's impossible," I said.

"Your blood is impure," Nezahual said. "My mother, Ixtar, who was born in the sea beneath the burning rock, lay with the Great Serpent. From their union, I was born. My brothers, too, and my sisters. From us, our children were born. All generations come from Ixtar. Even Medhya."

"I did not know . . . I did not think . . ." I felt confusion as he spoke. How was this possible? How could there be vampyres without the Threshold of Death? Mortals became immortal when they returned from that doorway. I did not understand how vampyres could be descended directly from the Great Serpent—a god that I had thought of as unseen in creation.

"It is because you are of the dead," he said, shaking his head, derision in his voice. He spoke his native language to the others, and there was much discussion among them. "Your mind could only grow from mortal understanding. You mentioned Pythia. You have come here to find her?"

I nodded.

"She is gone this night," he said with no further explanation. "My kin will not harm you. Rest with us, drink blood with us. Come, let me show you the rest of the palace." He leapt down like a cat from the throne, landing on all fours just in front of me. He stood, snarling words to his brethren, many of whom moved back away from us. "We welcome our kind here, even the bastards," he said as he drew me toward the corridor just beyond the throne's stair. He glanced back and barked orders to his guards and to the vampyres, and as we passed the priests at their seats, he whispered some words to them. They stood up and scurried off down another hall, as if their lives were at stake.

✦ 6 ✦

W E walked together through a hallway of crystal skulls, all stacked as if in catacombs. He lifted one from the pile and told me of the history of the maiden who had brought it. "She was sixteen years and covered with flowers. She was the daughter of a king of men, from a city to the north. Her blood was sweet, and as the priests held her before me, I drank her life force with respect for her offering. See how beautiful the handiwork is?" He passed the crystal sculpture to me, a perfectly smooth skull. "All of them, brought here as part of the blood offering. The priests present the most beautiful youths and maidens to me. The skulls are offered that we remember the lives they gave to the gods."

"Have you been to my country?" I asked. "You speak my language as well as any and better than most."

"Do you think the Son of the Serpent would not know all the tongues of the Earth?" he asked. "We are not human, Aleric. If I have drunk from men on every continent of the Earth, do I not know their tongues as well as their blood? For I have been on this Earth when the seas above ground were lakes, and when the Great Serpent wandered the lands to bring wisdom to the mortal realm."

After a moment, he slung his arm over my shoulder. He whispered to me, "The others do not like your being here. Many have been captured by the enemy, and mortals choose sides between my brother in the distant jungles and me. Our watchers spied you three nights ago across the great sea. It was only my intervention that kept you safe." He drew away from me, keeping his hand on my shoulder, looking me in the eye to see my response. I felt as if a spider had just drawn me into its lair and held me with invisible strands.

"Where is Pythia?" I asked again, unsatisfied with his earlier response.

He gave me a haunting stare, as if I scratched at a wound with the question. "Who are you to her?"

"I am one she made," I said.

"Yes, the undead become attached to the ones who kill and revive them," he said as if I were not there. "Well, she hunts the mountain villages. You will see her by dawn. You are here for her alone?"

"I am here not for myself, but for others," I said.

"The mask."

"The Gorgon Mask," I said.

"I think you will find it before the night is through," he said. "Do you know where you are?"

"Aztlanteum," I said. "Land of the Ketzal."

He laughed. "That would be the name the priests gave us." He pointed to the obsidian statues of creatures with two heads, or a woman whose face was like a dog but who held a child in her hands with the wings of a bat extending from his small arms. "These statues . . . these are of ancestors, born of Ixtar, my mother. They left our city to rule other kingdoms. My brothers and I remained." We came to a dark stone statue with eyes of jade of a goddess with terror in her glance. I recognized her instinctively.

"Medhya," I said.

"Three daughters born from my mother as serpents from her womb," Nezahual said. "Mictlya, Zabatzan, and Lamixtara." As he said the names, I knew the names of these three goddesses of our tribe: *Medhya, Datbathani, and Lemesharra.*

"We are told that they are three in one," I said.

"She slew her sisters. *My* sisters," he said, touching the onyx hand of the statue of Medhya. "Their destruction increased her dominion. She took from the Serpent Goddess the golden mask you seek and a sword of fire. From Lamixtara, whom you call Lemesharra, she acquired a staff of conjuring." He turned to me. "They exist still, though their flesh and blood are usurped by others. The priests of the tribes from which you and your mongrels are descended used tortures and sorcery to extract that essence of youth and immortality that keeps you from crossing the Threshold to death. You do not die, but you extinguish. That is the mark of a mongrel vampyre." He drew closer to me, pressing his face into my hair, inhaling deeply. The heat of his hands upon my shoulders and the warmth of his skin at my scalp reminded me too much of nights with Ewen. I pulled away from him. He smiled sadly. "I smell your lineage in you. Not the Sacred Kiss. But your birth. I smell a mother from a tribe of mages. And I smell your father. He was one of them."

"*Them?*"

He raised his hand to quiet me. "You really are of bastard blood, in both mortal and immortal life. I mean no offense. He was one of the thieves. I smell him on your skin. You are special among the mongrels? For your birth was no accident for a Priest of Medhya to bring birth to you. Few of them had the ability to do this. Only a powerful mongrel priest could do such an act."

As he spoke, my mind raced as I wondered if Merod himself was my father; or one of the other Priests of Blood I had not known; or even the Nahhashim priests. All I knew of my natural father was that in some way, he changed the course of my mother's life for the worse. "Who was my father?"

"A mongrel like you, but a priest of my sister's tribe," Nezahual said. "You were created in mortality to fulfill some destiny, my friend. No priest known to me could have fulfilled the prophecies of your tribe, and yet I smell that priest upon you as I smell your mother. You are made by a mongrel priest who carried the Serpent's prophecy within his seed. You are a Maztera." *Maz-Sherah,* I thought as he said this.

"Maz-Sherah, yes," he said, as if he had just read my mind. He gave me a knowing look. "Your kind has endless life, even in a kind of living death. There is no savior for that, I think."

"And you?" I asked, suppressing my anger. "You must also enter the Extinguishing if someone put you in the sun, or pressed a sharpened spear into your heart."

"They have tried." He smiled. He reached over and combed his fingers through my hair. When he withdrew his fingers, he sniffed them as if seeking my scent again. "You do not understand what our purity is, Aleric. The pure ones may walk in the sun. Its light exposes us to mortals in a way that the night cannot, so we do not choose it often. Yet it does not harm us. The stake in the heart—it pains us. Chop us into pieces, and our hands will find our arms again, our heads, our necks. But it does not extinguish us. You are imitations of the gods. We are the gods themselves."

"Then there are no gods," I said.

"And yet we create them from those with greater power, or greater sorcery," he said. "We have gods here, mongrel. We know our mother. She exists. She protects us with her sorcery. With her eternal life."

I did not ask what I wished—for I began to be curious about how these immortals might be destroyed if not by sun or stake. What other powers did they posses? I felt such a strong pull of the stream here, and yet I could not communicate as I could with my own tribe. It was as if I felt pressure along my spine, while my head throbbed from a constant ache. The thickness of the stream's current made me feel heavy and slow.

I followed him out to a parapet overlooking the city. The torchlight seemed like a thousand candles in the city below us, while the stars flickered above. "And as gods, do you perform miracles?"

"I wish I could," Nezahual said, sadness in his voice as he looked out over the city. "Our time here will pass one day, whether it is from these wars my brothers wage, or from invaders from the northern mountains."

"If you are immortal, what do you fear from men?"

"My sister had her cloak of flesh torn from her and her blood stolen through ritual and ceremony. She exists, but beyond the Veil. So the twilight of our kind will take us there, for mortals learn rituals and capture the gods they once worshipped." He shook his head slightly. "Even the gods fear men, mongrel." He lifted his arms up to the night wind, which was light and warm. "We felt the changes that those shadow priests of my sister brought into this world from the Veil. Our mountains erupt again with fire, mortals grow fearful and bring war. The western sea is slick with ash from the burning earth beneath the water. Heat is in the air all around us. The earth has trembled, and we have felt it in the caves beneath this city. Your kind brought this upon the Earth through that ancient thievery. The unmaking of the world is at hand. Even you, the harbinger of the end of times, Maz-Sherah. Savior. Messiah of the Damned. Children are born without life. Men murder their families in madness and fear. Gods do not die from disbelief or forgetfulness. But they may be trapped, or driven to places far from this Earth, beyond the Veil itself."

"Then you were wrong," I said, looking out at the flocks of vampyres as they moved like dark birds across the moonlit night. "Perhaps it is not like the Extinguishing my tribe faces. But it is just another kind of Hell. None understand it, for your priests are not like you. They are mortal. The gods do not inform them of your afterlife."

"Stories of priests. It is all made up, Aleric. All I know of the world is here. And the tens of thousands of years of my life, born not a mile from where we now stand. The mortals who worshipped me at my birth, and those who worshipped my brothers and sisters, as we worship our mother. I am Lord of Death and Life here, to those mortals below. I am the Son of the Serpent and King of Miclan, the Land of the Dead. I am the son of Ixtar, the Queen of Eternal Life, not the goddess of death. Not the Queen of the Undead, as you might find in some great mother goddess. No, our gods exist, and their lives are never-ending. Yet . . . yet we have all felt the shaking of the earth. Volcanoes that have lain sleeping for hundreds upon hundreds of years begin to awaken since the Veil's tearing has begun," Nezahual said. "It is those priests of my sister's kingdom who have brought this to the world. And you have come for a mask of the ceremonies that will hasten the end of all this." He looked across the expanse of light and majesty, his gaze stony and his jaws clenched. "These mortals that surround us still believe we can save them. But all we can do, my friend, is wait for what will come."

"A kingdom of vampyres," I said, in awe of all of this, despite the dismissive tone he had taken with me. "It is like the legends of what Alkemara once was."

"Our concerns are not yours," he said, with more kindness than he had offered since my arrival. "You are here to find the vampyre who made you." He looked at me, and something in his glance softened. "I do not blame you, Aleric. I wish my sister Medhya had never created her kingdom of priests at Myrryd. I wish I had stopped her from leaving her home."

"They say a war is coming in my own land," I said. "A war of vampyres and mortals, also. I am the Maz-Sherah, but not only of the Priests of the Kamr and the Nahhashim. If you . . ."

"I have war enough here," he said. "I have brothers who jealously want the old kingdom. The nest. The river of life that lies beneath this city. I have lost ten thousand mortals from my kingdom in one night when Aquil's slaughter took them. I will lose a hundred thousand more. One night, Aquil and Kulcan will unite, and my granddaughter Pacala will bring her armies, and they will overrun my beautiful city. I will watch the end of things from the highest temple, and then I will leave this place. I will abandon it to its fate.

"If I travel with you to fight the shadows of my sister's wrath?" he asked. "What will it gain? My own kingdom will fall, for none of my kin will stay and fight. This is the ancestral city, and my birthplace, Aleric. I already feel sorrow for it, for I know the night will come when all will end for us here."

We stood there silently for a moment, then he said, "Come, it is a quiet evening. I sense no battle tonight. All are weary. Look, below—see how the people carry their dead to the canals? They set them on barges, surrounded by flowers. They believe they go into that sacred sea beneath the mountain. They believe they, too, are Ixtar's children. But they are not."

"Still, it is a beautiful ceremony," I said as I watched the long, flat boats, torches along the canals, and the red and yellow and purple flowers spread out across the bodies of the dead. "Mortals find comfort in such ritual."

"And you seek the mask that you may perform a ritual, as well," he said. "Do you understand what you would unleash with this mask?"

I shook my head, trying to read his thoughts. He was impenetrable.

He glanced up at the stars and sighed. "I have much to show you."

· 7 ·

H E led me to the edge of the terrace. He pointed across to the high mountain ridge just to the south of the city. We will go there, but from the underground passage." We climbed down along the steps to the middle platform of the temple, planted with trees and flowers and strange, beautiful plants. I followed him into an inner corridor, and from this a stairway down through the center of the pyramid itself. We passed carvings of skulls and serpents and bats and jaguars as we raced downward. He leapt upon the encircling wall like a spider, with his hands and feet upon it. After nearly an hour, we came to the bottom of the stairs. We entered through the cave doorway, and down its path we went, spiraling as the path turned this way and that.

Finally, the path opened onto a high chamber of rock and another carved stone stairway down to what looked like a shoreline below us, and a river. "This subterranean channel feeds the mortals of our city, and is the path of Ixtar herself as she wanders beneath the earth," he said. "This was once a burning mountain. It cooled when my mother was born from the subterranean sea itself as the lava cooled within it." He pointed into the distance and bade me fly to the far end of this cavern.

When I reached the other side, still with the river to my left, I saw a statue of a goddess as tall as any castle, and surrounding it a shining yellow brilliance as if fire protected Ixtar.

It was gold, so much of it that it seemed as if the treasuries of all the kings of the Earth had been raided and brought here.

CHAPTER 14

THE brilliant metal shone like the noonday sun at her face. Piles of coins and swords, battered and long; small statues of women and men and dogs and deer; vessels and round calendar stones made of gold bedecked the black onyx platform that held Ixtar's statue. There were hundreds of these, some buried in the sand with only a head or a spear end sticking up, some piled at the corners of the rock platform. I lifted a few of these in my hands—a miniature statue of a rabbit, a pitcher made entirely of gold, a sword so heavy I could barely lift it.

"Gold is sacred to her," Nezahual said from behind me. "She brought it beneath her fingernails when she came up from the mountain to the mortals of the Earth."

"This is wealth beyond measure," I said. "I had thought your people were primitive. I had thought this land was full of savages and ignorance among the mortals."

"Who are the savages?" he asked. "Those who have built the great cities of the Aztlan and the Tihuac and the Cuz? Or the ones who come here to take what is not theirs?"

I glanced up at Ixtar as I set the gold pieces back down along the platform upon which her talons curled.

She had been carved from onyx of varying hues—her body was black, and her face, brown and white; her wings seemed made of a marbled red onyx stone. Yet the effect was that she was carved from one great stone, a many-hued travertine rock that had withstood centuries. Her features were nearly worn smooth, as if this chamber had been completely submerged for long periods. The nipples at her breasts were rubbed away, and her eyes seemed round and hollow but as if they had once been made with great detail, for there were lines here and there indicating an iris and an eyelid. Part of her face was obscured with long, tangled hair carved from white onyx. Her throat was smooth and perfectly made, and a ring of skulls encircled it as a necklace. Her arms were elongated and bent upward, spread apart. The wings of a bat spanned from her talonlike fingers down to her hips. Barbed thorns thrust from the ridge of her arms, carved to perfection and smoothed down only slightly with time. Yet another smaller pair of arms were connected at her shoulders with her arm wings. In her left hand she held a round orb and in her right, a crystal skull. Her breasts were pendulous and heavy as if with milk. Despite the strangeness of her figure, she had a sensuality to her curves and the upturn of her breasts, as well as the curve of her arms, that offset the alien nature of her body. A wedged carving instrument had made what seemed like scales from around her breasts down to her shapely waist, for she had great sexual beauty in her torso, though her body seemed monstrous in every other way. Jade had been inset about her lower waist, just about her thighs, as if highlighting the sacred space from which she brought life into the world. There, beneath this, her labia, made of jade, spread apart. From that opening of her thighs, carved serpents flowed from her, and along her thighs, the etchings of flowers and creatures wandered down her legs, spilling, presumably, into the world. On the statue, they spilled across her knees and her clawlike feet. She was a mother of monsters—of vampyres, of creatures with the bodies of serpents and scales that seemed like feathers, as well as a serpent-bird that reminded me of the cockatrice and gryphon formed on the helm of Artephius. What little of her face I could see was covered in jade and obscured. She looked very much like the legendary harpies of the Greeks, those women of wing and talon.

"Queen Ixtar," he said as he leapt up alongside me. "Mother of the pure race. See her face? She is like the moon beneath the earth it-self. Her breasts bring the seas to the surface of the land. Her thighs bring pleasure to the Serpent, and from them, we have come."

This face, with round, vacant eyes and lips parted to reveal the split tongue of a serpent and the fangs of a jaguar, seemed as if it were from a more savage place within the vampyric lineage. Was Ixtar the purest form of the vampyre mother? Before the resurrection of those of us of mixed blood, was she some beast-mother bringing creatures that mimicked the look of mortals and grew from babies to children, suckling at the teats of wet nurses whose blood flowed into the young mouths? Surrounding the statue were a hundred skulls and the bones of the dead—none made of crystal, these were offerings to her. The blood of many stained her knees and thighs from the blood sacrifices.

I thought of the statue of Lemesharra in Alkemara. I thought of all the gods of the Earth, carved in stone. Did any exist in flesh? Was Nezahual truly the brother of Medhya?

Was Ixtar ever in the flesh, or was this a fanciful rendering of some idea of Nezahual's? Her name was so much like the Egyptian goddess, Ishtar, and Astarte—had these all once been the same crea-ture? A fertile mother monster? Even then, I believed in the gods, for I had seen too much as a vampyre not to do so. Yet I did not believe they had ever crossed the Veil. Yet, Medhya was both the mother of my tribe and its destroyer. She had once ruled Myrryd in the ancient times, and her priests had torn her flesh and blood to exile her spirit beyond the Veil. How could these ideas have flesh? How could this stone have ever lived?

I looked at Nezahual—his unearthly beauty was a costume, a skin to wear in order to attract mortals for feeding. Was he a friend? Was he a potential enemy? Were these the lies of his tribe, as I heard legends of ours?

How could one vampyre, of mongrel blood, perform ceremonies of these ancients and hope to do more than this Lord of Vampyres ever could?

Even as I thought these things, I saw in his eyes that he had invaded my mind. He could read thoughts, and I would have to be careful. A sly, almost sweet smile played at the edge of his mouth. "I did not think mongrels were so . . . fearful." He reached over to me, pressing the palm of his hand upon my forehead. "Your thoughts are like raindrops. They fall quickly and quietly." He brought his hand back, pressing it to his mouth and nose as if smelling my thoughts. "You wonder if I am a friend. You fear me, Aleric. You doubt your own path." He nodded. "I terrify some. It is what kings do best. But you. You are like my brother. I smelled the mongrel blood on you, yes. But I also smelled your benevolence, friend. I do not often sense that from my kin. Pythia has none. She has passion. She has desire. But not benevolence. I did not expect you to have it within you."

"Benevolence?"

He nodded, and then looked up at his mother's statue. "She had benevolence, as well. Her children have little of it. Even I have barely a cupful. But I recognize it in you. It's in your speech. It's in your thoughts. It's from the careful breeding that brought you into the world as the Maz-Sherah of your tribe. Blood may tell much, and the smell of yours has this benevolence within it. I respect this in you,

Aleric. Mortals who become immortal rarely bring it with them. It is hard to have goodness when thirsty for blood."

"Others are like me," I said. "We must survive, but we respect the mortal world."

"Because you once were mortal," he said. "My kin have no such attachment. We need our mortals. They worship us. We bring them a glimpse of eternity. We are their continuity, their history. Their visions of magnificence. They touch the gods when they come to us with their offerings. We are their justice, as well, and their mercy, though merciless we must be to them. We tear the throats of their enemies that they will bow down to us and create these cities to our glory. But we bring no goodness to them, my friend."

"The Priest of Blood, Merod Al Kamr, has charged me with the guardianship of the mortal realm. We drink from them, but we protect them as well."

"Protect them from what? Ah, the pure ones," he said. "My sister exists past the Veil, but her hounds enter the world to return her flesh and blood, stolen by your priests. This is why you fear me. For I share blood with my sister, and it is in you. You should be my enemy, mongrel. But I do not feel that. I admire your feelings for mortals. My sister's war is not my war."

"Then we may be friends," I said, hoping he would honor this.

"Yes, we are friends," he said.

You have mortal children, he said. Had he even said this aloud? He spoke within my mind as he said these words, although his lips did not move.

Yes, I answered silently. *They—and many others—will be destroyed if I do not bring the ceremonies of the priests into the house of my enemy.*

"I have had many children, but that ended . . . long ago. I understand how you must protect your mortal children. I have not always been able to protect my immortal ones." He pointed over to the river. "When I was born, this was a sea that carved out these chambers. Before my birth, it was a great ocean under the burning mountain. But when the lava came within the hollow of the mountain, the ocean burned away into obsidian, and the sea was formed. Now, it is a river, and one day, it will be a stream. When it dries, I will no longer exist. We do not extinguish here, Aleric. But like the giant dragons and serpents of the world that existed when my mother came into being, we will one day be gone. My sister hastens this. She does not care for her own kin. She only seeks destruction."

He took me over to the river's edge. It was deep as it ran along the bank of the shore, and its water was clear. There, within it, as he pointed to rocks beneath the water, I saw several vampyres with tails like eels and serpents, their long hair flowing like eelgrass down their backs, their skin a gray-blue. I had seen such creatures before—those water maidens of Alkemara, who drank from our kind.

◆ 2 ◆

THESE vampyric maidens swam with the current, following the river where it sank beneath a rock canopy at the end of the chamber. They undulated beneath the water as they went, wiggling like snakes. I could not forget those who had torn at one of my companions, for these drank from vampyres as well as mortals.

Nezahual drew off his cloak and let it fall to the ground. He stood there in his loincloth, the jewels shining along his body like a constellation of stars in the heavens. "If we follow the river for several miles, beneath the ceiling of rock, I will show you a city older than any other. It is Ixtar's nest, and mortals who have seen it call it Miclan or Xibal, but it is the womb of Ixtar herself."

"I am weak in water," I said, watching as one of the eely vampyres slowed near the shore, watching us as she raised her head above the surface of the water. She opened her mouth, showing the ridges of gray shark teeth, her eyes yellow and gray. She moved toward us, and

I stepped back from the river. She climbed up on a perch of rocks, clinging to them. She watched me, and looked as if she were about to scramble from the river up the bank and attack me as a wild animal might. But Nezahual barked at her in a language she understood. She slipped beneath the water and continued on her way.

"Like you, these are mongrels, as well," he said. "For some of our kind have mated with mortals. It does not work well with us. The serpent or the bat become too strong in the blood, and these throwbacks to unknown ancestors survive the womb, though they eat their way into existence through a mother's body."

"I have seen them before," I said. "In the waters of Alkemara."

He stepped into the shallows of the river. He offered his hand. "They will not harm you, though they do like the taste of mongrel blood."

"A friend was devoured by creatures such as these," I said, looking down at a young male vampyre whose crocodilian tail slapped at the surface as he glanced at us on his way along the current. "His Extinguishing grieves me still."

"I will protect you," he said. "Take my hand, Aleric. If they detect your fear, they may go into a frenzy. You must be calm when you enter this river. Be at peace with them. Only their prey fear them. If you fear them, you will become their prey."

"The water takes much from me," I said.

"Your fear is what takes from you. I will carry you on my back if necessary," he said.

I drew off my shirt, and stripped to my waist, dropping cloak and clothing on the pebbles by the water's edge. I took a step into it. I did not feel that disconnection I had felt before near water. This was clear and clean, and felt more like the stream itself.

I took his hand as he stepped into the current.

"Yes, one more step," he said.

He dragged me down into the rushing water. Two of the serpent maidens swept by us, and I saw their terrible gray teeth, like a shark's with the maw of a lamprey. Yet I saw the beauty of these women, for their faces were lovely and their complexion gray-white, like the underside of a shark. I felt that fear of them, yet they ignored me as they swept by us. Their bodies undulated as they moved, their figures athletic and perfectly formed. Still, the memory of my friend Yarilo being dragged to his death by several of the Alkemars who drank from their own, filled me with slight dread.

Nezahual's grinning face put me at ease. He told me to wrap my arms about his neck and he would swim for me.

We passed beneath the rock ceiling and moved through a narrow passageway that became a tunnel. I felt the slimy forms of the lamprey-creatures as they moved alongside us. I began to relax as they passed, for they showed no interest in attack. When we emerged, he brought me up from the river, whose current had slowed. As I broke the surface, I glanced about and saw that we had come to a calm pool, while the river rushed to the left and right of it on some other course. A great waterfall spilled before us, over a rock cliff. I followed him through the narrow cave that had been formed behind the waterfall, and as we came through to the other side, I saw a great triangle of rock, high as a castle tower at its peak. Through its doorway, a corridor of gold set in plates along the walls and floor. The shape of the triangle held as we walked along it, and upon the flattened gold plating were painted many images of the vampyres of Ixtar's nest. They had the bronze skin and features of Nezahual and the other vampyres I had seen here. The sons and daughters of the sea with their eel-like bodies and lamprey mouths full of gray fangs were painted here also, as they were borne away upon a current represented by wiggles and curves of lines. The Great Serpent's body ran along the left wall, and upon it, the history of the Earth. Nezahual pointed to the dragons of the air and sea. "These were the giants of the first age, and from them, the Great Serpent came and lived beneath the mountain seas themselves, while the sun died above and the giants died with it. Then, see, the monkey comes, and jaguar, and they live upon the lands where the sea dried. From them, Ixtar was born, within the hollow mountain." He pointed out a volcano, within which the Bat Goddess lay as from her womb came those serpents and monsters into the world. On the right-hand side of the gold wall were paintings of the Age of Mortals, and the great kingdoms of the Earth were there marked—Ixtar, and Alkemara, and Myrryd, and four others in lands I had never known or heard of. The art was rendered crudely, but I could see the history of Nezahual's family as they emerged to rule the world of men. "Here is how my people see us," Nezahual said as he traced the line of a painting on the golden wall of a feathered serpent. "Bird-serpents. We fly across the night sky, and yet we come to them with fangs and venom to drink as a serpent does. They love us and fear us. We bring them treasure and beauty, and when there is famine, we fly across the mountains to return with game and fruits of the earth that they might live. And in return, they make offerings of their finest to us. This is how it should be. Your tribes of priests have changed this. The theft of my sister's power has doomed your kind."

Finally, at the end of the triangular corridor, a crude stone stairway made of slabs of red stone piled almost like rubble led upward through a spiraling opening in the rock. Nezahual stepped ahead of me as we went up this, and after nearly an hour, we emerged onto a plateau. Above us, cliffs and ledges curved about the inside of what seemed a hollow mountain. At the top, an ellipse that opened into the starry night above.

We were inside the center of what had once been a volcano.

• 3 •

UNDER the volcano's rim, were cliff dwellings along the rock ledges, and on the plateau upon which we stood, a city of black stone. Obsidian had formed this underworld. And yet as I walked toward it, taking it all in, the temples and cathedrals of it were part of a great facade that was a city unto itself—a city pressed into a mountain. Beyond it, caves of crystal and obsidian and onyx, as if a rock had been split in two to reveal a sparkling dark surface within. The spires of its pagan cathedrals rose upward like the stalagmite spines of a cavern. The structures had been carved from an outgrowth of the black shiny rock.

The place seemed empty, yet I saw shapes and shadows through the slightly translucent stone, so I knew that other vampyres were in their chambers and palaces, at their temples, a far remove from the temples of the city above ground. Here, the walls were smooth and black, and the towers rose up to meet the lower ledges of rock inside the volcano. The doorways were low and curved, and, above each level of housing or palace, were arched doorways in the wall. It rose up like sheets of dark glass, its towers square, its spires like spearheads at the top of the towers. It was like smooth black ice, but with spears of towers that stretched high above us. As it loomed above, I saw many columned terraces and dwellings. I saw shadows moving behind the black glass, and now and then saw a maiden vampyre or a youth stretch leathered wings across a doorway and climb along the sheer face of a wall like a spider moving upward into its nest.

Nezahual walked ahead of me, following the narrow pathway between buildings. Within them, were tombs and catacombs lining the obsidian walls. These, he told me, were where all of our kind slept, for they did not even trust their own priests. "Mortals fear us, but they cannot help hunting us when we are most vulnerable."

"Yet you may go about in sunlight," I said.

"All creatures need sleep, and daylight brings rest to us," he said. "Our potency returns at nightfall. Priests wish to be the gods they serve. Medhya's priests betrayed her when they could. She trusted them too much, and grew too close to mortals in the kingdom she established. She was blind to the mortal heart, which is more ruthless than ours. Priests seek power. They seek to claim the place of the gods. Yet, they also propitiate us, they organize and rule mortals in daylight that we may feed and prosper."

"And you are safe here?"

He nodded. "Look up." He pointed out the ridges that were miles above us, along the rim of the opening into the hollow mountain. Several vampyres flew in a flock upward in a spiral, one following the other into the night. "Mortals have tried to come here, but all fall to their deaths when they make the attempt. To enter through the river of Miclan is to risk drowning, or our sisters and brothers of the waters. Still, when the plagues swept through this land, many tried to come here for treasure or to destroy me. But no mortal has ever left our nest with his life."

• 4 •

W E walked up a low stairway as if to a public building. Two enormous black obelisks stood like sentries at the entrance. Upon them, the ancient writings of these vampyres. Past them, a grand hallway that seemed as if it had once housed a greater civilization. Thousands of columns held up its ceiling, a hundred or more feet above us. As he guided me along a passage between rows of columns, Nezahual told me of the slaves who had worked in the glass to create the city. "They were invaders from the east, come in ships four thousand years ago," he said. "Their country had been destroyed by their gods, and they sought our home. They possessed great talent, and industry, and their artisans knew how to carve beauty from rock."

"And you fed upon them."

"Some, yes. Others are still in the city above us, in the blood of their descendants," he said. "These were times of great peace for us. The arts thrived. My brothers and I had no quarrels. It was a golden age. That has ended now. One cannot return to it."

He drew me back through a series of narrow pathways, we came up a courtyard surrounded on three sides by high black walls, reflecting us in the dark glass. He brought my attention to a ledge high above us along the obsidian wall. There was a cave opening there, ringed along its crumbling edges with skulls. "You see? There is the original nest. And from it, I was born."

There was a light mist in the air, as if the spray from another waterfall was nearby.

Golden bowls with grills upon them had been set into the crushed pumice that made up the floor of the courtyard. Within them some fungal root burned, giving off a scent that reminded me of roast boar. Thin tendrils of smoke slowly rose, twisting almost imperceptibly, dissipating in the misty air.

At the center of the courtyard was a monolithic sarcophagus raised upon a staircase that surrounded it. The tomb was a yellow-white stone of some kind, as if it were aged ivory. Incongruously, it was surrounded with chains and ropes, as if to keep something or someone from escaping it.

"It is made of bone," he said. "Softened with acids from the sap of the *copalli* plant for years. It is a sacred to Ixtar. Our best artisans carved the figures upon it long ago."

Stepping up the slabs of steps to the sarcophagus, I saw it was covered with reliefs and inscriptions. The figures of the Great Serpent and the Bat Mother, Ixtar. Additionally, there were beheadings depicted along its lid, and on its edges were strange geometric designs that turned and twisted in such directions in the carvings that it seemed to me they moved slightly as I watched them.

"She still exists?" I asked.

"This is her city. It would not exist without its queen."

"You keep her prisoner here?"

"Is that what you think I would do to my mother? To the mother of us all?"

"Why is it locked?" I grabbed a chain and pulled at it.

"No lock could hold Ixtar," he said. "She is not like us. She may pass through locks. She may slip through doors as smoke through a keyhole."

For a moment, I thought I heard a sound from within the tomb, though it was faint.

He grinned and let out a roar of laughter, baring his dark teeth. He leapt upon the lid, and did what seemed like a strange dance upon it. Then, he crouched on all fours, finally lying down upon the tomb's lid. He stretched his arms across the head of the tomb. He pressed his ear to the tomb. He rapped upon it. "Do you hear?"

I had not heard any noise, but he put his fingers to his lips for silence. As I listened, I heard scratching from within the massive coffin.

"There is an offering here for her. A sacrifice. This is her private chamber, and within it, she may do what she likes with them. She is not like us. She does not just drink from them, Aleric. She plays with them. She fondles them. She has a certain appetite for flesh," he said. "The tomb lid is too heavy for anyone to escape it. But when several are put there so that when she sleeps for a season, she has . . . enough . . . we need to keep them there until she returns."

"How long has he waited for his death?"

"A few nights. She does not come for them immediately. She likes their terror. It is a traitor." He stood up and rose several feet in the air, his arms outspread. "It is justice to sacrifice to our mother, for her tastes are particular. She feeds off her own children."

"She drinks vampyre blood?"

He returned to the top of the sarcophagus. "I smelled the same quality within you. You have fed from a vampyre. It is the one great forbidden rule of our kind. Do all mongrels do this?"

"I tainted my blood with an elixir from a sacred flower. I drank that my friend would drink from me, and we would sustain ourselves during a terrible captivity. We did not devour each other as the river vampyres do. Or as this mother vampyre does."

"Did it bring you strength to taste his blood?"

"It nearly destroyed us both. But we survived. We lived for years in this sorry state."

"Where is this friend?"

Ewen's face appeared in my mind. *Be safe. Be safe.* "He is a captive, still."

"Ixtar thrives upon the blood of her children," he said. "As my sister Medhya will thrive on yours one day, mongrel. Ixtar enjoys the flesh as well. She protects our city so long as we bring her sustenance. Just as mortals make offerings to us, we, too, must offer our blood to her in certain seasons."

I looked at the great sarcophagus and wondered about the vampyre within. What traitor was this? Who had done something so terrible in this city that he—or she—would be trapped in the tomb of their own mother?

"I do not throw the undeserving there," Nezahual said, eyeing me with suspicion. "Those who betray me, those who spy or seek to overthrow the city for Aquil or Kulcan, or my dear nasty granddaughter, Pacala, will find themselves locked in Ixtar's tomb. She does not return to it every night. But when her desire for vampyre blood grows thick on her tongue, she comes here like a spider returning to the fly that had tapped at her web. She takes him into her arms, and brings her venom to him that he might not fight her. Then, slowly, while the offering is conscious, she begins to drink from him. She begins to tear at bits of his flesh to satisfy her hunger. It is terrible for a vampyre to be devoured like this, I think."

"Yes." I could not tell if he carried a threat with these words. But I would not test him, nor would I be any but a visitor here. I knew I would leave by the next night and would do nothing to jeopardize this. I came for but one thing. The Gorgon Mask itself. The wars of Nezahual and his brothers and granddaughter here did not interest me. The savagery of sacrificing vampyre brethren to a mother vampyre was not my concern, though it brought a nameless dread to me. All life, I knew, devoured life. All creatures fought and warred for supremacy. It was the horror of existence. I had seen it among mortals and immortals. Medhya herself would eat her children in order to regain her supremacy in the world. She would tear off our skins to create her own flesh if she had the chance.

Wars brewed in my homeland, and the deaths of children and friends were closer to my heart than vampyres who did not get along in their own countries.

"Would you like to see Ixtar herself?" he asked.

"She is here?" I asked, and I saw by the look on his face his confusion at the question.

"All I have told you is true," he said. "She is. She is eternal. As long as she is alive, our kind will live as well."

"I did not think gods dwelled upon the Earth," I said.

"Mongrels," he said, chuckling to himself.

* 5 *

H E guided me up to the cave of her nest.

As I landed upon the rubble of skulls at its mouth, I smelled the awful stench of rotting flesh and the waste of animals. We both had to crouch as we went along the darkening tunnel. Water dripped from its ceiling, and the floor of it was slimy and uneven so I had to spread my hands to the cave wall to keep my balance as I went. Finally, the narrow opening expanded into a rounded chamber that was nearly as hot as midday sun. The place reeked of foul odors, and the humidity from the nearby river and falls brought steam from the rocks. The wet floor was covered with bones and skulls, many of them with the long, sharp teeth of vampyres.

There, cloaked only in steam, she lay upon a bed of dirt.

It was difficult to reconcile this creature with the Ixtar depicted upon the statue I had seen. None of the feminine and sensual nature was there in the sleeping figure. She was at least eight feet tall if not taller. Her skin had been dyed with red dust of some kind so that she seemed as red as blood itself. She lay upon her back, her arm wings stretched out far. They were leathered and scaly, and were more like a large bat's than a dragon's. Her red-painted face had whorls and designs tattooed upon it, and from her lips, two twisting tusks grew. They could not properly be fangs, for they moved outward from her face, cutting through her lips to escape her mouth. Her nose and mouth were more animal snout than human. Her lidless eyes were wide, as if she stared at the ceiling of the cave, yet the sounds of her breathing revealed that she was in a deep sleep or a trance. Her hair was black and thick, but also powdered with this red dye as if it were some ceremonial makeup that could not be removed. Her hair was plaited at her scalp, yet a wild tangle as it grew outward, uncut and allowed to grow so that it was like a blanket beneath her as she slept. Her breasts were large and long from age, and her belly thick and round and lightly furred with brown hair, though much was obscured by the red-powder dye that had been spread upon her. I saw that the red powder had spilled from her body in certain places, revealing patches of chalk white skin. Her arms—beneath the set of winged arms—were thickly muscled and had scales upon them and ended in claws with long, curved talons. One hand was outstretched in that rictus of sleep; the other was tucked beneath her breasts, in this hand she clutched an obsidian globe the size of a man's fist. I had seen this before—it was an orb of some power, and though I knew scryers of the Forest used crystal formed in such orbs to see into the future, I did not know the magick of this object. Yet, I saw shadows moving along its curve, as if something alive dwelled within the dark glass.

Her loins were uncovered and revealed thick, curly hair that ran from her belly to her thighs. Her legs were bent slightly as she slept, and seemed small and slender for supporting her upper body. The remnant of a tail—just a thick stub—was also slightly visible.

I shuddered as I beheld her, some nameless dread rising within me, as if I had stepped from a dream into a nightmare.

"Shall we wake her?" he whispered. "She will rise before dawn to eat the captive in the tomb below us. If we wake her now, we may watch the feeding."

"No," I said, stepping back to leave the sleeping chamber of the creature.

"I have watched a thousand of my brothers and sisters come from her. I once slipped from between her thighs, one of many of the children of the Serpent."

I turned to leave Ixtar's nest. I felt a pounding in my heart. I could not account for the rush of fear I felt. It was as if I beheld some primal terror that I had recognized on sight without knowledge of what within her form inspired such horror. She lay there in that chamber, and in her face, I saw what monsters we were more clearly than I had seen in Artephius's mirror in the dungeons of Taranis-Hir. Ixtar was an abomination upon the Earth, a mistake of the gods, bound to eternal life, bound to produce the creatures who feed from the blood of mortals. The Serpent and this Bat Goddess, the two most vile creatures of the ages, mating to produce a race of creatures who looked mortal but were not. The youth and beauty of vampyres was a trick to seduce and nothing more—it was the web of the spider.

Even as I felt the confusion of these thoughts, I knew why she had terrified me on sight.

She was a spider herself. She was a spider in its trapdoor, its web moving outward. The obsidian city was part of her trap, and the city of Aztlanteum was a web that stretched across the Earth's surface. We were not gods. We were not men.

We were night creatures, parasites, preying upon mankind. And those of us of the mongrel blood would suffer more than Nezahual and his siblings in their wars. I cursed the Priests of Blood and the Priests of Medhya's flesh and all those who had brought the bloodline of this alien creature from Hell into the realm of mortal life. In my mind, I cursed the gods and God that could not exist if such monsters were the source of all sorrow and war.

Nezahual followed me to the mouth of the tunnel.

♦ 6 ♦

I crouched and put my hands to my face trying to wipe the memory of seeing Ixtar in her bed. "We believe we are beautiful," I said. "But we come from that."

"She was once beautiful, as well," Nezahual said with scorn in his voice. "And when she has fed, the youth of her early centuries returns. A flush comes to her face. Her breasts become round again. She has a glamour like no other creature on Earth when she has devoured the offering."

I could not look at him. "You are part of . . . I am part of a race of monsters."

"That is the mortal in you who speaks like this. If you were pure, you would see the beauty of her form. You have been corrupted by mortal life."

"Do *you* even look as you seem to me?" I asked, looking over at him. His face, so masculine and strong, so swarthy and full of life. He was every inch the ideal of what a king of a great land would resemble. Was this he? Or was it a disguise of sorcery to trap mortals?

He spat on the ledge in anger. "You are a corpse who walks. You will not be a judge for us, or for our mother, Ixtar. Were your powers to fade, Aleric, would we not see the skull beneath the skin? Would that thick bristle of hair not be thin strands on a dead man's scalp? Would this"—he grabbed my throat and held tight—"not be a chain of bones—no, perhaps even dust and ash—if you were left in the sun for a day?" He let go of me, as I coughed to catch my breath. "How many years of life did you have? Eighteen? Nineteen? And how many years dead are you? Ten? Twelve? You are still in your own mother's womb as far as I am concerned. You have barely cut your teeth on mortal blood. You have no experience from which to speak. Do not judge the ancients, for the ages of the Earth take much from them. She is your ancestor, even in your mongrel blood. She is your true mother."

"My mother was a beautiful woman," I said. "But that . . . that is a demon."

"I will not argue further. It is because you are still young. When you pass a thousand years—if you survive that long—you will come to see our great mother as possessing the true beauty of this world." When he had calmed, he slung his arm over my shoulder, and whispered to me, "It is a strange new world for you here. It is not the lie you have been fed by your priests. Mongrels steal and lie. You are different. You are not like them. You must not listen to their lies."

I had many questions to ask him, so we sat there for a while as I asked about the Great Serpent and Ixtar and her children and the bloodline to which I had been born, though mingled with the mortal world. Finally, I asked about the black orb I had seen. "Is it for scrying?"

"She is the Night-Bringer," he said. "Sister of the moon, the mortals have called her. That is what she holds—night, in an obsidian stone. It is called the Serpent's Eye, and within, she watches over us." I could tell by his tone that he was weary of questions. Still, I had seen shapes move within that orb, and it looked enough like the black stone orb I had seen in a vision of Datbathani that I grew more curious about this object that Ixtar clutched even in her deepest sleep.

Then he got a sparkle in his eye. "She awakes tonight for her feeding."

"This is why you show me her nest," I said.

"You will see the mother of us all feed upon her young."

Even as he said these words, I heard a scraping along the rocks down the tunnel. Suddenly, a sharp keening sound echoed through the tunnel.

Nezahual grabbed my arm, "Come quick. If she sees us in her lair, she will devour us. She is blind, but the Serpent's Eye guides her."

• 7 •

H E drew me up the wall to a ledge far above her nest, looking out over the towers of the obsidian city. The tomb below seemed a small box. We nestled down against the rocks, peering over the edge to watch her.

Bleating cries came from her lair. I heard another noise nearby— a dozen or more vampyres took flight from the dark towers up into the midnight blue sky, through the opening of the volcano. He pressed close to me, wrapping his arm about my shoulders. "None of my brethren wish to be here for this. They fear her. But she only seeks the offering. She may go many nights without one, but in these times of war, there are always vampyres to be caught and offerings to Ixtar entombed for her pleasure."

I could not help feeling that he took pleasure in the fear I felt as I heard the scraping and bellowing as if some bull had been awakened, the howls and screams that were nearly human as Ixtar moved through the tunnel unseen.

And then, after several minutes, I saw her head thrust out, then her wings. She looked from our height like a giant bat emerging from its cave. Yet she did not fly. Instead, she began crawling down the flat surface of the black wall, like a spider moving toward its prey. In her lower left hand, I saw that orb again, and she held it before her as if it guided her downward toward the tomb.

"Some believe our mother is one of a race that vanished when the giants and the dragons left the lands, when the seas rose and the sun fell to earth," he whispered. Did he watch me and not her? I could not tell, for I could not look away from her as she slowly moved down the wall, her legs and arms moving out to the side to hold on. Her arm wings stretched out and bent, while their claw hands seemed to touch down upon the wall, and she would pull herself along as her legs and other arms scrambled along. Her keening continued, echoing up the mountain. I was filled with revulsion—in her sleep, she was monstrous, an abomination upon the Earth, but in waking—in her batlike crawling, her spidery movements—I thought of my ancestry through the Sacred Kiss. If the breath of Medhya was within us, then the mother Ixtar also was in our blood and flesh.

As I watched her crawl across the floor, faster now that she had left the obsidian wall, another thought came to me. How was Nezahual human in appearance? How were any of these vampyres connected to humanity? I had been mortal, so my appearance was mortal. But Nezahual as an early child of this creature—where had his human features come from? Where this mortal beauty upon this immortal king?

Was the Serpent himself in the form of a man? For if the Great Serpent were a python encircling the Earth, why were these creatures possessing the youth and beauty of the mortal realm? Why did they not more closely resemble the snake and the bat?

I watched as she delicately lifted the heavy lid of the sarcophagus and gently laid it down against the side of the tomb. I could not see her hapless victim within the tomb, but I heard his cries of terror. She pressed her head inside the tomb, and a terrible sucking sound echoed through the courtyard. It was as if she were kissing him and smacking her lips as she drew his blood into her snoutlike mouth.

I looked away as she drew him out of the tomb.

"She is beautiful," Nezahual said.

I closed my eyes, hearing that sucking, reminding me of the first mortal I had taken down—a maiden whom the other vampyres around me had thrown to me, a bone to a dog.

Monsters. All of us. We could pretend we were gods. Pretend we were here to guard the mortal realm. To protect the weak species of men. But we were the monsters of their nightmares. We were the beasts of legend, not the lords of the Earth.

Nezahual whispered to me. "Do you see how she grows more beautiful in his blood? In his flesh?"

I opened my eyes as he spoke, and saw the hideous Bat Goddess rip the remaining leg from the vampyre's torso and shake her head violently as she pulled flesh from bone.

◆ 8 ◆

WHEN her feeding had passed, she crawled again up the black wall, holding the Serpent's Eye ahead of her, as if it were her only sight.

Nezahual turned to me, and whispered, "Do not feel compassion for the prisoner. He knew the punishment for his crimes before he committed them."

◆ 9 ◆

WE returned down the dark streets and paths of the obsidian towers. "Even your blood carries the memory of this place," he said. "From these rocks, the Serpent came to the river, to Ixtar, and here was I born. And my brothers, before me. And my sisters. And from us, the generations of vampyres have come into the world. This is the nest and source of the breath that is in your body. This is the vein of blood that nourishes you. Though your blood is mixed with mortal flesh, you are my brother." He embraced me, kissing my cheek. He called to others who were hidden in their lairs among the great buildings and the ledges within the hollow mountain.

I met a multitude of those pure vampyres who had only met one or two other mongrel vampyres in their lives. They sniffed and combed me, and snarled and embraced me.

In a great hall of obelisks, we feasted upon villagers who had been brought down to us from the night's hunt by flocks of my brethren.

When dawn came, Nezahual brought me into an alcove of the obsidian city. There, fresh earth had been laid about a recessed stone bed. I lay down in it. He laid cool palm fronds across my body and brushed strands of hair from my eyes as if I were his child.

"I thought I would send you to your Extinguishing when I first heard you were coming," he said. "But I cannot blame you for the crimes of my sister or those crimes the priests of Myrryd committed long before your birth. You have come to find Pythia, but she escaped us tonight. Tomorrow night, we will hunt her, for she has stolen something precious from me. She is always stealing. Yet she always returns."

"What has she stolen?"

He offered a wry smile. "It is a secret thing. But she will return it."

I took a breath, wanting to ask him more about her, wanting to find her and get the mask she had in her possession.

Beyond the city of Ixtar, the sun had begun rising, and I heard the cries of the birds of the morning from the rim of the mountain.

One night had passed. As I fell asleep for the day, I counted the days left until the solstice. I thought of my daughter's face as she slept in her bed; of my son looking down at me in my coffin. I could not spend another night waiting for Pythia. She had the mask, and I needed to take it from her.

When I awoke, Nezahual and two other vampyre guards took me farther up into the nest where these vampyres slept.

"Where are we going?" I asked.

"You are here for Pythia," Nezahual said. "The hunt begins."

· CHAPTER 15 ·

· 1 ·

WE flew over the mountains in the south, past the smoking volcanoes that loomed like sleeping giants at the outer edges of the valley. Nezahual motioned for me to follow him to a series of spiked mountains that overlooked a vast desert terrain. There along the peaks, he pointed to a mountain lake at the center of a high plateau covered in sparse forest and mud-and-straw settlements. "My spies told me she had hunted there, killing villagers who brought me tribute. She probably slips into the crevices of the mountainsides, or among the snake nests at the edge of fields left unfarmed since the battles here began."

He spoke no more of this, but flew across the expanse of valley, and I followed him. We came upon the mud-and-grass houses of the village by the great lake, its harbor with empty boats floating. The stench of blood and the dead was everywhere.

He lifted up a dead child who lay near a dry field, his hands still clutching a small toy—a pottery dog. He held the boy close, kissing his forehead. "It is not our way to drink from children. This is what mongrels do."

"I have never killed a child for sport or thirst," I said.

He laid the boy down upon the straw mat in the humble house that reminded me so much of the hovel I had lived in as a child. The boy's mother had been killed behind the house, as she had been baking. The clay oven was still warm to the touch. He turned to me, and said, "You see what your kind does? When we hunt, we kill. But we do not kill mothers or children. We accept the tribute of villages like this—they choose their sacrifices. We do not slaughter entire families at once. How can I love this animal? This mortal mongrel vampyre? I have many lovers in my city. I should not care for her. I should throw her to Aquil for his armies to tear her apart."

He ran from the house and moved into the sky.

In my mind, he whispered, *She is near. We will find her tonight.*

◆ 2 ◆

WE followed screams coming from the far rim of the lake. I found her leaning over an old man, his throat torn, his legs still jerking, and his hands shaking as she held him tight.

When she turned to face me, I did not recognize her.

Yes, her hair was that golden color of the sun, and her skin was alabaster in the moonlight.

She wore that golden mask I had seen in visions—the face of Datbathani upon it. It was the mask of the Lady of Serpents—the Gorgon Mask. It began at the peak of her hairline and ran down along her forehead as if it had been poured molten upon her skin. It clung to her features, and did not obscure them, yet it inlaid another face onto her own—the face of the goddess of our tribe, who had once possessed this mask herself. A sister of Medhya. A sister of Nezahual. In that moment, I was awestruck by the ancient story. I had come to a place of the gods of our tribes—and the mask itself was the face of

Datbathani superimposed in gold over Pythia's features. The mask did not seem secured by any cord, but simply had been pressed against her face, molded to it, down to her nostrils and over her cheeks. Her lips and chin were free of it and streaked with blood.

She snarled as Nezahual drew her off the dying man.

Her fangs snapped at the air. She reached back and scraped her fingers across Nezahual's face. Four thin trails of blood followed where her nails had gone into his cheek, but they healed as rapidly as the skin had been torn.

Her wings shot out from her back, and she crouched down, a wild cat ready to leap upon us. Her tunic was shredded and dark brown from blood and viscera.

"You disgust me," he said.

She wiped her hand across her lips, smearing blood along her cheeks. "Your brother does not feel this way."

He leaned down and slapped her hard across the face. A sound like a tiger's growl came from her. She drew her wings back in along her shoulders and stood up. "You would hit the mother of your child," she said.

"*If* you had new life in you . . ."

"Perhaps your brother is better at siring sons than the great Nezahual, king of all vampyres."

"Perhaps you should see the inside of Ixtar's tomb that you may tell her of her sons Aquil and Nezahual," Nezahual countered. Then, calming, he said, "My brother will find you. He will destroy you. You belong to me. Do not be so ruled by your desires."

"Am I your prisoner, then?" she asked.

"If you go to my enemy's camp, then yes, you are my prisoner while I have you," he said. "Do not forget who protects you. Do not forget who took you from the burning sun of the desert when you came, running from your crimes. Do not forget . . . your lover."

I stood there, bewildered, looking at the two of them.

She glanced over at me, her eyes seemed to burn with fury. "You followed me here. You will die here, Maz-Sherah. You will die in the bowels of the earth as I should have let you die in the towers of Hedammu," she snarled. Other vampyres following our scent found us, and Nezahual had his guard bind her and carry her back to Aztlanteum.

• 3 •

AT the palace of the vampyre city, Nezahual brought her to the priests. Much of the fight had gone out of her, and she seemed vulnerable and hurt. Yet I remembered this same appearance when I came upon her in the towers in my youth. How she had seemed innocent and in pain. How she had played me as if I were the greatest fool among men.

He spoke in soft tones to the priests, yet there was violence in his glance as he pointed toward Pythia. Then, turning to me, he told me not to feel sympathy for her. "She is not like you. She has no goodness in her. We supply her with many mortals for her hunger, yet she escapes and slaughters those whom she should not. Those villagers would alert us if my brother's armies were to cross the hills. And she has taken them, without mercy or justice. She has taken them without honor."

"What will you do with her?"

He did not answer immediately.

"Will they torture her?"

"My priests do not like her," he said. "They have ways of subduing her that are abhorrent to me. But sometimes these things must be done. Do not be afraid for her. She slaughtered the priests of the Temple of the Ketzal when she arrived here more than a decade ago. None have forgotten the site of that temple, flowing with the blood of the sacred priests. If I had not intervened, she would have been fed to Ixtar by now or left out in the sun to burn. She is protected, but she pushes me too far. She cannot control her impulses. My own guards do not like seeing the mask upon her face. They see my sister in it, and they fear her, as well. They fear mongrel sorceries. Pythia asks many questions of our kingdom, and steals what she is not given. During these times of unrest, I wonder why I do not just throw Pythia into Ixtar's tomb and be done with her."

"But you keep her here, a prisoner. For more than ten years. What possible reason do you have for this? Why not set her free?"

He glared at me. "Do not question me, mongrel. You have not seen all she has done."

"But you have not destroyed her."

"She is a monster among us. No one can trust her. No one. Not even . . ."

Even as he said these words, it occurred to me that he truly loved her, and he truly hated her. I had felt the same way toward Alienora as she had become Enora. She, too, was a monster. Yet I could not help but feel pity and sorrow for her, for I had known what she once had been. What was it in Pythia, who had come between brothers to bring war in these kingdoms, that had also inspired such feelings? Was it the mask itself? Was she such a powerful vampyre that he bowed to her in some way, though she was mongrel blood?

Or was it purely love? And mingled with love, its own mongrel blood, the hate and fury that came with the possession of the beloved?

"She was our prisoner for many years. But I have tried to give her some freedom here. To her, freedom is an excuse for slaughter and thievery. For her, freedom is for dividing our people and dishonoring the temples. Do you understand me? It is my fault she has remained here so long. It is my fault that I did not see who she was the moment she killed the Ketzal priests. I cannot . . . I cannot destroy her. I cannot set her free." He closed his eyes as if wishing away the world. When he opened his eyes again, it was with resignation. "She heard of your coming. You are the one, I think, she feared, although she did not name you. In you, she sees the end of her own existence. She had run from someone else, as well, someone who had betrayed her in love."

I repeated my question. "Why do you keep her here?"

He looked as if he wished I had never asked again. "When she came here, I knew she could bear children. Our women have not borne offspring in centuries. Ixtar, too, is barren. She will have my children. Or she will be sent to her Extinguishing. She is a vessel for my seed. Nothing more." There was a lie in what he said, though I did not know it.

"Let me take the mask from her then, and I will leave," I said.

"That," Nezahual said, "is impossible."

♦ 4 ♦

I flew down onto the lower temples of the city, crouching upon a domed roof as I watched the mortals below, many of them warriors, sharpening spears and swords and playing war games among themselves. The whores of the city paraded through them, and some of the men grabbed a wench and drew her into the shadows to satisfy their lusts. I thought too much of Pythia, even now. She was a monster. I remembered well seeing the child's hand in the straw at that tower of Hedammu where she took me. I remember that little boy who looked up to me as a father once—a boy left to the hell of war by his family and their poverty, who had followed me to my despair's edge. I had felt such love for that boy, as I did for those children of mine I had barely even seen. I did not believe that vampyres needed to slaughter the innocent. I did not understand the slaughter of life itself, though I had participated in it more than many others.

Life itself was drenched in blood, whether from my thirst or the thirst for power and dominion that Enora had sought, or any man who fought in battle for ideals while cutting down the enemy. We, the vampyres, were soaked in the blood of mortals, and we had no redemption as men did.

I had learned that Medhya was no goddess, but simply a vampyre of the pure races from whom we had taken our existence. Yet, was there a goddess? A god? I had been raised to believe in Christ, in God, in Christendom; my mother had wandered to the Old Ways of the Great Forest, and the goddess and god of that realm. And yet, what was this existence but flesh warring with spirit? What was beyond the Veil besides the monsters of creation? Was there some goddess there who might redeem us? Was there a god who could bring us to our higher natures?

I watched the mortals below me in their passions and pleasures, in their scuffling and frustrations as they prepared for the battles that were not even of their making. They would come up against the two Lords of the Dead here—Nezahual and his brother Aquil. In nights to come, his brother Kulcan, his granddaughter, Pacala, and perhaps even one day Medhya if she moved across the sea to conquer the world of her birth.

Sometime after midnight, I saw fires out along the low hills beneath the ridge of mountains. A great cry went up from some distance, a horn of some kind sounded an alarm. Below me, the men discarded their women, some of whom also picked up weapons. The men had stripped naked, their bodies oiled and ready for battle as they quickly organized themselves along the city walls. Beneath them, at the canals, fires were lit.

A battle came near us that night. I spread my wings and flew over the buildings, following the flat barges along the canals that were being filled with warriors as they moved down to the southern tip of the city to prepare for siege.

Vampyres began emerging from the city temples, and from that hollow mountain on the ridge, I saw dark shapes also fly into the night sky.

I passed many vampyres who went down among the mortals to fight alongside them. This would never have happened in my homeland, where we were devils to one and all. I looked up at the dark palace at the top of the tall pyramid behind me. I headed back toward the palace to find Pythia.

• 5 •

NEZAHUAL was on his throne, speaking with the priests. From his agitated tone, I could tell he was not happy with the developments of the night. He glanced over at me and dismissed the mortals. He drew me over with a gesture. "You have seen war?"

I nodded.

"Then fight with us tonight."

"Nezahual, I came here for one thing only. A mask that I might fulfill that destiny foretold by your sister in a vision. Foretold by Merod, a priest of my tribe."

"Fight with us," he said. "And you shall have your mask by dawn."

"You said it was impossible to get it from her."

"All masks may be removed," he said, as if he had made some harsh decision that he had not wished to make. "She has brought this battle to us with her mindless slaughter. She will pay for it."

• 6 •

I had no love for war; but as I returned to the wall at the southern tip of Aztlanteum, I felt that surge of strength that occurs in the field of battle when you are surrounded by other warriors. The battlements of the city were taken up by vampyres whose wings were spread, and who crouched down as they, too, lifted spears and swords toward the enemies who were already at the gate by the time Nezahual and I reached them. Nezahual had passed me a spear he called the Bloodseeker. "I have slaughtered many with this," he said.

"Killing mortals, I understand," I said. "But the vampyres? We may wound them, but that is not enough."

"Eh," he said, spitting. "They fight like dogs at our throats. Ignore them. Do not let them catch you, Aleric. It is the mortals who are with them who must be killed. Take many lives tonight. Spear their hearts, drink from them, but kill all those who seek to overthrow the city of Ixtar!"

• 7 •

THE enemy below us had already begun burning brush and trees along the perimeter of the city. Smoke blanketed the air, and the war cries were many.

This was not like the battles I had gone into against the Saracens of the Holy Land.

This was wild and unguided.

No knights or kings rode horses into the fray; instead, vampyres dove from the sky, swooping down to lift several warriors at once and drop them or throw them back into the enemy's fiery attack.

I flew into the thick of the smoke, dragging out a mortal whose three-edged ax swung against my thigh, cutting deep. The pain burned, and I fell to the ground; but another vampyre had come down and stolen the ax from him, leaving the warrior to me. I lunged at him, taking him to the earth, neatly snapping his neck.

I flew up again, staunching my wound with my hand.

As I reached the top of the city wall, the blood had stopped pouring from me. My skin healed swiftly as I stood there watching the warriors at each other's throats in the sky, or the mortals on the ground slicing with their thick swords and the two-handled blades cut through a man's neck with great precision.

Again I went down, raising the spear called the Bloodseeker, and drove it through a man's chest just as he was about to attack a woman who held her dagger up to cut his throat. Then another warrior came at me, and another. I used my wings to slap at those who came too near me when I was in the middle of a kill. I had little time to look around at the hillside or back to the city once I had gone farther along the enemy line. There were hundreds of warriors on the attack. The grass that grew thin in this hot climate blazed, and the grains that had been planted in the villages had caught fire.

The night itself seemed to burn, and I saw the shapes of my vampyre brethren slaughtering alongside me.

We were attacked from the skies by Aquil's vampyric warriors, and I dropped my spear as two great creatures dragged me into the sky. I struggled against them, one with a double blade with tiny razors upon it that cut jagged tears along my chest, as it sought my heart.

Suddenly, a sword burst through the chest of this aggressor.

Behind him, Nezahual who had seen my plight. He and I fought the other vampyre away, as well—my teeth dug into his thigh, ripping away at my enemy. Nezahual was at his throat, and we all three began to fall to earth.

We landed, crouching, and the enemy ran off into the smoke.

Again we parted, and I went through the line of the siege three times more, until another cry was heard from a distant hilltop. I saw a phalanx of vampyres moving swiftly through the air toward us. It was as if ships sailed in the skies, for their wings seemed the body of a ship. Above them, a single vampyre with spear in one hand and sword in the other moved; like Nezahual, he did not need wings for his flight. It was Aquil, and I saw Nezahual go to him as if in conference, also accompanied by a flock of vampyres in a nearly military formation.

I rushed upward to help Nezahual, but two vampyres held me back. They growled and snarled and snapped as they fought against each other, far above the human battlefield. It was as if two wolves tore at each other. And part of me wondered if this was over Pythia herself. Had she somehow created these wars through her very presence?

I was more afraid of that which was beyond even Pythia's touch. I was afraid it was the ripping of the Veil itself, the Myrrydanai shadows come into the world from Medhya, that had brought pestilence, famine, and rivalries between these brothers.

I feared that the tearing of the Veil had begun destroying all the kingdoms of vampyres, and this would not end until our race was obliterated.

After the brothers tired of their fight, the enemies of Aztlanteum ran toward the southern hills. Nezahual had prevailed that night. The mortal warriors chased the invaders, and when the smoke cleared within the hour, I saw hundreds of the dead on the earth, their blood staining the walls for more than a mile. It was not like the battles of the Crusades, where the siege would last for weeks or months.

It was brief—but a few hours of the night—and settled with a fight in the air between brothers.

• 8 •

"A skirmish, nothing more," Nezahual said. His wounds had already healed, although I saw a small thin line just below his right eye from his brother's deep clawing.

We were in the great hall of the palace, drinking blood from goblets. Prisoners were tied together against the columns. Many were half-dead; some were tied to those who had already died. I guessed that a hundred vampyres were gathered, and they tore the flesh of their enemies, pouring the libation into the gold cups. Many boasted in their language of exploits in those hours of the fight, or mortals killed, or the vampyres torn.

Nezahual, upon his throne, his face smeared with grease and blood as he drank, beckoned me to his side. I sat at his feet, an honored guest. "This is a distraction. He wanted Pythia tonight. He called to her. He is furious we have not given her to him. He is up to something, though I do not know what." He reached over and patted me on the shoulder. "And you, my friend. Oh, you were magnificent. Did you kill fifty? One hundred?"

"Not so many," I said.

"You are truly a friend of our kingdom," he said. "You are better than any mongrel could be. No wonder you are the Maz-Sherah. You should consider remaining here, Aleric. I cannot trust my family. But you—you I may trust with any treasure of my kingdom."

Yet I knew that as dawn approached—if I did not leave with the mask at the next twilight—I might not return to Taranis-Hir in time. Nezahual sensed my discomfort. "Our wars are not yours," he said later, after the hall had cleared and the bodies of the enemy dead had been thrown over the city walls. "But rest here one more night. Know that no harm shall come to you in my city. You are a hero to us. You risked your existence for our people."

"Where is she?" I asked after several more gold cups were brought to us, and I had begun to feel drunk from the blood.

"I have had to lock her away. She stirs many passions among mortal . . . and immortal. Taming her has been like forcing a wild pig to eat from one's hand." He laughed. "But I cannot resist her. My brother Aquil wishes the same as I—to possess her."

"But she is . . . to you, she is a mongrel."

He nodded. "But I will have sons by her, my friend. She is fertile with life as none of our women are."

I could not ask him how this was possible. The resurrected dead could not have children. It was impossible for us. My only children would be those I had fathered before death. Pythia, who had been dead for thousands of years, could not possibly bring a child into the world.

"I will take you to her," he said. "She has this mask you seek. You will stay until tomorrow night? My friend? Ah, good. Good. I would not wish for you to fly tonight with but an hour or two left before sunrise. But Aleric, remember. You cannot trust her. Remember those she has betrayed. Remember the evil she has wrought upon even her own kind. My guards would like nothing better than to tear her limb from limb. Her presence has brought darkness."

"And yet, you keep her here. You allow her to roam."

"You do not understand, friend. You do not understand," he said.

• 9 •

WE walked along the corridors, past several rooms with the doors closed and barred. Finally, he led me down a brief flight of steps. Four guards stood here, crouching on their haunches, swords in hand, as if ready to strike dead anyone who came. They nodded to their king and allowed us to pass to the locked chamber.

"You guard her like she is your prisoner," I said. "Not as a lover."

"She brought the battle to us this evening," he said. "I must show my warriors that punishment follows disobedience. Even to those I love."

Then he unlocked the door and pushed it back against several serpents within the chamber that had blocked it. "We have had to secure her here," Nezahual said to me, as I turned my back to him to enter the chamber. "Do not be frightened by what we have done. The guards do not like the mask. They do not like her presence. If we did not treat her as an enemy, some here would destroy her. She has been covered that none may look upon her." He passed me a key. "I do not like to think of her so restrained, but my priests are terrified of her, for she does not honor them."

Nezahual did not enter the chamber with me. He turned away, shutting the door behind him.

I was locked in with her, and I began to feel just as I had when I entered that tower of Hedammu in a country distant from this and saw a damsel who would bring me into the immortal realm.

· CHAPTER 16 ·

· 1 ·

THE room was long and narrow, and its stones had inset decorations upon them of serpents and birds and jaguars frozen in a dance along the walls. An area for a bed lay to the right, a stone slab, upon which had been placed deerskin and cloth. The floor seethed with serpents, some with diamond shapes upon their backs and death rattles at their tails, some were thin and iridescent red and green, with long bodies that slowly twisted and curved as they moved, and yet others were thick and heavy snakes as none I had before seen — pythons that barely seemed to move at all along the floor. Three golden bowls filled with oil burned on pedestals about the room. Above each of them were small holes in the stone that smoke would exit, and air would enter the chamber. The smell of it was sweet — I assumed some aromatic herb had been mixed in the oil, reminding me of a sweet mint.

There, on the floor among the snakes, she lay as if sleeping among them. She was clothed in the raiments of the local goddess of the people—a serpent of ruby and emerald feathers, a queen of some ancient legend. Her wings extended from beneath the robe and cloak that covered her, as if they had been broken.

Nezahual's priest had placed a mask of tin upon her face, battered into the shape of twin gods—one like a jaguar, and another like a dragon with long feathers streaming from its wings and tail, and a crest like a kestrel might have upon its head. I went to her, moving through the vipers on the floor, which parted at my footsteps. I crouched down beside her.

I slowly drew the mask from her face.

Beneath it, the mask of Datbathani seemed like her real skin and no mask at all. These priests of Nezahual's kingdom had placed two flat round obsidian disks on her eyes that they might not see her when they imprisoned her—and that she might not see them and remember their faces. Yet she seemed to follow me with these eyes, as if they had some use for her. I removed them, and she looked at me as if wondering if I meant her any harm. Her hair had been darkened with a powdered dye, although it still had the wisps of straw color flecked among it as the starlight disturbed a darkened stream. Even the color of her hair frightened them, and they had covered it with the dye that had been used to cover Ixtar's body. Braided within her hair were long feathers that were brilliant red and sun gold and blue like lapis stone and green as the deepest emerald. Her lips had been painted with a dark red stain.

She had been draped with a magnificent cloth of gold, and upon it the markings of some jungle god, as well as the twists and curves of a local snake god. Feathers were wrapped about her shoulders and the skin of snakes wound about her arms with gold chain and cuffs at her wrists. The tunic beneath her royal robe seemed to be made of wisps of cobwebs enshrouding her form perfectly as if a nest of spiders had captured her and spun about her. The priests of Aztlanteum had made her this night into their Feathered Serpent, and had draped her wings with silver and obsidian jewels that she might not take flight from her prison.

At her feet, writhing about her, hundreds of long brown-yellow snakes, the ends of their tails moving swiftly, rattling. A yellow-green python, several feet in length and thick as a warrior's arm, curved about her hips, as if embracing her.

She looked up at me, surprised that I had come to her. "You see what he is like?"

"Once I found a maiden in a tower," I said, softly. "I thought to free her from captivity. Yet she turned into a dragon and tore at me."

She turned away from me, looking at the opposite wall. "And once there was a prophetess of an island, born from a man who would one day become a priest of monsters. And as she sat at her table and looked into the openings of the earth from which the gods spoke to her, she saw a youth who would be born in some future time. He would come to her twice. The first time, she would love him. The second time, he would destroy her. And that seer, that maiden of pythons, swore that she would never let these things come to pass, and if she ever met this youth who came to her, she would murder him before she could know him well enough to love him."

"If you were once a prophetess, why did you not foresee even this?"

"Prophecy gives us a tantalizing glimpse, then takes away our sight when the moment of destiny arrives."

I reached around her, pulling the snakes back that wrapped themselves about her shoulders and along her cloak. Her wings folded into her body slowly, and when she looked up at me again, the gold face itself seemed to be flesh, and seemed to be she, again, in that tower where I had first met her. I could not separate the emotions that flooded through me then from my thoughts—I remembered human love. Not the love of the eternal or of mortal or immortal. I remembered that place when I held her in my youth; when I held Alienora in her father's chapel; in those times of absolute innocence when I had not seen the mask of the world removed to show me the ugliness and death beneath it, the curse that lurked beneath the visage of blessing. She was but a woman beneath the mask, beneath the immortal life. I had seen her as a beast when Nezahual had found her along the lakeshore with blood smeared across her face and throat and arms and breasts.

I knew why Nezahaul could not give her up, despite what had followed her here and the terrible things she did.

Something in Pythia herself cried out to me. She seemed pitiable and yet strong. She was invincible and yet vulnerable. Savage, and yet somehow a victim of the gods themselves if any watched over us at all. I wished to protect her as I had felt when I first saw her. Even knowing what she had done to me, and to others—how she had betrayed her father and her people in Alkemara, how she had murdered me and resurrected me, how she had kept the secrets of the vampyres from the ones in Hedammu she had created—allowing them to go to their Extinguishings in a short span of years. Even knowing this, something within me was bound to her. Perhaps we are always bound to those who bring us back from death. Perhaps her breath within me drew me to her again. I did not understand the mystery of this, but when I held her there, among the serpents, I felt as if I wanted to feel her breath again in my mouth and press my lips to hers though I despised what she had become.

I removed all restraints from her wrists, as I had once before in Hedammu.

◆ 2 ◆

SHE looked up at me, the gold mask shifting and moving along her features as if it were liquid. "I have been afraid of you since my mortal life, Maz-Sherah. In visions I have seen the end of all times, at your hand."

"I have seen visions, too," I said. "Of your father, who calls to me to perform the ancient ceremonies of the Priests of Blood."

"He lives within you now," she said. "As Datbathani covers my face with her mask, so I feel him here, in your flesh. I fear him. I fear all that will come to pass, Maz-Sherah."

We spoke of those things that were confusions to us both—our visions, of Merod, of Artephius. On this subject she had few words. "I was his captive as I am Nezahual's. Artephius deceived me in his sorceries. I believed he would stop the prophecies, but he has incited them with his machinery and his magick. Do you understand who he is, truly?"

"I have only seen a skull wrapped in cloth beneath his visor," I said. "He is the walking dead—a ghoul or wraith."

"He possesses the great grimoire of sorcery, bound in Medhya's flesh."

"I have seen this book," I said. "In his study."

"Within it are words of blood, the sorceries of immortality," she said. "He used me to destroy my father's kingdom. He held me captive for centuries, tearing at my skin and stealing my blood to find the essence of life that he might bring Medhya over through the Veil. Do you not even know, still, who he is to you? Do you not know why you exist, Maz-Sherah? You are not here to save our tribes. You are here to bring about the wars of vampyre and mortal, and when they are done, she will come again, in the flesh. When you have performed these ceremonies of which you know nothing—*nothing*—you will bring her in the flesh again. You will hand the Alchemist you fear and hate those powers he has been denied."

"I do not believe you," I said. "Your father speaks within me. He wishes these ceremonies."

"My father is weak," she said. "Artephius is unconcerned with the ancient priests. He tried to destroy them once, and he will try again. He seeks Medhya. He seeks power over all. He seeks to be the only god of this Earth, and Medhya shall be his goddess. The ripping of the Veil you caused has done this. You are his instrument."

"No," I said, feeling fury at her accusations.

"You are the one who tears the Veil for him. Your ceremonies will bring these prophecies to an end. You are the flesh and blood of the prophecies of Medhya, Maz-Sherah. You are the embodiment of all that Artephius wishes to create on this Earth. You are . . ."

I wanted to cover her mouth to keep the lies from pouring out of her. I wanted to stop up her breath that she might never speak again.

"You are his *son*," she said, finally, and then as I sat there beside her, my heart thudding against my chest, pains as I had not felt since the torments of the Red Scorpion itself, she told me of those things to which I had been blind.

· 3 ·

"THROUGH sorceries, he brought seed from his body into your mother's womb. Do you think your birth was an accident of flesh? That your mother, the granddaughter of the Druid race, the mages of your land, who had fought vampyres for a thousand years in the forests that covered Europe before Rome itself had arisen, was not handpicked? From the mud, the prophecies said. From the lands of the west of the kingdoms. Where the Veil grew thin upon the Earth, there, a daughter of mages will be found. Through her, through mud and sorrow, the Maz-Sherah shall be born. And he will come to us from the despairs of the mortal realm. I had seen this, so long before your birth, that I had nearly forgotten its truth when you came to me in the tower of Hedammu. He had known I would be the instrument of your resurrection. There had been others we thought were Maz-Sherah. I had sent many of them to their deaths and Extinguishings over the centuries. But you, I could not do this. You filled me with terror when I breathed immortality into your lungs where I should have breathed fire instead.

"Did you not sense the Myrrydanai at your rebirth into vampyrism? Did you not hear their whispers? You were their gate. Your birth tore the Veil. Your resurrection ripped it further. You are the hope of Artephius, Maz-Sherah. He knew of your coming. He knew all of it. You think you escaped his clutches to come here so easily? He desires this mask as well."

As she spoke, all of my life seemed to move in confusion in my imagination. I could not understand how this could be. Why my mother would have been raped by the armored knight and not spoken of it. Why the mysteries of my childhood had not been explained to me by my grandfather, who, in his youth, had been trained in the Druid's science and magick.

"Your father would have told me," I said. "I freed him from his tomb. He gave me the staff. He comes to me in visions. He passed power to me, to all who are Medhyic vampires."

"Do you think," she said, "I would imprison my own father. My sisters. Destroy that Temple of Lemesharra and all its people—a great civilization fallen in a trembling of the earth, covered in the rubble of a cataclysm—because I am evil? Or because even the great Merod Al Kamr did not understand the workings of the Myrrydanai? You fulfilled the prophecy of devouring the last Priest of Blood, yet you do not understand the meaning of such an act. He is within you, still. He hears us speak. He is waiting to return. You are a pawn of these priests, Maz-Sherah. You were created for their wars. As long as you exist, you are a threat to this world. You are a threat to mortals. You are a threat to the Earth itself. The only ones you do not threaten are Artephius himself . . . and Medhya. Even my father was fooled. He seeks the wars of vampyres through you."

"The Great Serpent," I said. "What of him. I have felt him near me at times. He guards the Veil."

"The Great Serpent is a belief that has no flesh," she said. "You have seen his bride Ixtar below? You have *seen* from whence our race descends. We are not born of the dust of Heaven. We are born of creatures from Hell, Maz-Sherah. And you are the key to the doorway. Once turned, once your ceremonies are performed, the demons come. Demons worse than you or I. Worse than Nezahual himself. This doorway is meant to be locked, as my chamber is locked. You were never meant to be born, Maz-Sherah. I was never meant to resurrect you. If I could destroy you now, I would. If I could tear you limb from limb to stop this, I would." Tears had begun flowing from her eyes. "But it would do no good. Only you may stop this. Only you may end what began when the priests of Medhya bound her spirit and tore her flesh and blood from her, and sent her beyond the Veil into her exile. All the priests should be destroyed. All the sacred objects should be thrown into the sea, never to be found. Even this mask . . ." She touched the edge of her golden face. "Even this mask fooled me. I thought I would have power to end these things if I but wore it. But it does not bring power to its wearer. It takes from me. It is a golden leech upon me, sucking immortality itself from me as each year has gone by."

• 4 •

O N E of the flames from the golden bowls flared briefly and sent bright shadows across the darkened room. Dawn approached beyond the walls, and we lay together though I felt a terrible emptiness at the pit of my being. She combed her fingers through my hair and whispered to me words meant to comfort after such revelations.

After several seconds, she said, "I hate you, Maz-Sherah. I hate what I saw in you when I made you vampyre."

"You saw the ceremonies of the mask and the staff. You saw the visions of Alkemara and your father."

"I saw more than this," she said. "I saw my mortal death by your hand."

I could not help myself. I leaned into her and kissed her throat.

I smelled mortality there. I smelled the flesh of the living. I drew her up, and carried her to the slab that was her bed.

I lay beside her, my enemy.

My murderer.

• 5 •

"ALL is destiny," she whispered, a heavy sorrow in her voice. "You are not merely here for the mask of the Lady of Serpents," she said. "You are here for me. You are my undoing, Maz-Sherah. You are the end of my existence." She drew me into her arms and I went to her, frozen inside from all she had said, though I could not believe any of it. I could not believe that her own father would be deceived as well. I could not believe this lying harlot who had used so many men, so many kings and priests, and now was in my arms, using her own glamour to draw me back to the lips I had not touched since my body had died to the world.

"Do you remember our nights in Hedammu?" she asked, a sad smile playing along the edges of her lips.

"I remember."

I reached up and touched the edge of the gold mask. It seemed as if it were one with her skin. My fingers followed the contours along her cheek and nostrils and the gently sloping ridge of her nose as it spread upward to form her brow. I felt tingling in my hand, as if the energy of the Gorgon Mask had moved into me.

"You feel it," she whispered, her breath warm against my face, for we were close as I felt the contours of her face. "She is there. Datbathani."

I wanted to pull away but could not help myself. I felt a curious pleasure, a delicious shudder go through me as I touched the golden face.

"Do you feel how it wants you?"

I nodded, unable to keep myself from the mask. I felt that frisson

of sexual energy from the golden form, and my fingers made light in-
dentations in the soft material as if it were not metal at all. As if it
were a light, smooth clay, spread upon her face. I was only vaguely
aware that Pythia had wrapped her arms around my waist as I explored the mask. I began to see through the gold, through my own
reflection—not the image of death I had seen in the silver mirror of
the Alchemist but a sunlit place where I again had wrapped myself,
naked, into Pythia's body as if my flesh belonged there. In this golden
vision, she again had me in my youth, as I offered her entry into my
blood as she offered me the cup of her breasts, the roundness of her
small belly, the heat of her thighs.

I felt the other, watching us. The Serpent entwined around us in
this vision, and I sensed the other watching us. Datbathani, sister of
Nezahual, spying upon us even in a false vision.

And yet, as my fingers left the gold face, my hands held to her
throat as if to strangle; yet I caressed her. I could not resist, for the
hardness between my legs pushed outward, and my heart beat quickly
as I pressed my lips to hers. She seemed vulnerable to me, now, not
the cruel queen of vampyres, daughter of Merod, concubine of Nezahual, but a maiden again in my arms, a damsel as she had been when
I first felt her body pressed to mine in my nineteenth year.

My breathing was heavy as I kissed the gold face and pressed my
lips beneath her chin to kiss along her throat to her breasts as I drew
down her gown. To say I felt enchanted was not enough. A lustful
youth awoke within me, desiring this woman's flesh again, this creature of Alkemara who had taken my life, had tasted my blood, and had
brought me from the Threshold of death into the vampyric realm. I
had not felt such burning among my tribe, even pressed into Ewen's
arms, lying down with Kiya in the graves of Hedammu—even in my
mortal life with Alienora herself. Pythia awoke something within
me. The gold mask unlocked what I had kept safe from others—the
bull within me that longed to mate again, to mount her, to find

release within her, to escape those thoughts that threatened to drive me mad.

Before daybreak, I lay with her upon a bed of cotton blankets, woven by the people of Aztlanteum for their gods. She lay with her back to me. I looked at her hair, come undone from the tight braids, falling like yellow silk across her shoulders. The brand was upon her back—we each had marks upon us of some enemy. She had a cross with Latin words beneath it, a memento of the Crusaders who had caught her, briefly, before we had met. I had the mark of Artephius on my thigh, and the brand of the Disk itself on my chest. I lay there enjoying the view of her back and the perfect line of her spine that ran down to the gentle curve of her buttocks.

She was becoming mortal. The mask took her immortality from her.

A mortal vampyre.

She had already gone into the day's sleep. I sensed someone else in our chamber, and saw near a blue flame Nezahual watching us. How long he had been there, I did not know. I felt no panic from this betrayal, for he did not seem unhappy that she and I had slept together. Would he be jealous? He already saw us as a breed below his kind. "Mongrel blood," the words went through my mind.

Your blood, he whispered within me. *Your mongrel blood. Within her.*

When I awoke, he sat on the edge of the stone table that was our bed in the serpent chamber. His fingers combed through his beloved's hair. He leaned over, kissing the back of her neck, sweetly. When he noticed that I had opened my eyes, he slipped his hand beneath the back of her head and raised it up. Her eyes were still closed. He kissed her eyelids, then kissed her lips. The gold of her mask seemed to shimmer, and she opened her eyes to him. She reached up to wrap her arms about his neck, forgetting that I lay beside her. He reached over to me, lifting my arm and bringing my left hand across her stomach. She glanced back toward me, remembering and gaped, looking up at Nezahual. He leaned down and kissed her, then leaned over me and kissed me as well, as if we had been lovers. I drew in a deep breath, my mind still trying to understand this.

He called out in his language, and six vampyres came into the chamber, wading through the serpents. Three of them grabbed Pythia. I got up quickly, ready to fight. The three vampyre guards leapt upon me with a strength beyond those of my tribe. They held me against the cold stone wall, while Nezahual went to Pythia, whom the vampyres had suspended between them.

"Betrayer," he said. He leaned forward, his dark fangs bared as if to devour her face. Instead, he kissed her, but tore at her lips so that her mouth ran with blood. He slapped her across the face; I struggled against those who held me; she glanced at me with fury behind that golden face.

"Take her to the nest," he said. He came over to me and spat in my face. "You have brought this to my city, mongrel. You are the Maz-Sherah of your tribe of thieves. It is your priests who exiled Medhya through ceremonies of damnation into the realm of shadows. I should never have trusted either one of you. Thieves and mongrels. But you slip into her bed the moment I am gone. You are pestilence itself. It is not the tearing Veil that brings the unmaking of the world, mongrel. It is you. Your existence was preordained to this. You claim you think of your children, yet they will die from your actions. You claim you care for friends left behind. They, too, will be destroyed. You save nothing. You have nothing. I will put you in a tomb from which you will not escape. I will bury you that you will go to your Extinguishing slowly and without mercy. It is better for the Earth that you are no more, mongrel. It is better that your tribe dies. And when the twilight of existence comes with the great dust of the Veil, and when my sister Medhya turns the Earth to darkness and ice, I will remember you. I will remember how your very birth brought about the end of mortal life. As you lie in your tomb, think of the torments of this world. You and your kind have brought them. If you had never existed, the Veil would not be torn. You believe you are the guardians of mortals, but what have you guarded? How many mortals have died from plague? Whom have you saved, savior?"

I fought like a wolf against the guards, but their strength subdued me. Several more vampyres poured into the chamber. Each began biting at my legs and arms, pouring my life's blood out, weakening me further. I tore one vampyre's arm from its socket, but then others were at my throat, ripping the flesh with their talons.

They carried me out of the palace, flying out across the city, toward the hollow mountain.

My skin blistered as I felt the first rays of sunlight upon me before being lowered into the obsidian city.

◆ CHAPTER 17 ◆

◆ 1 ◆

BESIDE the river, at the place of the nest of vampyres, they laid me in the bone sarcophagus that was the feeding trough of their great mother.

Before shutting the lid, Nezahual stood over at the tomb's edge, looking down at me. "As you extinguish, mongrel, think of those you were meant to save. Think of your children in your homeland. Think of your friends. Think even of Pythia herself. When Ixtar comes to you, when her hunger is great, remember Pythia's face. I may forgive her this transgression, but you, whom I trusted, I cannot forgive."

◆ 2 ◆

I lay there many nights, clawing at the stone that surrounded me, scraping the nails of my fingers back, bleeding as I tried to push the heavy lid back to the tomb.

I thought of my children, who did not know me.

And Ewen. I prayed he had not been tortured into those slave vampyres of the Myrrydanai.

I tried to find Merod within visions, but none came. No voice spoke to me in that tomb. The lies that Pythia had told me—that my father was that creature Artephius? That my mother had spread her legs that a fleshless creature might give his seed into her? All lies, I was sure. Pythia had seduced me with sorcery, as she had the first time we had met.

She had intended to destroy me, and by bringing me into her flesh, she had ensured it.

Was it too late? I lost count of nights. My lips were dry and numb from biting at myself to draw even my own blood into my body for sustenance. I remembered the vampyres I had seen in the chamber of Extinguishing at Hedammu, so long ago. How they had not been able to drink blood. How they had just lain there, disintegrating after many years.

I felt that was my fate.

There would be no ceremonies. Enora would rise and, with Artephius, bring Medhya in the flesh, crossing the Veil itself, destroying it, unleashing forces into the world far greater than the plagues that had come.

Calyx, I prayed, as if she could hear me. *Forgive me. My children, forgive your father. Ewen, forgive me. I have failed. I have failed all. Merod, speak to me. Come to me. Show me how I might overcome this.* Had Ewen already become a Morn? Was Kiya a mindless slave of the Myrrydanai?

Did Calyx wait for me among the Akkadite Cliffs? Or had the Chymers hunted them down, or the Morns taken them prisoner to the Alchemist.

Are you truly my father? I imagined that man of silver and bronze. *Are these lies?* All I knew of my father was rumor. All I knew for certain was that he had been a foreigner whom my grandfather had despised.

All of these thoughts ate at my gut and tormented me.

I called within my blood to Merod Al Kamr. *You are inside me. Your blood runs with mine. Speak to me now. Rescue your Maz-Sherah. Show yourself to me.*

After a time, I began to curse the Great Serpent. Curse the vampyre race. Curse Medhya and Ixtar and Nezahual and Pythia. Curse every demon of our tribe.

But I remembered Ewen's face, the boy I had grown up with, the youth I had brought as my companion into resurrection. I could not curse him, nor could I curse Kiya, nor Midias.

I am Maz-Sherah for a reason. Pythia does not know all. Merod Al Kamr does not know all. Even Artephius cannot control what is within me.

In my mind, I saw the Great Serpent, turning at the edge of the Earth where the Veil was a mist across water. No words were spoken, nor did the Serpent look upon me.

But it was enough to give me some strange hope.

All was not lost. All was not as it seemed. I was not the doom of my race as I had begun to believe.

The Great Serpent still protected that boundary, and in the vision of my mind, I stood upon its back, riding it as it stopped the mist of the Veil from crossing onto the land.

Too many nights had passed as I lay in the tomb. I began to think of Ixtar, and wondered when her hunger would rouse her from sleep. When she would fly down from her nest and open the tomb and crawl inside with me to suck the marrow from my bones.

One night, I heard the lid of the sarcophagus being moved.

She is here. Ixtar has left her nest.

And then, another thought that was pure madness: *If I am to be devoured by the mother of vampyres, then I pray Pythia did not lie. I pray that my end will stop all that Artephius put in motion when the Priests of the Myrrydanai and the Nahhashim and the Kamr stole sorceries from the Queen of Myrryd.*

• 3 •

T HE heavy lid of the tomb moved. I thought of the vampyre I had seen as he was torn limb from limb by Ixtar.

Pythia stood there, soaked from exertion. She wore a torn and bloodied tunic, with a small round sack, like a purse, drawn about her throat with cord.

She reached in and grabbed me by the arm, lifting me up.

"The sky burns. The volcanoes erupt to the north and east, and ash spreads across the land. Aquil has brought his wars to the borders of the city for three nights," she said. "Many vampyres have been taken and bound by enemy priests. You are weak, but I will carry you until we find blood. Until then, drink from me. Drink. *Now.* There is no time to waste." I grasped her wrist and snapped my teeth down upon that flesh. Her blood burst into the back of my mouth, like a taste of heaven. *Mortal blood.* I sucked at her forearm until she drew it back from me with some force. "It will not heal easily," she said. She closed the wound with a strip of cloth torn from her tunic.

"Why do you . . . save me?" I asked.

She bared her fangs, the gold mask on her face placid as she pulled my body from the tomb. She cradled my head on her lap and combed her fingers through my hair. "Nezahual knew the moment he touched me. I am dead here. He will hunt us both. He felt the life inside me the morning he found us together."

"Life?"

"A child," she said. She seemed to be out of breath as she spoke so quickly and I felt as if I were being drawn into harsh light with her words. "He has tried to bring life to me, but he cannot. His seed is dry within him. Yours, Maz-Sherah, lives. Rise. I have slaughtered seven priests to get to you. I have taken something sacred from him. The confusion in the city is great, but it will end. Ixtar is awakening in her nest. We have no time. We have no time, do you understand me?"

She drew me up into the night, up above the river's edge, through the great hollow of the mountain. As we passed along the obsidian wall, I looked at that entryway into Ixtar's lair and thought for a moment I saw her, moving along the inner ceiling, crawling like a spider as if someone had disturbed her sleep.

And then I knew without even having to ask Pythia what had hung in the rounded purse at her throat:

She has taken the obsidian globe. The Serpent's Eye.

I heard the war cries and the smell of smoke in the air. She held me close as she flew upward into the smoke. We were clear of the war below us, but I heard the screams of men and the growls and snapping teeth of vampyres in their midair fights, the singing of swords as they cut the air and the whistling of spears and arrows as they flew beneath us. I could see the night emerge as she pushed farther toward the heavens—the stars were obscured by the gray-and-black plumes of smoke that rose from the earth.

We passed above the walls of Aztlanteum as the mortal vampyre raised me up, carrying me across the burning city, her mortal blood upon my lips.

In the distance, I saw the yellow-and-red sprays of lava burst from a ridge of mountains. The sky had gone gray and yellow at midnight.

I looked up at Pythia's golden face, like the visage of the statue of a goddess.

Datbathani has saved me. Saved us. She brings new life through us into the earth.

The Great Serpent lives.

I found the strength of my wings as they opened at my back.

I let go of her, and dropped, while my wings unfurled in the ashen air. I stretched my wings and glided at first. Far below, on the rim of the hollow mountain, I saw a dark figure that was too large for an ordinary vampyre. It was Ixtar, emerging from her home, clinging to the edge of the mountainside. I climbed upward along the wind to fly beside Pythia.

For a moment I saw the end of that great city below me, as burning gases from smoke devoured it, as flames ran along the canals and boulevards.

The sky had turned sulfurous yellow and black as pitch, and it seemed then as if the world would end, and the city of Nezahual with its great pyramids and temples would be devoured by the earth itself. The shapes of vampyre fighting vampyre, of the cries and shouts of the mortals who had not yet fallen beneath Aquil and his armies, the flocks of black-winged creatures who attacked each other like falcons fighting beneath us.

I turned and followed Pythia out to the western sea, away from the coming of dawn. Yet, I felt the stream as if it were the strands of a spiderweb, drawing at my wings.

Someone pursued us from the burning city.

Visit www.Vampyricon.com
The Vampyricon continues